DOCTOR WHO

CITY AT WORLD'S END
CHRISTOPHER BULIS

Published by BBC Worldwide Ltd,
Woodlands, 80 Wood Lane
London W12 0TT

First published 1999
Copyright © Christopher Bulis 1999
The moral right of the author has been asserted

Original series broadcast on the BBC

Format © BBC 1963
Doctor Who and TARDIS are trademarks of the BBC

ISBN 0 563 55579 3
Imaging by Black Sheep, copyright © BBC 1999

Printed and bound in Great Britain by Mackays of Chatham
Cover printed by Belmont Press Ltd, Northampton

Prologue

The force of the impact totally destroyed the asteroid and came close to splitting the tiny moon in two. In a fraction of a second, kinetic energy of motion was converted to heat, light and a scattering of X-rays. The combined flash was visible across half the stellar system.

A crater five kilometres deep and almost eighty wide was blasted out of the moon's surface. Fifty thousand cubic kilometres of rock were converted into an incandescent plume of vapour and semi-molten fragments and ejected into space at a velocity too great for the slight gravity of the moon to ever draw it back. In time it would form a ring about the moon's parent world.

During the days following the collision the outward effects of the cataclysm gradually subsided. The scar of the glowing crater that stretched across half a hemisphere cooled below red heat. New mountain ranges thrust up by the impact settled into equilibrium. The shock waves reverberating through its interior faded away, leaving only the steady whisper of thermal contractions within the surface rocks.

So the moon continued tumbling on through space – but no longer along the same course it had followed for the previous hundred thousand years. The impact had reduced its velocity, and in obedience to the laws of motion and gravitational attraction its orbital path changed.

The long fall had begun.

Chapter One
The City

'I don't suppose you've any idea at all where we've landed, Doctor?' Barbara asked the old man in the black frock coat. There was an edge of weary impatience in her voice.

The Doctor remained bent over the console, throwing switches and tapping dials, the cool white light of the control room gleaming off his flowing silver-white hair. 'The readings are not as clear as I might wish…' he said absently, 'but it seems we are a few thousand years beyond your time, Miss Wright.'

'Well, whenever it is, it doesn't look very prepossessing,' Ian Chesterton observed.

The TARDIS's monitor camera had completed a full rotation and once again displayed the first image they had seen after landing: slowly billowing fog almost obscuring a long curving chest-high wall topped by a wire mesh screen. The ground between the TARDIS and the base of the wall was covered in blackish mud dotted with puddles. The view had been much the same to either side. Behind them was the blank expanse of a taller dirt-streaked concrete wall that stretched as far as the eye could see.

'It does look pretty dismal, doesn't it?' Susan agreed, her bright intent face at odds with her words. 'But according to the instruments the composition of the air and the temperature are both fine.'

'So now I suppose you want to go outside and take a look around?' Barbara said.

The Doctor straightened up, hooked his thumbs under his lapels and thrust out his chin. 'And why should I not, pray?'

'Firstly, because there doesn't seem to be anything of interest there and secondly, because it's not where we want to be.'

'May I remind you,' the Doctor said testily, 'that I am not operating a taxi cab service. I promised to return you to your proper location in space and time as soon as it was practicable, but I refuse to leave this place without making at least a cursory examination. Who knows what strange and wonderful things we might find out there… just beyond that wall, perhaps?'

'And who knows what might find us,' Ian pointed out.

'You and Miss Wright are at liberty to remain inside the TARDIS if you wish, Chesterton,' the Doctor said dismissively, 'but I am going outside.'

'And me, Grandfather,' Susan said quickly.

The Doctor smiled benignly at her, good humour returning mercurially to his features. 'Thank you, my dear. Let us leave our unadventurous friends to their own devices. But perhaps we'd better wear our coats. It does appear to be rather damp out there.'

'I'll fetch them,' said Susan, stepping lightly over to the bentwood stand in the corner.

Ian caught Barbara's eye and she gave a little helpless shrug. They had been Susan's teachers back on Earth in 1963, but now, as her strange origins became more apparent, she was growing away from them. To outward appearances and in some mannerisms she was still a teenage girl, but Ian sensed a personality of great strength and boldness developing within her.

They said nothing as the Doctor donned his long cloak and muffler, while Susan put on a stylish raincoat and cap she had brought with her from England. The Doctor threw a switch on the console, the TARDIS's heavy outer doors swung smoothly inwards, and he and Susan stepped outside.

'There really isn't any point in arguing with the Doctor, is there?' Barbara said ruefully. 'I sometimes wonder whether even after all this time he resents the way we came aboard, and is determined to take us back home by the longest route he can find as a punishment.'

Ian smiled. 'You know him. He never minds where he ends up.' He checked the monitor screen which showed Susan and the Doctor examining the muddy ground. 'Still, there doesn't seem to be anything dangerous outside this time.'

Barbara saw the expression on his face. 'You're getting as bad as he is. You don't have to keep me company if you want to go outside.'

'I wasn't staying just to keep you company,' Ian protested. 'But as we're not going anywhere until the Doctor's ready anyway, we might as well take a look.'

Barbara sighed. 'I suppose it wouldn't hurt to get some fresh air and stretch our legs...'

As they stepped out of the narrow outer door of the TARDIS, which externally retained its disconcerting resemblance to a twentieth-century British police call box, Ian tasted the air. It was cool and fresh enough except for a faint tang of stale soot. Their feet sank into a thick layer of crusted black mud. Barbara grimaced. 'I should have worn wellingtons.'

The largely featureless wall behind the TARDIS proved to belong to one side of a round structure, broken only by narrow louvred windows and a solid metal utility door. Mounted on its roof was a heavy latticework girder mast that rose high above their heads. Extending from its sides were several oddly shaped mesh panels and dishes which Ian took to be aerials. The other wall appeared to surround the building entirely and was separated from it by the strip of level, muddy ground.

Ian and Barbara picked their way across the mud avoiding the puddles. The Doctor, still crouching beside Susan, looked up at them in satisfaction.

'Ah, so you've decided to join us after all, have you? Good.' He indicated the ground. 'What do you make of this, eh?'

'It's mud,' said Barbara.

'No,' the Doctor beamed. 'If you examine it closely you will find it is layered ash and soot. Clearly there have been several fires close by in the recent past.'

'I suppose nobody comes here very often,' Barbara said, looking about her. 'I can't see any other footprints.'

Ian made a cautious circuit of the open ground around the building, which was about twenty yards in diameter. 'There are no other doors,' he reported when he returned, 'or any opening in the outer wall. Just more fog beyond it.'

'Maybe there's a tunnel,' Susan suggested.

Together the four of them walked with squelching steps across to the outer wall and peered through the mesh screen into featureless swirling opalescence.

'Well, I don't call that particularly wonderful,' Barbara said, pointedly glancing at the Doctor.

But even as she spoke the wind was strengthening. An orange disc of a sun appeared in the grey sky, growing brighter by the second. The fog shredded and thinned about them. Suddenly a dramatic vista crystallised out of the haze.

'Don't you, Miss Wright?' the Doctor retorted triumphantly.

'Of all the places to land us,' Ian said with a chuckle, 'you had to pick the top of a skyscraper!'

They were looking out over a great city of similar buildings. As the fog rolled away they saw hundreds of towers thrusting graceful spires up towards the clouds. These were linked by an intricate web of enclosed tubes and aerial roadways that spanned the artificial canyons formed by the buildings' stepped walls of glass and stone. Streamlined vehicles, looking like scurrying beetles from high above, were speeding smoothly along the open ways.

'Can you see any people?' Ian asked after a minute.

The Doctor had taken a pair of folding opera glasses from the recesses of his coat and was peering about intently.

'Not at the moment,' he said, 'but then the inclement weather has no doubt been keeping them inside.'

Barbara pointed to their right. 'The city seems to stop short in that direction. Do you see between those buildings... is that a wall?'

The Doctor turned his gaze in the direction she indicated.

'It is indeed a wall of considerable height,' he reported. 'I can see a flat-topped tower built into it... there is some smaller structure mounted on its roof which I cannot identify.' He swung his glasses from side to side. 'The wall continues as far as I can see. Perhaps, like medieval cities, this one is entirely enclosed.'

'What's that beyond it?' Ian asked, narrowing his eyes in the silvery-grey light.

'A range of mountains,' the Doctor reported, 'running along at the back of the city...' He swung about. '...Which appears to be built on a promontory jutting out into a sea – or at least a sizeable lake. I can make out a wide shoreline running away to the horizon. Hmm. There is some object of considerable size lying part of the way along the shore. It does not seem to be natural... this is most annoying, I cannot quite make it out. Susan, dear... will you run back to the TARDIS and fetch the telescope?'

Susan was back in a minute carrying a long naval-style brassbound telescope of antique design.

'I left some very muddy footprints on the floor, I'm afraid,' she said apologetically.

The Doctor rested the telescope on top of the parapet wall and focused on the object on the shore.

'Most extraordinary,' he murmured.

'Don't keep us in suspense, Doctor,' Ian said. 'What is it?'

'See for yourself, Chesterton,' said the Doctor, relinquishing his position.

Ian focused the device and gave an exclamation. 'A flattened cylinder... a huge vessel of some kind, I think. Perhaps a submarine? It's split half open down one side. No, surely it's too big to be a submarine. A crashed airship, perhaps?'

'Don't let your imagination be limited by the capabilities of your own time,' the Doctor warned as Ian gave up his place so that Susan and Barbara could look. 'Who knows what devices the people of this world may be capable of building?'

'With those exposed ribs it looks rather like a beached whale,' Barbara said.

'An inappropriate if picturesque simile,' the Doctor replied. 'However, the object has certainly been badly damaged.' He tapped his chin. 'What fate befell it, I wonder? Unless it is a very recent tragedy, why has it not been salvaged?'

They made their way slowly around the parapet examining the sprawling cityscape. The boundary wall seemed to be continuous.

'What's it meant to keep out?' Barbara wondered.

The towers coming into view became steadily taller. Evidently the one they had landed on was situated near the city's outskirts. Now they were facing towards the centre, which had previously been hidden by the roof building.

Suddenly the Doctor halted: 'My goodness! How remarkable.'

Standing in the very heart of the city was a structure that dwarfed all the others around it. It rose in a series of graceful tiers and flowing curves and even through the hazy air it gleamed metallically. Beside it was a huge latticework tower of girders connected to the silvery form by numerous extended bridges and boom arms.

'It looks a bit like one of those rockets they launch from Cape Canaveral,' Ian said breathlessly. 'But this must be over a hundred storeys high.'

The Doctor, peering through the telescope, said: 'The upper sections of what I take to be support fins are just visible over the tops of the intervening buildings. It does indeed appear to be a rocket and launching gantry.' He then added with unexpected solemnity: 'Truly a ship worthy of the city giving it birth.'

'What was that about picturesque similes?' Barbara chided him gently.

'I was employing metaphor, Miss Wright, not simile,' the Doctor retorted. 'And there are times when it is fully justified.'

'But why build such a huge rocket right in the heart of the city?' Susan wondered. 'Launching it would cause terrible damage – unless it had a counter-gravity drive.'

'But the streamlining suggests a high launch velocity,' the Doctor pointed out. 'It may be propelled by simple nuclear transfer reactions.'

'But would they risk the pollution that would cause?'

'They may have mastered the use of the stable trans-uranic elements,' the Doctor speculated. 'Or perhaps a pulsed fusion system with a magnetically contained thrust.'

Ian was beginning to feel left out of the conversation and saw a glazed look in Barbara's eyes. Back at Coal Hill School on Earth he'd taught Susan science, yet the terms and concepts she was using so casually were far beyond his understanding. He coughed. 'Excuse us, but does it matter how it's powered?'

'You're quite right, Chesterton,' the Doctor agreed unexpectedly. 'The question of propulsion can be put aside for the time being. First we must determine its intended purpose. Something momentous I'm certain.'

His eyes were sparkling and Ian could almost feel the enthusiasm crackling from him. The Doctor began walking briskly back towards the roof building with Susan at his side carrying the telescope.

'Just a minute,' said Barbara, 'where are you going?'

'There must be a way down through this building to the first of those roadways,' he said. 'We may be able to utilise the transport system to reach the ship.'

'But we know nothing about the people who live here,' Ian pointed out. 'They might be hostile.'

'There is no indication that this city is dangerous,' the Doctor replied. 'Its inhabitants could not live in such an advanced society or co-operate in the construction of such a ship without having developed a civilised code of behaviour.'

'The Daleks lived in a great city, yet I'd hardly call them civilised,' Ian retorted.

The Doctor hesitated, but only for a moment. 'You can stay up here, but I am going. Susan, you may remain as well if you wish.'

'No, Grandfather, I want to find out more about the ship too.'

The Doctor smiled at her warmly.

How can he love her so much, yet allow her to take such risks, Ian wondered.

As they reached the TARDIS, Barbara said: 'Doctor, what about the people who live or work in this building? You think you can just walk past them? What if they're not even remotely human?'

'If I meet any local inhabitants I will be able to ask directly about the ship's purpose.'

'Would knowing that satisfy you... so that you wouldn't need to inspect it for yourself?' Ian asked.

The Doctor fidgeted. 'Perhaps,' he conceded grudgingly.

'Right,' Ian said. 'Let's hope we meet a friendly and well-informed local.' He looked at Barbara. 'It might be the quickest way to sort this out, then we can get going again.'

She shrugged resignedly. 'All right. Let's give it a try.'

They returned the telescope to the TARDIS and the Doctor locked the door.

Ian hoped the door set in the side of the roof building would also be locked but, though its handle was stiff, it grudgingly creaked inwards. Ian put his shoulder to it and suddenly it swung open all the way. He stumbled forward a couple of steps, then jerked back in alarm.

'Watch out!' he shouted.

Inside there was only a small catwalk suspended over a void fifty storeys deep. The building was a hollow shell.

'That gave me a bit of a start,' Ian admitted, wiping the back of his hand across his forehead. 'I expected a proper floor at least.'

The interior was crisscrossed with long beams and bracing struts. Where once there had been floors, there were now only ragged ledges running along the inside of the walls. Here and there long ladders had been slung between the supporting framework and the building's shell. Everything, including the rows of tall windows running down into the depths, was smoke-blackened.

'That explains where the ashy mud on the roof came from,' Barbara said. 'Obviously the building was gutted in a fire but they managed to save the outer walls.'

'Anyway,' Ian said with some satisfaction, 'we can't get down so that's that. Sorry, Doctor.'

But the Doctor was smiling impishly. 'Really, Chesterton? Do you see that pair of vertical beams in front of us? Note that they seem to run the full height of the building. I believe they serve as a lift shaft.'

'Not what I'd call a shaft.'

'Then what is this control unit for?'

For the first time Ian noticed a small box bolted to one of the stanchions that supported the catwalk handrail. The box had three large buttons on its front. Before anyone could stop him, the Doctor pressed the upper button.

Somewhere far down below them a motor hummed into life. A metal-frame lift cage rose out of the shadows, climbing rapidly up the vertical beams.

'It seemed logical to suppose that the people who worked on this building would have left themselves some means of ready access,' the Doctor said, beaming with overbearing self-satisfaction.

The lift halted opposite the catwalk. The Doctor opened the safety gate and beckoned them to step inside. There was another three-button control box within the cage. The Doctor pressed the lower button and they began to descend.

'Don't fret, Chesterton,' he said. 'Consider that otherwise we would have been reduced to climbing down the ladders.'

And Ian believed the Doctor might have tried it at that. He was aware that he could never underestimate the old man's stubbornness.

As they sank down between the maze of bracing struts, Susan said: 'I think those long translucent plastic rods must be temporary lights.'

Ian had already noticed them strung along almost every beam; trailing power cables that gathered into bundles which snaked away towards the lower levels of the tower.

'They're just work lights, I expect,' said Barbara. 'Maybe they're going to start rebuilding soon.'

'But why are there so many of them?' Susan wondered. 'And do you see, they're all set near the windows so that they would shine outwards. Wouldn't you want them facing inwards for working?'

The Doctor looked thoughtful but said nothing.

They stopped the lift cage beside another gantry landing. In front of them was a doorway set in the side of a rectangular box-like structure which ran through the middle of the tower.

'This must enclose one of the roadways we saw from the roof,' the Doctor said. 'We should be able to gain access to the transport network from here.'

'All right,' said Ian. 'We'll take a look outside. But at the first sign of trouble we go back up to the TARDIS, agreed?'

'Yes, yes,' said the Doctor impatiently. 'I'm not a fool you know, Chesterton.'

They opened the utility door carefully. There was a narrow raised pavement beyond, flanking a stretch of black-topped roadway. They slipped through into the tunnel and closed the door behind them.

'There's a car coming,' Susan said almost at once.

Ian tensed as the vehicle approached almost silently, with only the faintest hum of an engine, on large balloon tyres. It was painted a bright metallic scarlet and was the size of an average saloon car, but streamlined into an aerodynamic teardrop. Through a lightly tinted side window Ian glimpsed the head and shoulders of a perfectly ordinary man sitting behind the wheel. The car passed them without even slowing down.

'You see, Chesterton. Nothing to worry about,' said the Doctor.

They walked along the pavement into the grey overcast daylight and out across the dizzy heights of an aerial roadbridge. Framed between the towering edifices to one side of them stood the gleaming form of the great rocket ship.

Viewed from twenty floors lower down the city was even more impressive, yet somehow not overpowering, Ian thought. The soaring lines of the buildings were softened by fluted vertical mouldings, strongly sculpted cornices and ornamental friezes, avoiding the stark bleakness he so disliked in modern Earthly tower blocks.

Half a dozen billboard-like panels mounted on stanchions rose above the roadside railings. As they got closer to the nearest of them they saw that the images displayed on it were moving.

'They're giant television screens,' Barbara exclaimed.

Within a few feet of the nearest screen, sound suddenly cut in to accompany the pictures. A neatly dressed woman was sitting behind a desk, apparently reading a news report with calm deliberation.

'...lost contact with our automated monitoring station in Arishia,' she said. 'The last telemetric readings received showed the land had been completely submerged by a series of tidal waves.

'Once again we remind you that there are still approximately thirty-four days to go until Zero Day. The mayor's office also confirms that the final tests on the Ship are proceeding to schedule. On launch day the evacuation warning will be transmitted over all the usual channels, allowing ample time for an orderly embarkation. Meanwhile, go about your business as normal.

'And now we have this message from Bishop Fostel.'

The image changed to show a middle-aged man dressed in dark blue robes richly decorated with silver and gold thread, standing behind an altar decked with burning candles and gem-encrusted icons. His mouth, under the shadow of a hawkish beak of a nose, split into a beatific smile and he opened his arms wide in greeting. Multicoloured light radiated from behind his head to create a scintillating halo.

'Peace be upon you, Brothers and Sisters, followers of the One Maker,' he intoned solemnly. 'My message is simple. If you hold to those truths we know to be absolute and inviolate, you shall be saved!

'Meanwhile, I ask you to show compassion to those of our fellow citizens who have not yet found the One Path, and to remind them there is still time to embrace the only truth. Lead them into the light and their salvation will also be assured, joining the chosen who will rebuild the church anew on another world...'

They stepped back from the screen and the sound muted once more.

'Well, I think that explains the purpose of the ship,' Ian said. 'Some disaster is threatening this world and they're planning to leave. And so should we.'

'Quite so, quite so,' said the Doctor absently. 'But there's no need for haste, my boy. As you heard, they do not expect this calamity to strike for a month or more. But what is its exact nature, I wonder? There are still so many questions that remain unanswered.'

'For instance,' said Barbara unexpectedly, 'why several cars have passed since we've been standing here but not a single driver or passenger has even glanced at us.'

The others looked at her in surprise.

'Because we resemble the local inhabitants,' said the Doctor.

'But they haven't looked at the screens either.'

'It's good sense to keep your eyes on the road ahead while driving,' Ian said.

'Including the passengers?' Barbara persisted. 'Then why have the screens here at all? It can't be for the pedestrian traffic.'

'Barbara's right,' said Susan. 'There's nobody else in sight. We should at least get a glance.'

They all turned to watch the next car. It had a bubble top and they could see the driver clearly. His eyes, too, remained rigidly fixed on the road as he passed them.

'He appeared to be somewhat preoccupied,' the Doctor admitted, 'but no more than that.'

'We'll show you,' said Barbara, and whispered something to Susan.

The next vehicle to appear seemed to be a light delivery van, closed at the back and with a separate driver's compartment. As it came towards them, Barbara and Susan began waving wildly at it. Just as it came level Susan parted her coat and stuck out her leg provocatively.

'Susan!' the Doctor exclaimed, as the van sped past.

'Sorry, Grandfather. But did you see… he didn't take any notice of us at all!'

'They're right, Doctor,' Ian said. 'That was pretty odd.'

'Hmm.' The Doctor's face creased in thought. 'Perhaps if we…'

He was interrupted by the strident blare of a siren, issuing from the row of information screens. The images and muted voices had been replaced by large red arrows pointing back along the bridge and flashing urgently.

'Alert, alert!' boomed a harsh voice. 'Class seven meteor storm detected. City defences activated. All citizens to shelter positions. Repeat: all citizens to shelter positions!'

'Back to the TARDIS, quickly,' Ian shouted above the clamour.

They started back at a half run, letting Susan and Barbara set the pace in the lead. Ian was appalled to see how far along the bridge they had come from the mouth of the tower tunnel and suddenly felt horribly exposed.

On the city wall a searing white fireball blazed into existence and leapt into the sky, followed by a second and third.

'Interceptor missiles,' the Doctor said. 'It must have been their launch installations I saw on the wall towers.'

'Explanations later, Doctor,' Ian shouted.

The clouds were lit up from within by multiple silent explosions – the sound would take long seconds to reach them. Out over the grey ocean an incandescent thunderbolt lashed down from the sky and exploded in a towering fountain of boiling water. A second bolt struck the beach.

Then the heavens opened and it seemed to rain fire.

From the city walls narrow threads of light flickered and stabbed upwards in response. The sky filled with vaporising rock and metal.

'Laser cannon,' the Doctor panted.

A meteorite fragment slipped through the overloaded defence screen and smashed into the upper levels of a tower not a quarter of a mile away, blowing out all the windows. The air filled with the curious crescendo of its supersonic descent.

Then a car emerged from the tunnel ahead and drove serenely past them; the driver was apparently quite oblivious to the destruction pouring down from the sky.

'The fool!' Ian gasped. 'What's he think he's…?'

There was a blaze of light and a shocking raw thunderblast of sound. The surface of the bridge rippled and bucked under their feet, sending them tumbling.

Ears ringing, purple after-images floating before his eyes, Ian struggled to his knees and looked around. The others were also picking themselves up, stunned but apparently uninjured. A hundred yards behind them smoke was rising from a cratered hole, punched clean through the structure of the bridge.

Balancing on its very brink was the car that had just passed them.

'Barbara, Susan… get back to the lift,' Ian said, struggling to his feet. 'Doctor… we've got to try to get the driver out.'

The two men stumbled through the pall of smoke as scattered fragments of concrete ground under their feet. They reached the car, its gleaming sides now torn and buckled and its windows cracked and starred. Ian fumbled with the unfamiliar handle on the driver's door for a moment, then with a jerk it fell open.

'Are you all right…?' he began, only to feel the words die in his throat.

The driver was strapped in place by broad belts that crossed his shoulders and waist. His hands were still clasped around the steering yoke, while his eyes stared sightlessly ahead. But he had no legs. His torso ended in a flat plate that rested on the seat.

It was a dummy.

For an instant Ian's eyes met the Doctor's, which reflected his own utter astonishment.

Before they could speak there was a booming explosion from high above.

They spun about to see that the top of the tower where the TARDIS rested was surrounded by a spreading cloud of blast fragments. The roof deck seemed to fold in upon itself and then dropped down through the hollow shell of the building into which Susan and Barbara had run only seconds earlier.

'No!' Ian cried out in fear and despair.

He had managed just three futile strides when the road tunnel, crushed flat by the avalanche of falling debris, vomited a plume of dust into his face.

Chapter Two
The Mayor of Arkhaven

Brantus Draad's skycar circled the remains of the tower twice before receiving clearance from the reconstruction squad ground team. The pilot set the car down gently on the elevated road, on the far side of the tower from the damaged section, and Draad climbed stiffly out. Supervisor Curton greeted him and they walked clear of the wash from the car's idling fans.

'How does it look?' Draad asked.

'The shell's going to need a rebuild, Mayor. The foundations may have been damaged as well, but we can't tell until we excavate the wreckage down there.' Curton looked at Draad uncertainly. 'This close to Zero Day, I was wondering if we couldn't just make it safe and leave it be.'

Draad sighed. 'Yes, that would be the sensible thing to do, wouldn't it, Mr Curton? But you know it's not as simple as that.' He suddenly felt very tired. 'However, I'll see what I can do. Meanwhile, what was this you said about finding some NC2s up here?'

'That's right, Mayor. They're over here.'

Curton led him across to the small cluster of emergency vehicles.

Beside an ambulance a couple of city guards were watching over two strangers, both men, one with flowing grey hair, whose odd clothes showed they were not citizens. A young woman, hardly more than a girl, was being loaded into the ambulance on a life-support stretcher.

'The men had just pulled the girl from the remains of the tunnel as we arrived,' Curton explained. 'Apparently there's another NC2 woman still missing. They think she may have been in the service lift when everything collapsed.'

'How did they get out of the camp and find their way up here?' Draad asked. 'I wasn't notified of any recent escapes.'

Curton hesitated. 'In the circumstances I haven't pressed them about it yet. They seem pretty confused by what's happened and too worried about the condition of the girl and the other woman. Sorry, Mayor.'

'Even NC2s deserve our compassion,' said Draad. 'But we have security to think of, especially at times like this. What about their registration cards?'

'I asked for them, but they didn't seem to understand what I meant.'

'Thrown them away and thought they could pass themselves off as citizens, I expect. They must have been hiding out here since the last break-out, waiting for a chance to get closer to the Ship.'

The medics were trying to close the ambulance doors, but the old man seemed to be protesting, even as the younger man seemed to be trying to reason with him. The guards held him back as the doors closed and the ambulance lifted into the air, warning lights flashing urgently.

The two strangers watched it recede into the distance until it was lost in the city haze. Then they turned back to the wrecked tower, and Draad saw the bleak despair on their dirt-streaked faces. Well, they had certainly paid the price for trying to escape. He'd prefer to simply have them shipped back to the camp immediately, but there were questions that had to be answered first. He gestured to the guards to bring the men over to him.

'You realise this is a restricted zone, and you could be punished for being caught here,' he told them when they stood before him. 'However, if you co-operate, I may decide to be lenient. First, tell me when you escaped from the camp.'

They looked at him blankly, as though he was talking complete gibberish.

'Do you understand me?' he said slowly. Perhaps they were island-dialect speakers. 'Are you from the Ferren Islands?'

'We understand you perfectly,' the old man said, his voice dulled by exhaustion. 'I wanted to travel in the ambulance with my granddaughter, but they wouldn't let me. Where have they taken her? I must be with her!'

16

His fear and concern were so palpable that Draad found himself saying reassuringly: 'She'll be taken to City Central Hospital. Don't worry, she'll get the same care as any citizen. When she has recovered she will be brought back to you. Meanwhile, you will answer my question. When did you escape from the camp? Who aided you?'

The old man rubbed a shaky hand across his forehead.

'Camp! I don't know what you mean about any camp. We have just arrived here, my granddaughter is seriously injured, my friend is missing. I have no time to answer your foolish questions.'

'You'll speak politely to the mayor,' one of the guards said sharply.

'You're the mayor?' the younger man said, as though waking from a daze. 'Look, you must get more men here. We've got to try to find Barbara!'

He looked as though he wanted to go back into the ruined tower and start moving the rubble with his bare hands.

'I assure you everything will be done to find your friend,' Draad said. 'Heavy excavating equipment will be here very soon. We don't leave anybody unaccounted for after a meteor strike, even NC2s. Now, for the last time, when and how did you get out of the camp?'

'We have been in no camp,' the old man snapped back. 'We are travellers, wanderers in time and space. We arrived on this world no more than an hour ago. Our craft landed on top of this tower... I suppose it is now buried somewhere amongst the rubble. It appears externally to be a large blue box. If your men come across it –'

'Doctor!' the younger man interrupted angrily. 'Forget about the TARDIS!'

The old man looked contrite. 'Of course... I'm sorry, Chesterton. The shock. Naturally we must think of Barbara first.'

'Your, ah, spacecraft, landed on top of the tower?' Draad said slowly.

'Only in a simplistic sense,' the old man said irritably. 'But my friend is right – you must concentrate all your efforts on finding our companion. If she remained inside the lift cage there is a chance, a good chance, that she has survived.' The younger man hung his head, looking sick with worry. 'No, never despair, Chesterton. I'm sure they'll find her.' He turned back to Draad, his eyes burning fiercely. 'You promise every effort will be made, sir?'

'Yes, every effort will be made to find your friend,' Draad replied simply. 'I promise.'

'Good, good. The TARDIS can wait. It is very robust. I'm sure it has survived the fall.'

Draad's heart sank in exasperation and not a little pity. There was little point in questioning them any further. The two men were obviously delusional. Mental disorders were not uncommon amongst the last refugees they had taken in. Many of them had been convinced the world was going to be saved by divine intervention or superhuman aliens – though these were the first he had encountered who actually thought that they themselves came from outer space.

'I'm sure it has,' Draad said lightly. 'Meanwhile, let the guards take you back to the camp. That's where all newcomers to Arkhaven go. You belong there. They'll see you get new registration cards and then you can draw your rations and have a rest.'

'But I must stay here,' the younger man said.

'No, you can't do anything more here,' Draad said firmly. 'We have plenty of experience in this sort of work.' He heard the hum of powerful engines, and a large transporter rolled up. 'Look, the heavy equipment has arrived.'

The side of the truck split open and unfolded to form a ramp. From within came the whine and hiss of machinery powering up. Fluorescent orange and yellow metal limbs unfolded and wheels turned as the robot squad disembarked and marched and rolled purposefully towards the tower. Claw hands flexed and cutting beams flared as they awaited their assigned tasks.

The two men stared after the excavators in surprise, almost as though they had never seen anything like them before. They are far gone, Draad thought. The drone of a skycrane passing overhead made them look up. A bucket grab was already being lowered from its main body, supported by six multibladed fan units.

'You see, we've got every tool we need,' Draad said. 'I promise that as soon as we find anything, you'll be informed. And also about your granddaughter's condition,' he assured the older man.

The two men didn't protest further. Their evident shock and exhaustion made them tractable.

'Treat them gently,' he murmured to the guard sergeant as they were escorted away.

'Poor devils,' Curton said as he watched the guards' car depart. 'They behaved as though they really believed that nonsense.'

'I think many more of us may go that way before the end,' Draad said bitterly. 'And I don't mean just NC2s. So you'd better get this mess tidied up as soon as possible. We'll maintain the illusion a little while longer.'

Almost two hours later Draad's skycar landed him on the roof pad of the city hall. A short descent by lift took him down to his private office in the residence, which occupied most of the tenth floor.

'You have calls waiting for you, Mayor,' said Monitor as he entered. 'I judge the two most urgent are from Lord Vendam and Bishop Fostel. Shall I inform them you are now available to interface with them?'

'No. Hold all calls for a minute, Monitor.'

Draad poured himself a drink from his cabinet, swallowed a pill with it and then stood for a moment staring out of the window.

Once the view would have been of the lake and gardens of Hub Park. He remembered one hot summer night in his student days when he and a group of friends had swum in the lake and looked up at the stars. And they had laughed and joked and talked of their hopes and plans for the future, not realising that the future would turn their dreams to dust.

How could he have wasted such golden moments of peace so idly? Yet what else were such times for?

Now his friends were gone and the lake had been buried under concrete, ringed about by machine shops and site offices. Within this ring, supported by its skeletal gantry and squatting over its cavernous blast pit like some silver monster, was the Ship.

It had been known as the 'Ship' from the start. It had never needed a proper name because it was unique. The tiny probe rockets that had preceded it simply did not compare. Nothing like the Ship had ever been built in Arkhaven, or anywhere else on Sarath, as far as anybody knew. Perhaps the Taklarians had tried to construct something similar in their homeland during their last days, but by then it had been too late. No other country on the planet would have had the necessary technology even to begin such a project. The Ship would be the first and last of its kind.

To view it, Draad had to lean into the window bay and tilt his head back to see its nose cone. Each of its four outflung landing-leg nacelles rose twenty storeys high. Draad often privately likened the monstrous fins that connected them to the main hull to the flying buttresses that flanked the city cathedral. But you could have rolled the nave of the cathedral through the arch of the fins with room to spare. In other circumstances the Ship's location, in a city centre, might have been oppressive – but not in Arkhaven. Here everybody lived as close to it as possible, not only because this was the most heavily defended area of the city, but against the time when they would be called upon to board it for the first – and last – time.

Draad thought once again of that carefree night in the park. There had been a girl in the party who had been more than just a friend to him. Halfway through the night they had slipped away together. What had been her name? Surely he didn't need to check the records… But it would not come. Perhaps he should ask Monitor to call up past college registers. No. That belonged to another life he dare not let himself think about now. Either there would be time for nostalgia later – or there would be nothing.

He finished his drink, sat at his desk, and faced Monitor. Screens and displays filled the rest of the wall around the computer's audio-visual receptor and vocaliser. The mobile camera eye set within the softly glowing green ring on the wall unit regarded him impassively. That was perhaps Monitor's highest virtue – he had infinite patience. Of course, that was the way he had been programmed. He served the mayor and city of Arkhaven with unswerving mechanical loyalty.

'The bishop and Lord Vendam are calling again, Mayor,' Monitor said, the green ring about its camera eye pulsing in time with its words.

'All right. Put them on together.'

Two screens lit up to reveal Fostel and Vendam.

'Gentlemen, my apologies,' Draad said quickly. 'I was out personally inspecting the latest damage. I understand you wish to speak to me.'

Fostel and Vendam both tried to speak at once before realising they were on a three-way link. Draad kept his face carefully expressionless as they apologised stiffly – both men heartily disliked and distrusted each other.

'Mayor Draad,' said Fostel quickly, holding out three pebble-sized blackened stones towards the camera, 'meteorite fragments actually struck the cathedral during the last shower. The transept window was badly damaged. This is not to be permitted to happen again. The people must not see that the last great house of God on Sarath is vulnerable.'

'The cathedral area has been assigned the next highest priority on the defence grid after the hospital,' Draad said. 'Only the Ship and the central zone have greater protection.'

'It is easier to heal wounds of the flesh than the spirit,' said Fostel. 'I suggest you revise your priorities.'

'Bishop, this was an unusually large and intense shower that struck us with little warning,' Draad protested. 'I'm sure it will not happen again.'

'Well, if it does, I shall hold you personally responsible,' Fostel warned him.

'When you've quite finished worrying about that archaic monstrosity of a building,' Lord Vendam said impatiently, a scowl contorting his long face, 'I've had news that this strike came very close to hurting real people in Feldor Avenue and Rinthian Prospect. Now, what are you going to do about that, Draad?'

Feldor Avenue and Rinthian Prospect were almost exclusively populated by families of the Elite class; descendants of the ancient royal lines of the North. Lord Vendam's family was first amongst them.

'I can only repeat what I have told the bishop,' said Draad. 'Of course, if more resources were freed from other tasks, we might be able to improve matters. As we are now getting so close to Zero Day, we might allow damaged buildings in the Outer Zone to remain unrepaired. Then we could build another turret on the wall to improve the siting of the interceptor units.'

'Can't be done,' Vendam said. 'We must keep up proper appearances. It's good for morale.'

'I must agree with Lord Vendam,' Fostel said reluctantly. 'The city must be preserved until the last possible moment.'

'But I'm sure if we explained to them –' Draad began. Vendam interrupted him:

'You're employed to solve problems and manage the city. That's what Functionaries do best. Now you know what's required, so don't bother us about the details. Just get the job done.'

And his screen blanked.

'Remember, the cathedral must have improved protection,' Fostel reminded Draad. 'Meanwhile, I expect a repair team to be here within an hour.'

Then he also vanished.

For a moment Draad sat staring into space. The selfish narrow-minded fools, he thought. How did we ever come to deserve such anachronisms? Tradition weighs us down like a yoke around our necks. Well, soon we'll have a chance to begin again – to build something cleaner and better.

'Monitor, link me with Professor Jarrasen.'

In a few seconds Jarrasen's perpetually distracted features appeared on the screen. Pale, dark-shadowed eyes blinked out from under a mop of unruly hair, now shot through with grey. When they had started the project, Draad recalled, Jarrasen's hair had been quite black. But then so had his own, and there had been far more of it.

'Hello, Tovel. How's the Ship?'

Jarrasen managed a thin smile. 'We can launch any time. Surviving the flight is another matter. There's so much we can't test down here.'

'What do you think our chances are? Honestly.'

Jarrasen shrugged. 'I think it's fifty-fifty whether we'll be dead on arrival or not.'

Chapter Three
The Wall Zone

Ian was too sick with worry over Barbara to notice their transport had reached the camp. Only when he and the Doctor disembarked did he take in their new surroundings. There was a strip of open land perhaps half a mile wide between the outermost city buildings and the perimeter wall. The ground had evidently been cleared some time ago, leaving it resembling a huge bomb site with straggling weeds growing between scattered piles of rubble.

It was obvious where the cleared material had gone. The massive concrete ribbon of the city wall towered above them. A walkway along its summit linked the towers from which the missiles and beams had been launched against the meteor shower. Nestling against its sheer inner face was the camp, enclosed by a tall mesh fence topped by barbed wire. Floodlights and cameras were mounted on pylons at each corner. Within the outer gates a cluster of simple frame buildings formed the administration and service quarters. A second inner gate opened on to a large compound that resembled a ramshackle tented army camp.

Over the main gate was the sign: NC2 INTERNMENT CAMP.

Ian and the Doctor were processed rapidly. They were photographed and fingerprinted, given identity cards, a pack of bedding, water bottles and plastic food bowls and utensils. A bored guard led them through to the inner compound.

'You're in row E unit 17,' he said. 'Think you can find your way?'

'Certainly, young man,' snapped the Doctor, having regained some of his spirit.

'You get water from a standpipe at the end of each row,' the guard continued, unperturbed. 'Three meals a day in the mess hall. Sanitary block's over there. Listen out if your number's called over the speakers.'

They walked along hard-trodden paths that meandered around old piles of rubble between the signposted rows of tents. People stared back at them, some curiously, others beyond caring. A few wore civilian clothes in various degrees of disrepair, others were dressed in utilitarian one-piece overalls. Some tents had been enlarged with rickety extensions built with improvised materials. Whole families seemed to be living in them. It was like a refugee camp with a thousand or more inhabitants. Over it hung an air of despondent resignation.

Tent 17 row E was just big enough for the two of them. It was not made out of canvas, but from light, rigid plastic panels that clipped together. Its sole furnishings comprised two low, camp-style folding beds.

They sat on them wearily, laid their meagre possessions out and stared at each other; trying to come to terms with what had happened. After a minute the Doctor cleared his throat.

'If you want to say something, Chesterton, you might as well get it over with.'

'What are you talking about?' Ian asked flatly.

'That we wouldn't be in this situation if it wasn't for my insistence on exploring this city. Susan wouldn't have been injured... and Barbara wouldn't be missing.'

Ian looked at the Doctor with as much dispassion as he could muster. 'Is there anything I could say that would make you feel worse than you do already?'

'No, Chesterton. It is my fault, I won't deny it.'

It was almost shocking to see the Doctor so contrite.

'Then I haven't anything to say to you,' Ian said. 'Just promise me that you'll help me get us out of this mess as soon as possible.'

'Naturally I shall do everything in my power to put matters right.'

Ian resumed his private thoughts about Barbara. Realistically he knew the chances that she was still alive were slim, but he could not let himself give up hope. If they had let him stay with the rescue teams he'd know at once if they found her – alive or dead. They had seen no trace of the lift cage itself during their frantic search through the rubble. If Barbara had stayed inside, and if the cage wasn't crushed, she might just have survived. Too many ifs, but it was all he had. The waiting and uncertainty would be the worst part.

He realised the Doctor was sitting on his bed grim-faced. He must be equally concerned about Susan, Ian thought. She had looked in a bad way when they pulled her out of the remains of the road tunnel. Half-conscious, she'd kept mumbling over and over: 'Barbara pushed me clear...' Ian looked at the Doctor again and sighed inwardly. He really shouldn't add to the old man's troubles.

'I suppose it might have been worse,' he said slowly.

The Doctor stirred slightly. 'In what way?'

'None of us would have objected to staying on the roof for a while longer. Then we'd have had no warning about the meteor storm. If we'd been on the far side of the roof when it hit, the building could have collapsed before we'd got back to the TARDIS.'

The Doctor brightened slightly. 'Yes, Chesterton, that is possible.' He appeared to consider for a moment, then said: 'I thought those excavating machines looked most sophisticated. Yes, I'm sure they'll have that wreckage cleared away in no time. They'll find Barbara very soon, you'll see.'

'And if their medical facilities are equally advanced,' Ian said reassuringly, 'then I'm sure Susan will make a full recovery.'

The Doctor smiled gently. 'Thank you, Chesterton.'

They sat in silence for another minute, then Ian said: 'I don't think the mayor believed who we were or how we got here. It must seem a pretty far-fetched story without any evidence to back it up. Maybe we're lucky he only had us sent here. It might have been an asylum.'

'Never fear, they will begin to recognise the truth when they uncover the TARDIS. Then they'll want to talk to us further.'

'You're sure the TARDIS will be all right?'

'Certainly. It will take more than a fall like that to damage it.' The Doctor suddenly seemed infused with new energy, and looked more like his irascible but indefatigable old self. 'Well, we mustn't stay here feeling sorry for ourselves, Chesterton. If we are to improve our situation we must learn more about this city. Were those meteors somehow linked with the doom that seems to be facing it? What is the social order here and where do we stand within it? We cannot make progress until we establish these basic facts.'

'Perhaps we should draw some water from the standpipe,' Ian suggested. 'That'll give us a chance to meet people and ask questions.'

'Capital, my boy. Let us do that very thing.'

It didn't take them long to find a suitable informant.

They had only been standing at the standpipe for a minute, slowly filling their water bottles, when a small wiry man dressed in a ragtag assortment of clothes appeared. At first he seemed to be walking past them with his head bowed, but then he took a few oblique steps, made a sidling half-circle and was suddenly at their side. Ian had the feeling he had already been sizing them up from afar.

'Haven't seen you here before,' he said with an ingenuous smile, as his sharp eyes flicked over them. 'Just got in, have you? Where you from?'

Ian decided to try the friendly approach, though he didn't like the look of the man. There was a distinct slyness about his eyes, which didn't quite meet his gaze directly. He smiled back.

'Yes, we've just got in. My name's Ian, and this is the Doctor. We... uh, come from the Ferren Islands.'

'And who do we have the honour of addressing?' asked the Doctor quickly.

'Gelvert. Harlo Gelvert,' said the small man.

'A pleasure to meet you, sir,' the Doctor continued smoothly. 'Actually, Mr Gelvert, being new here ourselves – as you so perspicaciously observed – and having travelled some considerable distance recently, we're rather out of touch with the latest developments in the city. Perhaps you could enlighten us as to the current state of affairs.'

Gelvert's smile became shark-like. 'You want information, you've come to the right man. But, you see, I don't give anything away, I trade. Know what I mean? What you got that might be worth something?' And he eyed the Doctor's sapphire ring meaningfully.

'Small, easily portable items of high value, I presume?' the Doctor said. 'Useful to barter for favours and considerations.'

Gelvert shrugged. 'A man's got to do his best with what he's got. Make living in this place a bit more comfortable. No harm in that.'

'None at all,' the Doctor agreed heartily. 'And of course such items are also useful for a man who has to move rapidly and unobtrusively… perhaps without official approval?'

Gelvert's face did not change expression, but Ian saw the tip of his nose and cheeks suddenly become pale as the blood drained away. The Doctor's speculative shot had struck home.

'What you saying?' Gelvert asked huskily.

'That you are involved in a plot to escape from this camp,' said the Doctor, beaming. 'Perhaps we should warn the guards of our suspicions. It might improve our standing with the authorities. After all one has to do the best with what one has, as you said. Don't you agree, Chesterton?'

'Absolutely, Doctor. Now, which is the quickest way to the guard hut?'

'All right, all right,' said Gelvert frantically, dazed by the sudden reversal of roles.

'Now, shall we trade information for our silence?' the Doctor asked.

Gelvert sighed. 'What do you want to know?'

'Assume, for the sake of argument, that we are ignorant of this world's recent past and current circumstances. Tell us what has happened here.'

Gelvert frowned. 'What sort of game are you playing?'

'It doesn't matter, does it?' the Doctor inquired. 'Humour us and you have our silence.'

Gelvert looked at them suspiciously, as though he doubted their sanity, then shrugged. 'Fine, if that's what you want. Uh, better sit down over here.'

They settled on flat slabs jutting out of a pile of rubble on one side of the main camp thoroughfare.

'First, what are NC2s?' Ian asked.

'Non-Citizen, Non-Conformist, of course. Get it? If you come from outside Arkhaven, or if you don't fit in with their class laws, or speak out against the Church, you're an NC2.'

'I see,' said the Doctor. 'And apart from internment, what else do they do to NC2s?'

'They don't have to do anything, they just keep us here until the Ship lifts.'

'Ah, would that be Zero Day?'

Gelvert laughed. 'Before then, unless they're stupid.'

'Why?'

'Why! Because that's when the moon's going to smash us. Where have you been for the last ten years?'

'Never mind where, Mr Gelvert,' the Doctor snapped. 'Remember our bargain. What brought about this unfortunate state of affairs?'

Still looking at them very strangely, Gelvert said: 'An asteroid knocked it out of its orbit so it came in close to us. The equatorial regions got hit by meteor storms from the small pieces the asteroid blasted free. The moon went on out into space again, only not quite so far as before. And its orbit got a little shorter. It goes the opposite way to the way Sarath spins. Every time it makes a close pass it loses more speed. Something about our magnetic field.'

'Of course,' said the Doctor, half to himself. 'Its core must have an unusually high ferrous content. That would slow it down far more rapidly than gravitational forces alone. How large is the moon?'

'Uh, hundred and fifty Ks across, maybe.'

'Too large to destroy or deflect by conventional means,' the Doctor said. 'Yes, the devastation would be tremendous. The crust of the planet might be split wide open!'

Ian felt slightly sickened at the thought. 'So what we saw today was just a foretaste of what's to come.'

'It would be like comparing a few tossed pebbles to a landslide that carries away half a mountain,' the Doctor said solemnly. 'This city has evidently been very fortunate, so far.'

'Well away from the worst of it up here in the North,' Gelvert said. 'Only get a few strikes like today, and the odd tidal wave. Before I got here, I saw...' he faltered, as though fighting against some intolerable memory, then anger took over. 'Doesn't matter what I saw. It won't happen to me like that!'

In the silence that followed Ian said: 'So the wall was built against tidal waves.'

'And the Bronzers,' said Gelvert moodily.

'Who?'

'The Taklarians. When the moon started falling and their lands were smashed they tried to move north. Overran everything until Arkhaven stopped them. That's the last of their battle craft out there on the beach. They wanted to take a ride on the Ship.' He laughed ghoulishly. 'Now all they've got is a pile of sand as a tombstone.'

Gelvert paused as a small powered cart appeared rolling along the path. Its open back was stacked with trays of assorted small goods. It halted a little way along from them and a man in a bright green coverall got out of the cab. Several NC2s emerged from their shelters and rapidly gathered about the cart, apparently negotiating to buy items from his selection.

'Back in a minute,' said Gelvert, and joined the back of the small crowd. He was the last to be served, and Ian noticed he spoke to the trader for significantly longer than the previous customers. Eventually Gelvert turned away, tucking a few small items into the inner pockets of his long, patched coat. The trader climbed back into his cart and it trundled silently away.

'Who's that?' Ian asked Gelvert as he rejoined them.

'Lesitor. He's got the franchise to supply a few luxuries to the camp. Keep back a few ration slips and you can buy fresh fruit, sweet bars, a warm coat. Get you anything for a price. Got an eye for a good deal, has Lesitor. He'll be trading right up to the day the Ship lifts.'

31

'Yes, the Ship,' said the Doctor. 'Where is it bound?' He quickly held up a hand to forestall another incredulous response from Gelvert. 'I know you cannot believe we need to ask, but tell us anyway.'

'Mirath, of course. Next planet out from us. When the moon started falling, Arkhaven sent an automatic probe rocket there. They found it was colder than Sarath, but it had breathable air and water and even some vegetation.'

The conditions sounded to Ian rather like those Mars had once been assumed to possess. 'What do you think about going there?'

Gelvert stared at them in frank disbelief. 'You really don't know, do you? Why do you think the people in this place look like they're already in the morgue?'

'Perhaps you would enlighten us,' the Doctor said.

For the second time Gelvert sounded angry and resentful, and a little colour came to his bony cheeks.

'When Arkhaven started building the Ship they designed it to carry their own people and the tools and supplies they'd need on Mirath, plus a bit of space for special cargo. But that was before the war refugees from the other cities started arriving. Now there's only room for a few extra people with special skills, or those the Elite families want as servants... slaves more like!

'The rest of us stuck in here,' he jabbed his finger, 'that's you and me, they're just going to leave behind. For a few days after the Ship lifts we'll have the whole city to ourselves. Then the moon'll hit.' Gelvert punched his fist into his palm. 'And the world'll crumble to pieces under our feet!'

Chapter Four
Underground

Barbara slowly recovered consciousness.

It was an effort to force open her eyes. When she did there was nothing but blackness and it took her several blinks to decide that her eyes really were open and that there simply wasn't any light to see by.

She was lying on her back with the taste of grit in her mouth. Her head was pounding and she felt dangerously sick. Every part of her body seemed to ache - but she was alive.

Stay still, she told herself. Get your breath back. Wait until everything stops spinning round.

She remembered the moments before the lift fell.

There had been a swelling roar as an avalanche of concrete filled the hollow shell of the building, smashing into the lattice of bracing struts and snapping them like matchsticks. Instinctively she had pushed Susan back through the door of the lift, even as its supporting beams shivered and then bowed outwards under the impact of the descending debris. Metal screeched as one set of lift-runners came free of their supporting beams, the sudden shock of separation jerking her off her feet before she could follow Susan. Some automatic safety brake on the remaining runners slowed the lift's fall, but to Barbara it still seemed to plummet like a stone. It struck bottom with enough force to drive the breath from her body, even as debris began to pound its metal frame.

Then there was a blank.

Now she lay in blackness, its silence broken only by the sound of her breathing. As her daze lifted she became aware of a length of ribbon twisted about her hand. It took her a moment to work out what it was. Mustn't lose that, she thought muzzily, and tucked it into the seam pocket of her slacks. Even this simple movement hurt.

At least the lift cage had protected her from being crushed. What were a few bruises compared to that? But she was still buried under many tons of rubble, somewhere in the lower levels of the tower.

She began to feel panic rising within her but firmly quashed the sensation before it had a chance to take hold. Losing control of yourself won't do you any good, she thought. Wait until you feel better before trying to do anything.

She diverted herself for a minute or two by planning what she would say to the Doctor when she next saw him. Still, she knew he would do everything he could to find her. Ian and Susan would see to that. Yes, they would all come for her eventually.

But how long would it take?

If only she had a light.

Wait a minute, she thought. Inside the lift cage beside the control panel there had been a tubular object held in place by a spring clip. She hadn't paid it much attention at the time but it could have been a torch. It made sense to leave one there. Now if only she could find it.

Feeling the wave of sickness slowly subsiding she tried to sit up.

'Oww!' she gasped and lay quickly back down again.

She had cracked her head on something no more than two feet above the floor of the lift. Cautiously she reached upwards and felt buckled metal mesh, that had been torn through in places by the broken edges of concrete blocks. It must be the roof of the lift cage. It had been hammered down almost on top of her.

How much weight must it be supporting – and how long would it continue to bear the load?

Again she fought down the impulse to panic. This was not the time or place. Later she would let her feelings out, but not now.

She reached out experimentally on either side. Her right hand brushed against crumpled heavy wire mesh. Yes, that must be the side panel of the lift cage. She rolled over, wincing as jagged shards of concrete ground into her, and pulled herself up to it. Now, feel along until you reach the corner post, she told herself. There it is. Now, if this is the front of the cage, the control panel should be up here and the clip should be to the right. Her questing hand ran across twisted mesh until it closed on what she sought. It was still in its place! She pulled it free, fumbled until she found a button on its side and pressed.

White light flooded the cramped space. Her gasp of relief was choked back as she saw the entire roof of the cage was bulging downwards to a frightening degree. The tilted and warped floor was already littered with dust and small fragments of stone that had apparently been driven through the many rents in the framework.

Somewhere in the mass of debris above her stone cracked and metal gave forth a rending twang. A dribble of dust and grit pattered softly on to the lift floor. She looked about desperately. The lift door was wrenched half off its hinges. Beyond was a crazy jumble of concrete blocks and a twisted length of metal beam. Between them was a narrow aperture framed by the dancing shadows cast by the torch.

Barbara twisted round and kicked at the door, bending it back far enough for her to squeeze through. The lift cage groaned and squealed and the roof sagged lower.

She forced herself through the gap between the twisted mesh panels of the door. The hem of her jumper caught on a snag of wire, pulling her backwards. She tore it free with a frantic jerk, ripping the yarn, and hauled herself clear.

She crawled through an arch formed by two crossed pieces of concrete beam and, at her heels, the cage folded up and was crushed flat. Immediately the arch began to collapse in turn as the pressure from above shifted to fill the new void.

Ignoring scrapes and grazes Barbara scrambled frantically along on her hands and knees, trying to hold the torch as she went, slithering into whatever gap next presented itself. All she cared about was getting clear of the settling mass of wreckage, driven by the horror that any second now it would all give way, trapping her helplessly as it crushed the life from her.

Her hands pressed down on a slab that rocked and then suddenly tilted upright. Before she could stop herself she fell forward headfirst into a black hole, taking a shower of loose rubble with her.

She struck the floor of a shaft running downwards at an angle of about thirty degrees. Its sides were wet and slick with slime and Barbara began to slide. She scrabbled frantically but could not find any grip to slow her descent.

Then the slope of the shaft abruptly flattened and she was shot out into a black void. Even as she screamed in utter terror she struck water with an echoing splash. Coughing and spluttering she surfaced, threshing about wildly for a moment until she found her feet were touching the bottom. She stood upright and found the water only came up to her hips, lapping about them under the impetus of a gentle current.

She was still holding the torch; locked in her clasp by the fear of being lost in the dark once more. She had to steady it with her other hand, and realised she was trembling violently. Its beam illuminated a ledge rising clear of the water just a few feet from her. Above it a dark wall curved up and over to form the roof of a large tunnel. She waded over to the ledge, hauled herself out of the water and lay there panting.

She felt cold, wet, miserable, bruised and frightened. She pulled her knees up to her chest and allowed herself to cry heartily for a full minute.

When it was done she felt better. She sat up, wiped her eyes, and then took a careful look round at her new surroundings.

The tunnel, perhaps twenty feet across, vanished beyond the range of her torch beam in either direction. From where she sat she could see three openings spaced along its sides, identical to the one she had emerged from so dramatically. She guessed she was in part of a storm-drain system. It was not the most pleasant location but she consoled herself with the thought that it could have been a sewer. The air was damp with the smell of mildew but the water seemed relatively clean.

So, what should she do next?

There was certainly no way she could climb back up the shaft she had come down. It might even be dangerous to try with all that wreckage up there. But when the Doctor and Ian and Susan came looking for her they would eventually uncover the upper opening. She would hear the activity and could call up to them.

But how long would that take? If the whole building had collapsed it might be days before they could dig down that far, assuming they could get help from the locals. They might think she was already dead. If she could get herself back up to the surface, then she could spare them a lot of needless anxiety.

Suddenly Barbara pounded the sides of her head with her clenched fists in disgust. 'Self, self self!' she shouted angrily, the words echoing down the tunnel.

She had been so wrapped up in her own plight that she had forgotten that the others might have problems of their own. Did Susan get clear in time? If there had been another meteor strike on the roadway while Ian and the Doctor were still out there...

She scrambled to her feet as rapidly as her stiffening and bruised muscles would allow. There was no way she could wait passively to be rescued. She had to get out as soon as possible.

If she simply followed the direction of the flow of water she would be bound to come to some sort of maintenance access point or to the tunnel's outfall. Then she could make her way back to the others long before they could reach her.

But, just in case, she would leave a sign.

She made her way along the ledge until she reached the point below the shaft she had fallen through. Grimacing, she slid back into the water and felt around with her feet until she found a fist-sized splinter of concrete that had come down with her. She pulled herself back on to the ledge and began scraping at the stonework under the lip of the shaft. In a few minutes she had marked a bold B-> in the wall, with the arrow pointing in the direction she intended to travel.

Then, torch shining hopefully ahead of her, Barbara set off down the tunnel.

Chapter Five
Hospital

The autosystem monitoring the new patient's progress beeped urgently, informing senior clinician Nyra Shardri that all was not well.

She left her station in the middle of the intensive care unit and crossed over to recovery tank five. She could have called up the information on her own console, but she liked to get close to her charges. Of course the machines did the actual work, but she felt human contact should be a part of the healing process. Theoretically, she could even take over if the machines and their back-ups failed. She had done well in simulated medical emergencies, but so far she had never been put to the test with a real person. A century ago practically all medical procedures had been performed by humans – their primitive machines were there only to assist them. Now nobody in Arkhaven would trust themselves exclusively to a human doctor.

Within the tank a pale-faced young woman dressed in a hospital gown rested on a contoured body pad. Robot arms had already put the usual support and monitoring lines in place. Re-gen pads on her head, chest, left arm and right leg indicated that major injuries were being stimulated into accelerated healing.

The display read:

NC2-Susan Foreman. Traumatic shock victim. No identity code/registration number. No previous medical history.

A list of her injuries was displayed:

Concussion. Minor depression fracture to anterior of left parietal bone causing pressure on brain. Major bone fractures: clavicle, right side (compound); third and fourth ribs, right side; radius, left side; ulna (two places) left side; tibia, left side (compound). Minor damage to thoracic vertebrae. Various puncture injuries and lacerations to trunk and left leg. Blood loss. Shock.

Treatment: Parietal pressure relieved and bone fragment set. Spinal column re-aligned and nerve regeneration initiated. Major bone fractures aligned and set, bone regeneration fields established. Wounds cleaned and tissue bonded, external derma dressings applied. Intravenous fluids and blood transfusion to replace traumatic losses and alleviate shock. Standard antibacterial and antiviral agents administered.

Ongoing treatment: Deep-scanning brain, spine and internal organs. Elevating body temperature to counter hypothermic fall.

The girl's core body temperature had been unusually low, Nyra noticed, which was quite common in shock cases. But it was not responding to the standard treatment of intravenous fluids and gradual external warming. Her pulse rate had also been very low, though steady, with surprisingly good blood volume in the circumstances. Now Nyra saw it too was not responding to the normal stimulation.

She consulted the cardiac display, noticing a curious double peak.

'Re-tune heart monitor to remove echo,' she ordered.

A message flashed up: *Monitor operating within optimum parameters. No echo detected.*

Nyra frowned. What was the matter with it?

Now she saw that the encephalograph was also displaying a strange pattern. It was not dangerous, so it had triggered no alarms, but it was, well, odd.

A message flashed up to show that the results of the blood and biopsy analysis were ready. Nyra examined them with a growing sense of disbelief. They made no sense whatsoever.

'Run self-diagnostic on sample analysis unit,' Nyra ordered. If the unit was faulty she wanted it replaced at once.

After a minute the message appeared: *Self-diagnostic confirms unit is operating within optimum parameters.*

That was ridiculous, Nyra thought. Nobody had a body chemistry like that. Except that it seemed at least one person did, and she was lying right in front of her.

Well, whatever the girl's peculiarities, she was still a patient in her care. Was the synthetic blood they were supplying her with compatible? It was multi-spectrum and non type-specific. But in any case they had nothing better. What else could she do? Nyra wondered. For a start, check for any other abnormalities.

She called up the results of the deep scan, only to stare in disbelief at the images on the screen. There were no internal organ injuries so the system had not initiated further treatment, thereby ignoring, with mechanical indifference, something very strange indeed.

What was that... or rather, what were those?

Susan's consciousness flickered in the depths of her mind.

She knew she had been badly injured. She sensed there was damage to portions of her brain and spine that had to be attended to at once, otherwise she would be forced to take the final option, which would be dangerously premature at her age. There was a way she could treat herself, but it was a skill she had never used before except in practice. She only wished her grandfather was there to guide her. Still, there had to be a first time for everything.

Warning lights lit up all over the tank's display panels as urgent messages trailed across the screens.

Brainwave activity diminishing. Body temperature decreasing. Pulse and respiration falling.

Nyra stared at them in horror. For no reason at all, it seemed her patient was suddenly dying. And no form of stimulation the tank could apply was halting the decline.

Inexorably Susan's pulse and respiration dropped below measurable values. Her brainwave activity was reduced to shallow flickering lines.

Nyra knew there was only one option left.

She hit a button initiating terminal emergency stasis.

The interior of the tank filled with chill white vapour, washing over Susan's still form and obscuring her from view. The body monitor readings abruptly fell to zero.

Nyra gave a little sigh of relief.

Death had, once again, been put on hold. The system had bought them a little time in which to find out what had – almost – killed her most unusual patient.

Chapter Six
Break-Out

A restless but unnaturally mild wind blew out of the night, tearing the overcast sky into racing tatters of cloud and revealing fleeting glimpses of the stars. There was no rain yet but Ian sensed it was building to a storm.

His mood darkened with the weather. Surely they should have heard some news from the rescuers at the tower by now. Always assuming the mayor's instructions had been passed along properly. He clenched his fists. He couldn't stand much more waiting. Another hour and he would go to the camp office and demand they find out how the work was progressing.

He glanced across at the Doctor, who was sitting on his bed staring at the city through the half-open door of their shelter. There was little else to do in the camp. Gelvert had been the most garrulous person they'd met. Others had responded to their inquiries in monosyllables or else ignored them completely, as though they had already given up on life and were merely marking time before the inevitable end. A few had hurled abuse in their faces. There had been a wild look in their eyes which showed how close they were to breaking point.

Ian understood now why the mayor had humoured the Doctor and himself. And he also knew that he would find it difficult to maintain an equilibrium if he had to live under effective sentence of death for months.

Yet he could not take in the full implications of the situation. The city around him, the very land on which it rested, was going to be destroyed by a cataclysmic event of such magnitude that it was beyond his comprehension. The death of an individual he could understand, but not the death of a world. He accepted the concept intellectually but not in his heart. Perhaps that was for the best. Otherwise he might end up like those poor wretches around them.

He thought of the handful of young children they had seen playing about the shelters and briefly his thoughts turned from Barbara. The children had seemed unaware of their fate and their play had brought forth the few smiles they had seen in the camp. It was heart-wrenching – whatever their parents might have done, they were innocents. Surely the city rulers could find room for them, at least, inside the vast escape ship, the illuminated spire of which was clearly visible from the camp.

The Doctor suddenly spoke up, intruding on Ian's reverie. He was pointing at the city across the waste ground. 'Chesterton. Tell me what you see.'

Ian couldn't understand the point of the question, but he gave a straight enough response.

'Lights… Windows and street lights, illuminated tube trains, a few moving cars. That's what you expect in a city at night.'

'Exactly,' said the Doctor. 'But can you see any people?'

'No, of course not.'

'Then how do you know they're there?'

'Well, we know they are.'

'Really. How many people have we seen so far, outside this camp? A dozen, twenty perhaps?'

'About that.'

'Then why do you presume there are any more of them?'

'Look, a city this size must hold millions of people.'

'Wrong, Chesterton. A city this size *might* hold millions of people. But all we see are lights. For instance, observe the windows of those buildings closest to us, as I have been doing for the past hour. Wouldn't you expect to see them turned off or on, or twinkle occasionally as curtains or blinds were drawn?'

'Yes, I suppose so.'

'Well, I have seen nothing of the sort. And recall the lights strung up inside the hollow shell of the building we landed on. They were designed to illuminate the windows to make the building *appear* inhabited. And what about the dummy driver we found in the car? What if all the cars we had seen were similarly arranged?'

Ian pinched the bridge of his nose, feeling his head throbbing. He wasn't really up to contemplating such puzzles at the moment. 'But why? What on earth would be the point of such a deception?'

'A few possibilities suggest themselves,' the Doctor said. 'But they will keep until the morning. You look tired, my dear boy. This day has been a terrible strain on both of us. We should try to get a little sleep.'

Ian knew the Doctor was right. 'Perhaps just for an hour or so. I want to check with the camp office later, to see if there's any more news.'

He turned off the dim, battery-powered light in the ceiling of the shelter and they lay down on their beds. He couldn't sleep, but it made sense to rest.

Ian must have dozed despite his anxiety, because when he was jerked back into wakefulness there was rain splattering on the roof. But it was not that which had woken him. There was somebody else inside the shelter with them.

He heard the Doctor give a shout of alarm even as a hand closed about his own mouth. He lashed out by reflex, felt his fist connect with a cheekbone and heard a stifled grunt of pain. Some blunt heavy object smashed into the side of his bed, missing his head by a fraction of an inch. In desperation he kicked out into the darkness, his foot catching one of his assailants in the stomach. He struggled to his feet, swinging punches at shadows.

Suddenly a pale grey rectangle of light appeared as the shelter door burst open. For a moment three figures were silhouetted against it, then they were gone.

He plunged through the doorway after them and ran a few steps beyond, but the rain-lashed night had already swallowed the intruders. Shaking his head angrily he splashed back into the shelter and switched on the light. The Doctor was sitting on the side of his bed, his clothing in disarray, cradling his right arm and flexing his fingers gingerly.

'Doctor... are you all right?'

'Thank you, Chesterton... yes.' The Doctor wheezed slightly. 'I think they were after my ring. Fortunately they did not succeed in removing it.'

'Was one of them Gelvert? Or friends of his, perhaps? He had his eye on your ring earlier.'

'I thought the voice of one of those you struck sounded familiar, but I could not swear it was Gelvert.'

'I bet it was. But as all they got were bloody noses I suppose it's not worth reporting.'

Ian righted his bed, which had been tipped over in the struggle, and sat down, brushing back his damp hair.

'But why bother stealing trinkets when the world, quite literally, is coming to an end soon? The only thing of real value left would be a ticket on that spaceship, and I don't suppose that can be bought with any amount of money or precious rings.'

'Not a ticket itself, perhaps,' mused the Doctor, 'but perhaps a step towards it...'

He faltered, patting his pockets with a growing sense of urgency. Now he looked at Ian in concern. 'Search the floor, Chesterton. I think they tore the TARDIS key from me in the struggle.'

They examined the floor and then turned the bedding inside out. There was no sign of the key.

'Well there's no point in looking outside in this weather,' said Ian. 'We'll have to wait until morning.'

'You understand we cannot get back inside the TARDIS without it,' the Doctor reminded him gravely.

'They probably snatched it thinking it was valuable,' Ian said. 'When they have a chance to examine it no doubt they'll simply throw it away. It can't be any use to them. We might still find it. If not, Susan's got one, hasn't she? It will be with her things at the hospital...' He trailed off as he saw the expression on the Doctor's face.

'Chesterton, do you recall seeing Susan's key when we rescued her?'

'Well... no. But I was hardly paying attention to a detail like that.'

'No, neither was I, more's the pity. But I do not think she was wearing it around her neck as usual. She must have lost it in the ruins of the tower. If that key is missing as well, then even when the TARDIS is recovered, we'll never be able to leave this world!'

For a moment they could only stare at each other hopelessly. Then the Doctor rose, his chin set at a determined angle.

'We must make every effort to track down our attackers. First let us alert the guards. They must search Gelvert's shelter... if it's not already too late.'

Holding the waterproof liners of their beds over them like capes, they left their tent and walked briskly towards the administration block.

'I can't blame Gelvert for wanting to escape from here,' Ian said. 'I don't like the idea of informing on him. We promised we'd keep quiet.'

'Any understanding we had with him is over,' the Doctor said sharply. 'We must make the most of the situation. Now it has become even more urgent to convince the authorities that we are not common refugees.'

They reached the guardhouse only to find that the sentry in the outer office was half-asleep before a bank of monitor screens. No wonder people are planning escapes if their guards are as slack as this, Ian thought.

'We have been attacked and robbed,' the Doctor told the man sharply, jerking him into resentful alertness. 'An item of some value has been stolen. I believe one of the thieves was a man called Harlo Gelvert. I demand that you check his quarters immediately.'

'You NC2s are always stealing from each other,' the guard replied irritably. 'Come back in the morning, make your complaint, we'll look into it then.'

A determined glint entered the Doctor's eye. 'You might be interested to know that Gelvert is planning an escape. In fact he may have already accomplished it. Now, what will your commanding officer say if he learns that you waited several hours before acting on our information?'

With a scowl of annoyance the guard unwillingly checked Gelvert's shelter number, detailed another sentry to watch over them, and stumped off into the rain.

He was back inside three minutes at a run and rapidly began punching buttons on the control board.

Additional lights came on all around the camp perimeter and a siren started to wail mournfully. Spotlights on the fence pylons flared into life and began quartering the waste ground.

'Looks as though Gelvert has done it,' Ian said to the Doctor. 'How did you guess he would go so quickly?'

'It was a strong possibility. I don't think he would risk such a blatant theft unless he was ready to leave. My ring was no doubt intended to top up his funds for use on the outside. When the attempt failed he suspected we might alert the authorities and so left immediately. From his behaviour earlier I suspect he has been planning the escape for some time. Ahh... I presume this is the camp commandant.'

A large red-faced man entered the guardhouse still adjusting his uniform. 'What's going on here?' he demanded.

'A complaint from these prisoners led us to investigate unit R8, sir,' the guard reported unhappily. 'All its occupants are missing. We believe they have escaped.'

'Turn out the camp for roll call.'

In minutes the camp was roused and every internee was paraded and checked off, shivering and bleary-eyed in the rain. Apart from Gelvert fourteen men and two women from four different huts were unaccounted for.

'Dismiss them,' the commandant ordered wearily when the roll was complete. 'Then start checking the fence and review the visual log.'

'What about the two who raised the alarm, sir?' the guard asked, indicating Ian and the Doctor.

'What? Oh no, it's best if you keep them here for the moment. I may want to question them later. Meanwhile I'd better alert the Watch.'

He walked heavily through to the inner office.

'He sounded fed up with the whole business,' Ian observed, as they sat on a bench in the anteroom. 'I would have expected him to sound less resigned and more angry.'

'Considering the lax standards of this camp I suspect this is not the first such escape he has been obliged to report,' said the Doctor.

A few minutes later a car painted military drab rolled in through the gates. A smart young officer in a dark green uniform emerged from it and entered the guardhouse. He glanced curiously at Ian and the Doctor before being shown through to the commandant.

As he rested his head on the adjoining wall, Ian found he could just hear what was being said within. He nudged the Doctor and they both listened intently.

'This is the fourth escape in three months,' the newcomer was saying. 'Haven't you been able to plug the gaps in your security yet?'

'I've done my best, Captain,' the commandant replied stiffly. 'But they don't send me the extra men or equipment I need. It's a matter of priorities, apparently, and right now NC2s are at the bottom of the list. If you think you can do better, you can have my job any time you want and welcome to it!'

'There's no need to take that tone with me, Breen. I'm just doing my job. When NC2s escape they become the City Watch's responsibility.'

'Yes, and how many do you catch and bring back? A handful, less than ten per cent. That doesn't sound so very efficient. When you start recovering half of them maybe you can start telling me how to run my camp.'

'What are you talking about, ten per cent?'

Breen smiled grimly.

'I keep records, you know, and I can count.'

'Well, I can't explain the numbers. I'm only standing in for Captain Terrel... he's off sick... and his squad reports directly to Commander Pardek. But I'll do what I can to get you the extra resources you need.'

'Thank you, Lant. I'd appreciate that.'

'Meanwhile we have your NC2s to find. Do you know how they got out yet?'

'None of the fence alarms were triggered. At the moment your guess is as good as mine. Frankly, we're still puzzling over how the last group managed it. We even had the compound scanned for tunnels, though it's bedrock only a metre down. There was nothing, of course.'

'I had no idea things were so bad,' Lant said.

Breen gave a hollow laugh. 'It's not been widely advertised. They don't want the populace alarmed. You know what most people think of NC2s. The few we do get back won't say how they got out, and we can hardly beat it out of them. What *can* we threaten them with? Probably they hope to use the same method again.'

'I'm beginning to understand your problem.'

'Well, try to impress it on the council. This sort of thing is going to happen more often when the NC2s accept that we really can't take them with us and they realise they've nothing to lose. We'll have to increase security soon or else they'll riot. If only they'd sent me the...'

'Time to make our move,' the Doctor said to Ian quickly. He got up, opened the door of the inner office and was halfway through it before the surprised guards could respond. 'Perhaps I can be of assistance,' he said to Lant and Breen amiably.

'Who are these men?' Lant asked, regarding them with deep intelligent eyes.

'They reported the escape. Go back outside, you two. I'll speak to you later.'

'But we overheard you speculating on the method by which Gelvert and his associates may have escaped,' the Doctor continued, 'and I thought you might benefit from our advice. But apparently I was wrong. Come on, Chesterton. It seems we are not needed.'

And he made to withdraw.

'Wait!' Commandant Breen snapped. 'Do you know how it was done?'

'I do not know from first-hand knowledge, if that is what you are implying, sir,' the Doctor replied with dignity, 'but I can deduce the most likely method used, bearing in mind the prevailing conditions at the time of the escape. Unless it is proven that the escapees simply walked out of the front gate past your somnambulistic guards, I can suggest the most likely section of fence to examine and save you much wasted time.'

He's got their full attention now, Ian thought. I only hope he knows what he's talking about.

'All right,' Captain Lant said, 'how do you think it was done?'

'First I must confirm that your security system works as I suspect. You have visual monitors mounted on the towers, infra-red sensors beyond the perimeter and the fence itself is no doubt alarmed? Come, sir, do not be reticent. Your security has already been breached. You can lose nothing by admitting the facts.'

Breen hesitated for a moment, then nodded.

'Then I can tell you what most probably occurred. Taking advantage of the downpour which obscured the cameras, Gelvert and his accomplices would have made their way to a point equidistant from the towers on the longest stretch of fence facing the waste ground. There they either cut through the fence themselves, after connecting bypass leads around the section, or else passed through a hole that had already been prepared for them...'

'What!' Breen exclaimed. 'You cannot be suggesting that a citizen helped them?'

'Very probably. To evade your heat sensors they would have needed thermal scattering blankets. Where would they get them from? Perhaps you should ask the trader, what was his name... yes, Lesitor. We noticed Gelvert talking to him at some length earlier in the day. Anyway, once clear of the camp they could have reached the edge of the city in five minutes. You really should level the intervening ground properly, it provides far too much cover.' Before Breen could respond, the Doctor glanced out of the window. 'Ah, I see the rain is easing off. Shall we examine the fence?'

It was just as the Doctor had said.

A corner of mesh panel, adjoining a stanchion post between two watchtowers, had been cut through and repaired several times with conductive metallic adhesive of a matching colour. The bulges formed by the adhesive on the mesh were so slight that they would have passed all but the closest inspection. A couple of lengths of wire with spring-clip ends remained in place across the cut section.

'They were too hurried this time to finish hiding their tracks,' said the Doctor. 'No doubt due to our prompt raising of the alarm.'

As Breen and Lant conferred, Ian said quietly: 'I'm not sure I like the way you've implicated that trader, Doctor. After all, he was only helping what amount to refugees and political prisoners to escape.'

'Lesitor was no doubt exploiting those he aided for his own ends, not acting out of some noble sense of altruism,' the Doctor replied brusquely. 'My ring was probably intended as payment to him. He was playing on the hopes and fears of vulnerable people. But was it simply for monetary reward? I suspect there is more going on here than meets the eye. These are not isolated incidents, there is method behind them. How else can you explain…'

He broke off as Lant came up to them.

'I want to know why you are doing this,' he said simply. 'If you hadn't pointed this escape route out, you might have used it yourselves.'

'Ah, but we have no intention of attempting anything so crude,' the Doctor said with a twinkle in his eye. 'When we leave here it will be quite open and above board.'

Lant frowned. 'Well, Breen's grateful enough, I grant you. No doubt you'll have an easy time here. But if you think this buys your way on to the Ship, I'm sorry but you're mistaken.'

'That was never our plan either. This little exercise has simply served to attract the attention of somebody in authority, such as yourself,' the Doctor explained with disarming candour.

'You have my attention,' Lant said. 'Go on.'

'We only ask three simple favours. First, would you please check on the condition of my granddaughter, Susan Foreman. She was taken to your City Hospital earlier today after being badly injured. I have not yet had any news of her.'

'I can do that. Next?'

'A friend of ours may be trapped in the damaged building where your people first found us... I do not know the address but I'm sure it is on record. Please monitor the progress of the work for any news of her. Also there will be a blue box, rather taller than a man, in the remains. It will be undamaged and you will not be able to open it by any means at your disposal. You may wish to bring its existence to the attention of the mayor, and to remind him that the explanation we gave when we first met was the truth.'

'What explanation?'

'Ahh, if I told you that now, without evidence, you would not believe me.'

'Really,' said Lant dubiously. 'And the third favour?'

'If you find the man Gelvert, he may have a key on him tied to a length of black ribbon. It was the item he stole from me. If you find the key, I will show you what is inside the box.'

Lant gave them a very searching look, then nodded. 'All right, I'll see what I can do. Meanwhile, I suggest you get back to your tent.'

The Doctor rubbed his hands together with satisfaction as they walked back through the darkened camp. 'Most promising, eh, Chesterton? Captain Lant's curiosity has been piqued sufficiently for him to co-operate. We shall soon be out of here, never fear.'

'Yes, Doctor,' Ian said grudgingly. 'Very neatly done. But what is going on here?'

The Doctor frowned. 'There is something very wrong with this city and this camp.' He gazed into the distance, musing half to himself. 'Escapes on this scale, primitive security systems... No, no. If it wasn't absurd, I would almost say somebody was giving these people a chance to escape.'

'But that's ridiculous!'

'As you say, my dear boy, ridiculous. But ask yourself; what happens to the nine out of ten NC2s that are not recaptured?'

Chapter Seven
End of the Tunnel

Laboriously Barbara scratched another B-> mark on the side wall of the tunnel. She was feeling desperately tired and increasingly dispirited.

As far as she could estimate, her watch having stopped, she had been travelling for six hours. It had been hard, slow going. The ledge pathway was narrow and slippery and twice she had fallen into the culvert stream, on the second occasion cracking her knee badly so that she now walked with a limp. In several places she had to work her way round piles of rubble from collapsed walls. Each time she glanced nervously up at the cracks radiating across the arched concrete roof over her head, hoping she would not bring it down on top of her.

So far she had found two ladders set in the sides of the tunnel, rising through shafts to what might have been manholes. But the heavy metal covers would not budge and there had been no response when she pounded on them and shouted for help. She had not expected when she set out that the only exits from the drains might be sealed.

Now she was wondering how far she could continue. Thirst would soon force her to drink some of the drain water and pangs of hunger were also making themselves felt. Meanwhile the chill of her damp clothes was steadily sapping her strength.

Then she became aware of a new sound beyond a bend ahead of her, rising above the soft lap and splash of the stream. It was an echoing rush of breaking water and was growing steadily louder. Could it be the outfall of the drainage system? She almost ran forward, slipping and sliding dangerously, longing for the first sight of daylight.

She rounded the corner... and her heart sank.

Three feeder tunnels, similar to the one she had travelled along, met in a chamber half-full of dark swirling water. On the far side was the low arch of the main outlet into which they emptied, but its mouth was closed off by a heavy grille of close-set bars that extended from the roof down into the water. Perhaps the stream did eventually lead to the outside, but there was no way she could follow it any further.

Barbara sank down on to the narrow ledge that skirted the edge of the chamber and buried her head in her hands. Either she would have to return to her starting point, or else explore the side tunnels. How many miles might they run? Would all their access shafts be closed off as well?

As she brooded she switched off her torch to save its battery. But after a few minutes the absolute darkness became oppressive. She began to hear words hidden within the rush and gurgle of the water and thought Ian was calling to her. She almost shouted back in response before she realised it was all in her mind.

She switched the torch on again.

The beam shone by chance at a low angle along the line of the ledge, and picked out imprints in the thin crust of damp silt that had been deposited over the years. She peered closer. There were unmistakably two sets of large, fresh bootmarks. One set headed in the direction she had come, the second overlay them and came back the other way.

Somebody had been down here recently, perhaps within the last few days. And if she followed the second set of bootmarks they must eventually lead to an exit. It might just be another one of those sealed shafts, of course, but what had she got to lose now?

Holding the torch low and moving in a half-stoop she set off, following the tracks down one of the feeder tunnels.

For a hundred yards the trail was easy to follow. Then it gradually began to be obscured by other prints, as though several people had walked back and forth over a short distance, treading the soil flat and hard. That sort of traffic would suggest a junction or place of special interest, but the tunnel was quite bare at that point. Biting her lip she pressed on, hoping the trail would become clearer.

And in a few yards it did, reducing to just two sets of bootmarks once more. Except that now the top set of prints was facing in the opposite direction.

Barbara frowned and went back to the point at which the tracks had become obscured. There was still nothing to be seen – but why the heavy traffic? She knelt down and examined the ground closely. Caught in the angle between ledge and wall were a few grains of pale grit and sand, distinctly lighter in tint than the concrete of the tunnel itself.

She looked up at the wall, holding the torch flat so that its beam skimmed the surface, and ran her fingertips over the harsh cold concrete. Very gradually she began to make out a disc a little over a yard across that was not quite flush with the surrounding wall.

Perhaps it was a maintenance hatchway of some kind, she thought. If she had been less weary she would have wondered why it was not marked more distinctly. But she was close to the limits of her endurance and all she could think about was finding a way out.

She banged on the hatch with the flat of her hand, then with her clenched fist.

'Hello!' she called out. 'Is there anybody in there? Please help me... I'm lost.'

There was no response or any sound to indicate anybody was on the other side. She banged again, beginning to feel desperate.

'Please answer if you can hear me. I just want to get out of here and back up to the surface.'

Without any warning there came a slight grating noise. The hatch disc moved smoothly inwards like a plug and swung to one side. In the darkness beyond she could just make out the vague form of a large man.

'Thank you,' Barbara gasped. 'I was beginning to...'

A gun barrel emerged from the shadows, there was a soft pop of air and Barbara felt something sting her neck. Instinctively she clawed at the spot and felt the end of a tiny dart protruding from her skin. She tried to call out but already an insidious numbness was spreading through her body. The torch fell from her limp fingers on to the ledge; coming to rest, it threw her shadow across the arch of the tunnel.

With an expression of wide-eyed surprise frozen on her face, Barbara silently toppled backwards into the black waters of the culvert.

Chapter Eight
Sport

Once the Sentinel Club had been the city rendezvous for the elite of Arkhaven, when they travelled to the capital from their country estates across the continent. When the war with the Taklarians had started the club had filled with men in uniform; discussing battles or preparing to join their regiments. Few had ever returned.

Now half its rooms were closed, roboservers gathered dust and only a handful of human servants remained. It had become the meeting place for the sons of those who had gone to war. The only uniforms to be seen were worn by the young men in service with the wall batteries. Though the batteries were essential to the city there was little satisfaction in the duty. Without the possibility of actual combat it was the sort of work that could be left to machines and Functionaries.

That was the trouble, the young men thought. There was no fun to be had in Arkhaven any more. All they could do was while away the days until the Ship lifted.

Settling on a new world would be an adventure of sorts, naturally, but for the first few generations at least life would be very spartan and basic. They would not be able to take the comforts and luxuries they would wish for with them, and so it seemed sensible to make the most of the freedom they had while it lasted.

Which explained the group of a dozen or so young men, together with three or four like-minded female companions, that was gathered in the club lounge in the small hours of the morning. A fair amount of drink had already been consumed and some people were already beginning to complain.

'Isn't your man ever going to call, Plax?' the Honourable Orm Herstwell the Third asked, one arm around his girlfriend, the other holding a glass.

'He hasn't let me down yet,' Plaxander Vendam reminded him. 'And if you want to drive straight for a change, hold back on the drink. I'm not having you spin me off again.'

'You spun into me!' Herstwell retorted indignantly. 'Just you choose the course and I'll race you, Plax. Tell you what, we'll both have a bottle of any brew you name before we start, then I'll show you I can beat you drunk or sober!'

There was a loud chorus of disbelief as his companions showed what they thought of his challenge.

Plax's personal phone rang. He waved the rest into silence before answering.

'Lesitor here, sir,' said a thin voice from the speaker. 'I thought you would be interested to know that a party of NC2s has just escaped from the camp.'

'Have they indeed? Will we find them at the usual place?'

'I'm afraid the Watch have already been alerted. I had to leave them in the warehouse at the back of the old Reliance building off Fourteenth Avenue.'

'I know it. How many?'

'Fifteen men and two women, sir.'

'A good field. Well done. Expect the usual consideration.'

He rang off and turned to the others with a broad smile on his face.

'The quarry is out of the traps and the hunt is on!'

His friends cheered. Glasses were drained and ceremonially smashed in the fireplace, where the last cords of timber that would ever be hewn on Sarath were burning. Then the young men snatched up their coats, and poured out through the lobby and down the steps to their waiting cars.

Doors were sealed and idling gyros were revved. Headlights flicked on. Bracing struts retracted, leaving the vehicles balanced on their single broad central wheels. At a signal from Plax the gyrocars rolled out of their parking bays. Reaching the main thoroughfare they turned away from the towering bulk of the Ship and raced down one of the long avenues that radiated out from the centre of Arkhaven. They were heading towards the sparsely populated and unfashionable suburbs and industrial parks, weaving in and out of the light night traffic, heedless of squeals of brakes and angry horns.

Private cars were another luxury the new world would not be able to support, so they might as well make the most of them. And what better way than a hunt for the most challenging prey Sarath could still provide?

The warehouse was a great echoing vault, its bleak expanse of floor broken only by a single central line of supporting pillars. It felt as though it had been deserted for some time. What it had formerly contained, Gelvert did not know. Now it was giving shelter to seventeen men and women who were huddled in one corner. After months in the camp the open space was intimidating.

Gelvert dabbed his bruised cheek with a moistened handkerchief once again. Trying to take that ring from the Doctor had been a mistake. Who would have thought the old man's companion would be so handy with his fists? And had the two of them also been responsible for raising the alarm so soon? The escapees had barely crossed the waste ground before the whole camp had lit up. Lesitor, who'd been leading them, had been dismayed at the rapid reaction – evidently he had counted on having more time to get clear. But he had found a truck and taken them away from the area the Watch would concentrate on.

Yes, Lesitor had fulfilled his part of the arrangement; but then they'd paid him enough. Still, he had got them to a place of safety which was all he'd promised. Once they were hidden he'd wished them luck and left. The rest was up to them. Over the next few days they would work their way closer to the centre of the city, spying out the land as they went. Apparently there was a huge repository near the Ship which housed the thousands of items of cargo that were steadily being loaded into its holds. If they could enter that unobserved and conceal themselves properly they would simply be carried on board. It would be an uncomfortable trip, but what did that matter as long as they survived? Over the last ten years Gelvert had lost his family, his land and his self-respect. Now he had only his own life left.

The thought caused him to glance across at Tressel, who was sitting next to him.

Tressel would be their guide. He knew the city. Unlike the rest of them he was a native of Arkhaven. He had been a middle-ranking Functionary until he had criticised the Church too openly. Now he burned with an inner desire to defy the system that had rejected him. Unfortunately he was no natural rebel and Gelvert wondered if he had the strength to see the thing through.

'We'll hole up here another half-hour then make a start,' Gelvert said. 'What's the best route that'll keep us off the main avenues?'

In the dim reflected street light Tressel's face was just a pale blur but his tone was unmistakably hesitant. 'I'm not really sure. I haven't been to this area before. I'll get my bearings in the morning.'

Gelvert sensed the others were looking at them. 'What do you mean you're not sure?'

'I've lived near the centre for eight years, like everybody else who could manage it,' Tressel said bitterly. 'We didn't travel this far out unless we had to.'

'Huddling close to your precious Ship for comfort, I suppose,' Gelvert said.

'Why not …? It was safer there. Listen, I promise I'll guide you as best I can, but I don't know every back street. It's a big city.'

Gelvert snorted in disgust, got up and went to a small access door set in the great slab of the side wall. Carefully he opened it a crack to let some light in. Across an expanse of bare yard was the long bulk of another building that he took to be a fabrication plant of some sort. A few of its roof lights were glowing. Rising above and beyond it were residential towers aglitter with shining windows.

Standing so that the others couldn't see what he was doing, he took out of his pocket the only item he'd managed to snatch from the Doctor and examined it by the city light. As he'd thought, it was just a key. It hardly mattered to what. He put it back in his pocket by reflex, though it was probably useless. Why couldn't he have taken something more...

The loading doors at the far end of the warehouse suddenly rolled aside and beams of light flooded the interior with stark brilliance. There came the hum of powerful motors and a cacophony of car horns. Wild yells rang out, echoing back from the walls:

'Spied them!' 'The chase is on!' 'I see game!'

Eight or ten racing gyros rolled into the warehouse, spreading out and circling towards the NC2s who scattered in alarm, half blinded by the lights.

Gelvert did not wait to see any more. He flung the access door open the rest of the way and plunged out into the night. Feet clattered behind him as a few of the NC2s followed his example. From the interior of the warehouse he heard cries and yells and the incessant beeping of horns.

Who were these crazy people?

The NC2s were only halfway across the yard when lights flared at their backs, throwing elongated flickering shadows before them. With whining motors three gyrocars bore down on them. As they sped past, Gelvert and the others fell flat and rolled aside.

He heard bangs as compressed air was released and a swish as something flew past him. One of his fellow runners was rolling on the ground entangled in a mist of netgun mesh. A second was clawing at a snag line that had adhered to his side. As the line drew taut he was pulled off his feet and dragged along the ground behind the car that had fired it.

Tyres screeched as the cars came to a halt and pivoted around, gyros buzzing in protest. Yells of triumph came from the drivers who had caught their quarries.

Gelvert scrambled to his feet and ran towards the corner of the factory building, desperate to get off the open ground. The third gyrocar sped after him. He saw the passenger lean through the side window and raise his weapon. Gelvert dived even as the gun popped. He was not quite fast enough. The soft ball of a snag-line shot struck him on the arm. The micro-encapsulated bubbles of adhesive within it ruptured and set on contact with the air, binding themselves to his sleeve. Before the line could tighten he tore off his coat, scrambled to his feet and dashed madly away in another direction.

A low wall marked the boundary of the loading yard, with a border of shrubs and low trees between it and the main road. If he could reach that...

He succeeded – just – vaulting the wall and crashing into a thorny bush even as the gyrocar braked at his heels, its wheel screeching in a cloud of rubber. Ignoring the scratches he hauled himself upright and plunged alongside the shrubbery in a crouching run, keeping close to the wall. The lights of the car blazed out of the loading yard and swung along the road after him. What would happen when he ran out of shelter? Suppose another car joined the pursuit and got ahead of him?

Fear lent Gelvert the courage to do the last thing his pursuers expected.

He bent down, scrabbled up handfuls of wet earth and pebbles, then leapt out into the path of the oncoming car. As its brakes squealed he threw his improvised missiles as hard as he could.

The wet earth splattered across the windshield, blinding the driver, even as pebbles clattered off it. One must have struck the gun-wielding passenger because he cried out and fell back into the body of the car. Dazzled by the brilliant headlights, Gelvert could only throw up his arms in a futile gesture against the seemingly inevitable impact.

The car swerved madly, a side fender practically brushing his thigh, veered across the road and crashed into the shrubbery. For a second the motor gave a shrill whine of protest then cut abruptly.

Gelvert turned and ran. A little way down the road, on the opposite side, was a tubeway tower. He darted across to it. Ignoring the escalator for fear of the noise it would make as his presence activated it, he pounded up the external footramp.

Panting, he stumbled out on to the elevated plaza deck with its tiny arcade of shops that flanked the tube station. As he had hoped it was deserted, the shop fronts dark and only a few lights shining around the station access itself. He edged into the shelter of a planter trough and peered over the parapet wall back towards the warehouse.

Gyrocar headlights illuminated the yard, their beams picking out moving figures. The distant sound of shouts and laughter drifted up to him. Bound forms were struggling on the ground while others stood over them, apparently teasing their captives and giving them the occasional prod and kick. Would their capture be enough to satisfy the hunters, or might they come after him again? Should he stay put while he had some cover, or try to put as much distance between him and his pursuers as he could?

Before he could decide flashing lights appeared at the end of the avenue accompanied by the growing wail of sirens. Gelvert shrank back into the shadows. Obviously somebody had called the City Watch. A patrol car and van appeared out of the night and turned into the warehouse yard, drawing up beside the cluster of gyrocars. Watchmen climbed out and unhurriedly went over to them. It all seemed very casual.

Feet pounded on the ramp below and Gelvert just had time to duck down as two figures appeared. Looking through the plants he saw they were Tressel and Semanov, one of the female escapees. They were glancing desperately about them as though unsure which way to go next. If they stayed there in the light for too long somebody would surely see them!

'Over here... and keep your heads down!' Gelvert hissed.

They joined him beside the wall. Together they peered down at the scene in the warehouse yard.

The prisoners were being untangled from nets and snag lines and marched into the Watch van. There were cheers and catcalls from those who had brought them down. Meanwhile torches flashed about the gyrocar Gelvert had caused to crash. With a whir of motors it backed out on to the road again.

'Who are those people?' Semanov asked Tressel in a whisper. 'What's their game?'

'From the look of their cars I'd say they were probably from the Elite families,' Tressel said bitterly. 'Youngsters with nothing better to do. You hear stories about them but the authorities don't usually do a thing about it. They've got influential parents.'

'They could have run us down – we could have been killed!' Semanov exclaimed.

'I don't think that bothers the Watch too much,' Gelvert said. 'Just a few less NC2s to take care of.'

'Did anybody else get away?' Tressel asked.

'Not that I noticed. Just hope that the Watch think we split earlier and don't find out how many were in the warehouse. Then maybe they won't bother searching further.'

'Don't you care about the others?' Semanov asked.

'No,' said Gelvert simply. 'And if you want to get on the Ship, you won't either.' He was looking up at the night sky. 'Still got your thermal blankets with you?'

They nodded. 'Why?' Semanov asked.

'In case they bring in a skycar for a search. We can hide from nightscopes easily enough, but we need the blankets to avoid thermal imagers. If you've lost yours keep away from me.'

'Maybe we should take the tube out of here while we can,' Tressel said. 'We've got the money cards we bought from Lesitor.'

'Yeah, and just a hundred credits on each,' Gelvert reminded him. 'We'll need them for later. Anyway, the Watch might check the tube records. You go if you want. For now I'm staying put.'

He was simply being pragmatic. Moving now might only get him spotted. If the men in the car he'd confronted had seen him running up here and had then told the Watch, the watchmen would probably assume he'd already taken the tube out. But he guessed, from what Tressel had just told him, that the kind of young men who'd chased him would not care to admit losing out to somebody on foot, whose only weapon had been a handful of earth and pebbles.

Tressel and Semanov stayed with him. After a few minutes the occupants of the gyrocars climbed back into their vehicles and drove off in a straggling column that vanished into the night. The

Watch van carrying the recaptured NC2s followed. The patrol car remained for a quarter of an hour, presumably to check the warehouse was secure, then it also left. No search of the area had been made and there was no sight or sound of any aerial activity. With a whisper of displaced air, a capsule passed along the tube into the station. They saw a handful of people inside it but apparently none were getting off so it continued on through the stop. Apart from the occasional car passing along the avenue all was quiet.

'Where to now?' Tressel asked.

'Nowhere far,' Gelvert said. 'Let the excitement cool down. We'll move off in the morning when there are more people around.'

Cautiously they made their way around the back of the small arcade of shops to a long wall housing a row of utility doors. Gelvert examined the lock of the nearest one, took a sliver of plastic from his pocket and worked it back and forth until there was a slight click. The door swung open.

'You're very good at that,' Tressel said, his tone reproachful yet with a hint of grudging admiration.

For a moment Gelvert hesitated, recalling a time when he would never have dreamed of forcing a lock, far less known how to do so. But he had learnt a lot of survival skills during his long journey to Arkhaven as civilisation had fallen apart about him.

'Nothing to it,' he blustered. 'You people make dumb locks.'

They stepped into a small backroom, piled with boxes and cartons of unidentifiable merchandise. It was lit only indirectly through a fanlight over the door.

'This looks good,' said Gelvert, running his finger across the dust on the top of the boxes. 'I don't think anybody comes in here very often.' He closed the door and settled down in a corner, pulling his thermal blanket out and spreading it over himself. Semanov shrugged and followed his example. Tressel remained standing, looking uncomfortable, as though afraid to touch anything.

'There's never been much crime in Arkhaven,' he said. 'Even less after the war. Not common breaking and entering or theft, anyway…'

'Shut up and get some rest!' Gelvert told him firmly. 'And don't start developing a guilty conscience now. The people of your fair city were planning to leave you behind to get smashed along with the rest of the world, remember?'

'He's right,' said Semanov. 'We don't owe anybody anything. Getting on the Ship is all that matters. Nothing's going to stop me, I can tell you that. Nothing!'

'Would you kill to get on board?' Tressel asked simply.

Semanov didn't answer.

Tressel crouched down in the opposite corner and covered himself with his blanket.

Gelvert felt desperately tired and sleep overcame him in minutes. But as he slipped away a small detail surfaced in the back of his mind.

Despite all the confusion in the yard, the gyrocar chase and then the arrival of the Watch, nobody had come out of any of the surrounding buildings to see what was going on.

Chapter Nine
Visitors?

'Excuse me,' said the watchman, 'but which way is intensive care? I can't get any sense out of the receptionist and the signs aren't that clear.'

Nyra Shardri paused on her way through the otherwise empty main lobby of the hospital and smiled at the smart young man. A captain, she noticed.

'Sorry, the receptionist keeps breaking down... it's only a simple model,' she explained. 'Priority maintenance goes to the medical units, and we're short-staffed. We can't get people to do the ordinary work any more. You know how it is.'

'I know,' he said. 'They've decided it's not worth the trouble because they don't believe the Ship will be ready in time...'

'Don't!' Nyra said quickly. 'Please. It's something I have nightmares about.'

He looked genuinely contrite. 'Sorry.'

Nyra renewed her smile. 'Anyway, I'm going to intensive care as it happens... it's this way.'

They rode up the powered ramp side by side.

'Are you visiting a relative?' Nyra asked.

The captain smiled. 'No. I'm doing a favour for an... uh, acquaintance. He wants to know how his granddaughter is doing. A Susan Foreman.'

Nyra started. 'Oh. I didn't realise. The council hasn't sent you, have they?'

'No, just her grandfather. Why should the council have sent me?'

They reached the top of the ramp and started down a long corridor.

'I'm sorry,' Nyra said. 'I thought you must know about her case.'

'What about it?' He looked concerned. 'She's all right, isn't she?'

'Well... she's a very unusual patient.'

'How do you mean?'

Nyra considered for a few seconds. 'I suppose I can tell you. Is her grandfather an NC2 as well?'

'Yes.'

'I see. I was wondering why she'd had no visitors.'

They reached the doors of intensive care.

'Look,' Nyra said. 'It's the start of my shift and I've got to take the report. When I've done that I'll explain. By the way, I'm Nyra Shardri.'

He gave a smile a little warmer than basic politeness demanded, which she found pleased her. 'Benadik Lant... Ben, to my friends.'

Lant waited patiently as Nyra checked in with her fellow clinician who was going off duty, and reviewed the night records and case notes. When they were alone again except for the silent occupants of the support tanks, she led him over to unit five. Together they peered down at the pale-faced dark-haired girl within.

'She's fine now but she had a bit of a crisis yesterday,' Nyra admitted. 'We don't know what went wrong but I had to put her in TES suspension for a few hours.'

He gave a mock shiver. 'I went though that myself a couple of years ago. A sizeable part of a building fell on me during a particularly bad storm. Still, you people fixed me up. But I felt cold inside for days afterwards.'

'Purely psychosomatic, I assure you,' Nyra said with a smile. 'Anyway, she's come through it well. We'll let her wake up naturally and move her to a recovery ward later.'

'She looks perfectly ordinary. What's so unusual about her?'

Nyra frowned. 'Let's say she's different from the norm. Very different in some respects.' She realised Lant was looking at her oddly. 'I've notified central administration and the senior physician, but nobody's replied yet. That's why I thought you might have been sent here to check on her. Maybe they all think it's a joke... or else I'm letting everything get to me. But I assure you it's absolutely true.'

She led him over to the central console. 'I've got her tests here. How much anatomy do you know?'

'Only enough to give first aid.'

'Well, her skeleton is quite ordinary. But her core body temperature and pulse rate have stabilised at ridiculous levels... which is maybe not surprising considering her peculiar blood chemistry and cell structure.' She displayed a whole-body scan on the screen. 'Most of her major organs are correctly placed... but look at this.'

Nyra saw the captain's eyes widen in amazement. For some reason it felt comforting to share the mystery with him.

Twenty minutes later Ben Lant left the hospital and climbed into his car, still deep in thought.

He understood the realities of the larger situation better than Nyra Shardri and wasn't surprised that central administration hadn't acted on her medical report yet. They were overstretched, simply with planning the exodus while keeping Arkhaven running. The physiological peculiarities of a young NC2 woman would hardly receive top priority, even if they were taken seriously. But Ben found himself wanting to know the truth, one way or another.

Susan Foreman was either a radical mutation or else she was not native to Sarath.

It didn't seem possible that she was a mutation. She was otherwise too perfect. Even the Taklarians' selective breeding programme had not changed their internal bodily make-up. So could she really be from somewhere else?

There were disparities in Sarath's fossil record, and genetic differences between a few of the less successful minor plants and animals and the others. Some scientists suggested that millennia ago the founding fathers had journeyed through space to colonise Sarath, while the Church said Sarath was settled directly from the Maker's holy garden of Matherath. The debate over the so-called 'Origin Question' had raged for years. Now Susan Foreman had appeared. What if she and her grandfather and her friends weren't just a few more refugees from beyond Arkhaven's walls? What if the colonisers' distant cousins had come to visit them at last?

'Where to now, sir?' his driver asked, and Lant realised with a start that this was the second time the man had asked.

'Carlson Tower, intersection of Fifteenth Avenue and orbital twenty-nine. You may not be able to get too close – it took some storm damage yesterday.'

Carlson Tower was a rapidly disintegrating stub less than half its former height. A squad of robotic cutters, grabs and excavators were dismantling the building's shell, while skycranes lowered rubble to a fleet of dumper trucks waiting at ground level.

The site command unit had been set up on an elevated road overlooking the remains. Ben introduced himself to Supervisor Curton and explained what he was looking for.

'A blue box?' said Curton. 'That old NC2 man was on about a blue box yesterday.'

'You heard him?'

'Him and his friend. So did the mayor.'

'But what did they say, exactly?'

Curton chuckled. 'Only that they came from outer space, and had landed their spacecraft on top of the tower, then lost it when the building collapsed. You have to feel sorry for them, I suppose.'

'I see,' Ben said carefully, feeling a thrill of excitement.

'We're still scanning for the NC2 woman they said was missing as well, but there's nothing so far. Still, we haven't found the service-lift cage yet so there's some hope. They're built pretty tough.'

Ben nodded, sobered by the reminder that another life might yet hang in the balance. 'Anyway, you'll keep an eye out for this box … just in case.'

'Look, any box of the size you say, spaceship or not, won't be much of a box by the time we dig it out… assuming it's there at all.'

Ben gazed about him at the demolition site. The moment of brief elation had passed and he was suddenly assailed by doubt. What was he doing here? Following up an old man's cryptic suggestions and mad stories. Just wanting to believe that something wonderful had happened, wouldn't make it so. Perhaps the girl's physical peculiarities had some other explanation.

His eyes unconsciously lifted to follow the progress of a skycrane as it passed close by with another load of rubble in its grab. For a moment he frowned at the corner of an object projecting over the side, then snatched at Curton's arm.

'Don't let them dump that load!'

'"Police public call box",' Curton said, reading the archaic script printed on the door panel with some difficulty. 'What's that meant to mean?'

Ben walked around the box once again. Dust still clung to its ledges, but it seemed intact. Cautiously he tried the door. It rattled slightly but would not open.

'Can you get a laser cutter over here? There's something I want to try.'

'It's a miracle it's survived as it is, and you want to cut holes in it?' Curton said.

'If what I've been told is correct, we won't do any damage.'

Curton shrugged and went over to the main console. A spiderjack ceased dismantling the wall it was clinging to into manageable segments, walked down the sheer side of the tower until it reached the roadway and clumped over to them on its suction-pad feet.

'Cut out a ten centimetre circle around the door lock,' Curton ordered it, indicating the spot on the box. 'Depth five centimetres, intensity setting three.'

The machine extended its legs and rose until it was positioned exactly before the box. A nozzle extended from under its sensor head and the tip glowed redly. Carefully it drew a circle round the lock as it had been instructed. The nozzle withdrew and one of its forward manipulator limbs reached over and tapped the lock. Nothing happened.

'Material is resistant to cutting beam,' the spiderjack said. 'Recommend increasing beam intensity.'

'Increase to strength seven,' Curton ordered. 'Better wear these,' he told Ben, handing him a pair of protective goggles and putting on a set himself.

The laser flared more brilliantly than before as it circled the lock again. But when it faded the lock appeared untouched. Curton stepped forward and cautiously touched the spot.

'It's not even warm,' he said. 'Some sort of superconducting surface, maybe. It dissipates the heat before it can burn through.' He turned to the spiderjack. 'Use saw blade one, same cutting parameters.'

A small circular saw extended on a jointed arm, spinning up until its teeth were a blur.

'This cuts through steel like butter,' Curton told Ben confidently.

The humming blade touched the door beside the lock. There was a shower of sparks and the box shimmered with a bluish film of light. The men ducked as the blade disintegrated in a flying cloud of shrapnel that ricocheted off the road and the spiderjack's tough shell.

'Cease cutting!' Curton shouted.

The humming motor died away and they cautiously raised their heads. There was not a scratch on the door or lock.

'Reporting serious damage to number one blade,' the spiderjack reported impassively. 'Replacement required.'

For a moment Ben could only gape at the incongruous blue box in wonder. With a shiver he recovered his composure. 'Just leave it right there,' he told Curton. 'I've got to call the mayor's office.'

Chapter Ten
The Survivors

Barbara awoke to the sound of booming voices. Two men were conversing loudly somewhere close by, but she couldn't immediately make any sense of the words.

She felt curiously detached from her body. There was a chemical taste in her mouth and her lips were dry, but she could not move her tongue to lick them. Memory returned in fragments. The tunnel... the concealed doorway... the figure with the gun. She had been shot with a dart. Evidently it had been drugged. Where was she now? Perhaps it would help if she opened her eyes, she thought muzzily. In her current state that seemed a daunting task. Then the words being spoken became intelligible.

'Please be patient, Prince Keldo. She will be ready shortly. The effects of the dart must wear off before we begin.' The voice was slightly cracked with age but still strong.

'We must know what she was doing down there, Thorken,' replied the second, younger voice. 'Our egress point was hardly completed when she discovered it. Was this simply ill fortune or will others follow her?'

'If more come we shall not need to risk moving above ground in search of agents, Prince.'

'Perhaps... if she is suitable.'

'Look upon this female's arrival as opportune. She can be our first test subject.'

'You assured me the process was already perfected, Thorken,' the prince said with a suspicion of anger behind his words.

'It was perfected by the College of Science back in the homeland, Prince. We lack their resources. Of necessity some of my equipment has been improvised. But it will work, I promise.'

'It had better, Thorken. We need agents in the city to be our eyes and ears and more. When the time comes they may mean the difference between triumph and disaster.'

Barbara managed to force her sluggish eyelids open at last and her surroundings came slowly into focus.

She was in a room with smoke-stained metal walls, lit by harsh, white, coiled tubes. Cabinets and shelves held jars containing coloured powders and liquids. On battered tables intricate assemblies of frames and clamps supported laboratory glassware, together with the festooned cables and angular forms of electrical equipment. She blinked. Unaccountably it seemed as though all the tables were leaning slightly to the left. Then her sense of balance tried to tell her that the floor, and the rest of the room, was in fact tilted to the right. For a moment she felt sick until she noticed the tables had wedges under their legs to level them.

The two men broke off their conversation as they realised she was awake and strode over to her. Their appearance was so striking that Barbara drew in her breath sharply so that it rasped through her sore throat.

They were both at least seven feet tall and proportionately strongly built, with bronzed skins that seemed to shimmer in the light. The older man's hair was shot through with grey, but the younger one had a mane of golden hair that contrasted startlingly with his dark skin. In both, hawk-like noses dominated angular faces. They wore suits of what seemed to be finely woven metallic mesh. Silver for the older man and scarlet for the younger, who also wore a metallic scarlet band across his forehead.

'She seems to be conscious now,' the younger man said, regarding Barbara with clinical interest. 'Question her first about her presence in the tunnel.'

But Barbara was shaking her head in fear and confusion. She tried to protest, but all that came from her lips was a dry croak.

'Give her water, Thorken. She must be able to speak.'

The older man filled a plastic beaker and pushed it against Barbara's lips. She drank greedily, feeling the sensation returning to her mouth and throat. Automatically she tried to take the beaker in her own hands, but for some reason she could not lift her arms.

She looked down.

She was sitting in a large metal-framed chair, held in place by straps about her wrists and ankles and across her chest. Fear dispersed the last lingering traces of the anaesthetic, and she pulled desperately at her bonds.

'What are you doing? Let me go!' she choked out.

The man called Thorken reached out a huge hand, closed it about her cheeks and squeezed, spreading her jaws apart as the flesh was forced between them until she whimpered with pain.

'You will be silent unless spoken to, woman. Then you will answer all questions immediately and fully. Sensors built into the chair will detect any falsehood. If you refuse to answer or attempt to lie you will be punished until you co-operate. Understand?'

The hand was removed but Barbara was so shocked that she could only nod dumbly. There was no doubt in her mind that he meant every word he said, no more, no less. Protesting at her rough treatment was pointless.

Thorken and Keldo stepped over to a small console mounted beside the chair, and the older man threw some switches.

'We begin: what were you doing in the drainage tunnels?'

Barbara gave a stumbling account of her experiences after the meteor strike, which seemed to satisfy the two men. Then Thorken asked: 'What is your function in Arkhaven?'

'Sorry... I don't know what you mean. Is Arkhaven the name of the city?'

Thorken frowned and tapped the panel before him. The prince's face contorted into a scowl of anger that made Barbara shiver with fear.

'She is clearly lying, Thorken!' he boomed. 'Yet your devices do not register the fact. They are faulty.'

'With respect, they are not in error, Prince. But they only detect the physical symptoms of anxiety associated with the act of lying. Evidently she does not know what Arkhaven is.'

'Explain yourself, woman!' the prince said, addressing Barbara directly for the first time.

'I... I'm not from this world. We, my friends and I, travel in a machine that moves through space and time...'

They let her finish, though the scowl on the prince's face grew steadily deeper. Thorken looked up from the console. 'She is relating the truth as she believes it, Prince.'

'But it is madness; the stuff of myths and legends!'

'Quite so, Prince. Her answer is nonsensical, therefore she is evidently deranged. We theorised that many Arkavians might be driven to this state by their confinement in the city and the pressures of war, if you recall.'

The prince's expression cleared slightly.

'Ahh.. of course. The lesser races do not have our strength of will, that is known. But can she still serve? Will this interfere with her conditioning?'

Barbara's head jerked up. Conditioning? That was a term used in brainwashing. 'What are you going to do to me? Please don't...'

Without looking round Thorken touched a button on the console. Barbara gasped as an electric shock briefly jolted into her through the frame of the chair. It had been the most casual of warnings. She knew the shock could have been far worse. Trembling and desperately frightened she clamped her lips shut, not daring to utter another word.

'I see no reason why it should, Prince,' Thorken continued. 'Indeed, any slight behavioural inconsistencies induced by the process might be explained by her mania.'

The prince nodded. 'Then begin the procedure immediately. She must be returned to where we found her as soon as possible. Have you found a suitable item in which to conceal the sender?'

'She was wearing this primitive timepiece, Prince,' Thorken said. Barbara saw he was holding her watch and realised for the first time that it was missing from her wrist. 'Perhaps it is an antique. The sender can be fitted to it without interfering with its function.'

'Good,' said the prince, examining the watch with interest. 'You are sure she will recall nothing of this meeting?'

'Nothing, Prince. There will be a blank in her mind as though she had slept. Any dislocation of her time sense will be put down to the privations she has suffered in the tunnels.'

Thorken stepped up to Barbara and swung a metal arm out from a stand behind her chair. Mounted on the end was a large many-lensed lamp, rather like a smaller version of those used in operating theatres. This he positioned carefully a couple of feet in front of Barbara's face so that she was staring into the array of lenses. Each lens was tinted a slightly different hue and their surfaces were engraved with intricate patterns of lines arranged in rippling waves and spirals. They seemed to flicker before her eyes, making them water. She had once seen something similar in an exhibition of modern art. There had been something compelling about the images even though they'd given her a headache...

She turned her head aside. This was the brainwashing device!

But Thorken forced her head straight again, extended clamps from the headrest and secured it in place so that she faced the lenses.

'If you close your eyes there will be more shocks,' he warned her, 'each more intense than the one before.'

He returned to the console and operated the controls.

The lenses began to pulse with soft light. A droning electronic hum, rising and falling in synchrony with the lights, issued from concealed speakers close to her ears.

She had to fight it! Think of something else. She began counting backwards softly to herself.

'A hundred, ninety-nine, ninety-eight, ninety-seven, ninety-six – ahh!'

Another jolt of electricity coursed through the chair. Thorken had guessed what she was doing. She must be silent. She must count in her mind, she must...What number had she reached? She had to start... to start...

The sound and light seemed to bore into her brain, blotting out every other sensation. The fine patterns on the lenses swirled to fill her mind. She felt herself falling into an infinite void.

Then there was nothing.

Chapter Eleven
Puppet Show

Morning rush hour came and went. Gelvert, Tressel and Semanov did not see another living soul on the station plaza. The tube capsules passed through more frequently, but when they stopped nobody got on or off.

'What's going on?' Gelvert demanded of Tressel. 'Where are all the people?'

Tressel could only shake his head in bewilderment. 'I don't know. This is all wrong.'

'You don't think the evacuation has started already?' Semanov asked.

'No. The alert would be broadcast over every public screen. We couldn't have missed that.'

'Anyway there are people still riding the capsules,' Gelvert pointed out. 'They don't seem to be in any hurry.'

They looked down to the street below. A steady stream of vehicles was passing under the tubeway tower, but there were no pedestrians.

'Why didn't Lesitor warn us things were like this?' Gelvert began, then cursed loudly. 'He set us up! That's how they found us last night. We even paid him for the privilege...'

He regained his self-control and glared into his companions' confused faces. 'This area must be abandoned. Maybe it's still contaminated by weapon residue. We'll stand out like sore thumbs if we try to move around. Let's get out of here.'

'Do we risk taking a capsule?' Semanov asked.

'Yeah. At least there'll be a few people to give us cover.'

The station gateway credit-slot was not working, but it still let them on to the platform.

'Nobody's troubling to maintain the place any more,' Gelvert said. 'Still, at least it means we can travel free and save some credits.'

The next capsule came to a halt and the doors opened. They stepped inside and dropped into the nearest seats, carefully avoiding eye contact with the other passengers. They did not want to draw more attention to themselves than absolutely necessary.

After half a minute the capsule pulled away again. Gelvert let out his breath. The dozen or so people in the capsule were either gazing out through the windows or had their heads buried in newspads. None of them seemed to have noticed them boarding at a deserted station. In fact none of them had so much as glanced round...

Gelvert felt the hairs on the back of his neck rise.

Their fellow passengers were absolutely still and completely silent. Not a twitch or a sigh. Not even a breath.

Only now did Gelvert notice the thin film of dust over their clothes. He saw Semanov's and Tressel's eyes widening in alarm. Slowly he leant forward and prodded the shoulder of the passenger sitting in front of him. The man rocked slightly in his seat then settled back into perfect immobility.

'It's a dummy,' Gelvert said. 'The whole capsule's full of dummies!'

They were just that: mannequins, with realistic features and correctly articulated bodies - but utterly lifeless.

Semanov turned to Tressel looking frightened and angry. 'What is this? What's happening here?'

Tressel could only clasp his head. 'I don't know, I tell you!' As though in desperation, his eyes fastened on the illuminated destination board mounted at the end of the capsule. 'Look, Penko district is a couple of stops along. That's famous for its street markets and eateries. There'll be people there.'

'There'd better be,' said Gelvert.

They passed through the next station almost as still and silent as their dummy companions.

As the capsule pulled into Penko they looked down at a long tree-lined street flanked by broad promenades and laid out with market stalls and tables. A crowd of people was bustling about them. The escapees left the capsule and hurried down the ramps. Even Gelvert felt eager to be among people again. After months in the camp he had become used to company.

Their steps faltered as they reached ground level.

People sat drinking coffee at café tables while others bargained with stallholders. Children tugged excitedly at the arms of their parents. Dozens of mouths were moving – but no words came forth. The only sound in the street was the patter of heels on the pavement. A man and woman approached them walking arm in arm, staring into the middle distance with fixed smiles on their faces. Even as Gelvert flinched away some proximity circuit must have cut in for the couple turned smoothly to avoid them. Their movements had that repetitious precision and regularity that separated the mechanical from the living. They were simply amusement park animates. As they passed, Gelvert saw that their clothing was stained and sunbleached. How long had the two automatons promenaded up and down this road wearing those meaningless smiles?

He glanced at his companions. Tressel could only shake his head. Semanov simply shrugged. They walked slowly through the crowd like interlopers on a mute stage.

Then they began to notice the scars.

Tressel stumbled over a paving slab and they saw that large sections of the pavement had been poorly relaid and were now settling unevenly. Several slabs were cracked. The ghost of a jagged smoke-blackened line across a nearby facade showed where half the building had been replaced. Gelvert tapped the new section and found it was moulded and textured plasterboard, not stone. Semanov reached up to an overhanging branch of a shade tree and crumpled the leaves in her hand. When she released them they sprang back into perfect shape.

'Artificial,' she said with disgust. 'Just like everything else around here.'

The sky, which had been steadily darkening, suddenly dissolved into a torrential downpour. In seconds the pavements were awash. As though a switch had been thrown, the automatons ceased their play-acting and headed for the nearest doorways. Shivering, Gelvert led his companions after them and they crowded into a restaurant. Neither diners nor staff took the slightest notice of this sudden influx of dripping figures. The other animates lined up mutely against one wall. He could smell damp mould on their clothes.

Gelvert found a free table and slumped into a chair. Tressel and Semanov wearily copied him. Semanov drew her fingers pointedly through the thick layer of dust on the table-top. Tressel looked dazed. About them simulacrums of diners were going through the motions of eating, handling their cutlery with mechanical precision. But there was no food on the plates. A waiter solemnly filled empty glasses from an empty bottle of wine.

'Tell us…' Gelvert said to Tressel, anger and contempt in his words, 'tell us how you come not to know half your city's dead!'

Chapter Twelve
The Deception

Captain Lant returned to the NC2 camp before noon in an aircar. He brought documents with him releasing the Doctor and Ian into his charge. From his manner it was evident their status had changed. Lant looked as though he wanted to ask a lot of questions, but was constrained by protocol.

'I have been instructed to escort you to the mayor's office,' he said, formally.

'And about time, young man,' the Doctor said mildly. 'I see you have followed my advice.'

'Yes. We've found your, uh, machine. It was undamaged, as you said.'

'And Susan? You visited her?'

'She's out of danger and recovering well,' Lant assured him, a very curious expression flitting across his face.

'Any news of Barbara?' Ian asked anxiously.

'Not yet, I'm afraid. But they haven't found the lift cage, so there is still a chance.'

Ian could only nod sombrely.

The Doctor accepted their evident advancement with slightly overbearing self-satisfaction. He beamed condescendingly as he boarded the aircar, like some monarch triumphantly returning from exile.

The Ship grew ever larger as they approached the heart of the city. It was even more massive than they had originally thought.

'Extraordinary,' the Doctor said, gazing at it intensely through the aircar window. Ian could think of no better description of its overwhelming presence.

A fierce rainstorm blew up out of the lowering sky as their car set them down on the roof pad of a large municipal building. As they landed they noticed the TARDIS resting on the flat roof beside the pad, with a soldier standing guard over it.

'You see, Chesterton,' the Doctor said as they scrambled out of the car. 'I told you the ship would come through unharmed.'

'This way, gentlemen,' said Lant, ushering them out of the rain into a roof lift. 'The mayor would like to ask you a few questions.'

It was a very different meeting from their first encounter.

They were shown into the mayor's office. Draad greeted them cordially, invited them to sit in comfortable chairs and offered drinks. Lant refused refreshment and sat to one side. Draad returned to his seat behind his desk and regarded them intently for a moment before speaking.

'I have seen a blue box which you claim is some kind of transport,' he said. 'That in itself I find hard to believe. However, this selfsame box apparently cannot be opened or even scratched by any force at our command.

'I have also read a medical report on your companion, Susan Foreman, which I find equally hard to believe, but which has been double-checked and fully corroborated. I am prepared to accept the explanation you gave for your presence here with, shall we say, a more open mind.'

'Then you must first accept,' the Doctor began, 'that there are millions of worlds beyond your own, populated not just by humanoid life forms, but beings of every imaginable form...'

As the Doctor spoke on, Ian saw Draad and Lant grow steadily more fascinated by the tale of their wanderings though time and space. Lant's face shone with barely controlled wonder while the mayor's reserve gradually faded into deepening interest. Both men listened intently as the Doctor speculated that Sarath had been colonised thousands of years before by space travellers who might have originally come from Earth. Finally the Doctor finished and beamed at his enraptured audience.

Draad slowly shook his head, as if to bring himself back to reality. 'That is quite incredible. There are such theories about our origins which many people said were just legends. But now your presence seems to prove the matter.'

'You do believe us then?' Ian asked anxiously, worried that they'd be sent back to the NC2 camp.

'I do, Mr Chesterton,' said Draad slowly. 'There seems no reason for you to lie now we have seen this "TARDIS" of yours.' He smiled. 'It really is larger inside than out?'

'Certainly,' the Doctor assured him. 'A simple application of the laws of fifth-dimensional physics.'

Draad smiled again, though more wryly, at the use of the word 'simple'. 'But you say both its door keys have gone missing.'

'Regrettably yes. Unless Susan still has her own key with her.'

Captain Lant spoke up. 'After I checked your granddaughter's condition, Doctor, I took the liberty of examining her clothes and possessions which the hospital had stored. There was no key of any kind amongst them.'

The Doctor frowned. 'Then the man named Gelvert has the only key. You must find him.'

'Can you not open your craft in some other way?' Draad asked.

The Doctor tapped his chin, lost in thought for a minute. 'It is just possible that, with the right tools, I might be able to duplicate a key. It is more than a simple piece of metal, you understand. There is a unique pattern embedded within its molecular structure that the lock mechanism reads. I would have to re-create that to atomic levels of tolerance.'

The mayor looked at them both very thoughtfully for a moment, then said: 'Would you please wait in the outer office with Captain Lant for a minute? I have a proposition I want to put to you, but I must confer with somebody first.'

While they waited the Doctor said earnestly to Lant: 'You will make every effort to find Gelvert? Even with the finest facilities at my disposal, I am by no means certain I can create a duplicate key successfully.'

Lant smiled. 'I'll do my best. I'd like to take a look inside that craft of yours myself. I'll check how the search is progressing now if you like.'

He stepped over to the window, drew what Ian took to be a small two-way radio from his pocket and held it to his ear.

As he was making his call, Ian said to the Doctor: 'This isn't the first time this sort of thing has happened to us. Only having two keys is risky. It might be an idea to arrange some other means of getting inside the TARDIS in an emergency.'

'Perhaps you're right, Chesterton. I promise I'll give the problem my fullest attention, as soon as we have sorted our our immediate problems.'

Lant rejoined them, still holding his radio phone.

'It seems some NC2s were recaptured late last night,' he said, 'but Gelvert wasn't amongst them. I've asked them to be checked over for the key just in case, but I don't think you're going to be lucky.'

'I see,' said the Doctor. 'Well, thank you for trying, Captain.'

'I haven't given up yet. I'm still waiting to hear about the ongoing search. The trouble is I was only assigned to this squad temporarily, so I don't know how to get the best out of them yet.'

He moved aside again, putting the phone to his ear.

Another matter had been troubling Ian. 'What was it about Susan's medical report that has them so puzzled? If they're originally from Earth, why should we seem different to them?'

The Doctor gave him a peculiarly penetrating look, then sighed. 'Evidently you have not yet fully grasped the facts about our antecedence, Chesterton. A pardonable mistake in the circumstances, perhaps. You see, Susan and I are not actually…'

Mayor Draad opened the door of his office: 'Please come back in again, gentlemen.'

One of the screens on the office wall now displayed the image of a tired-looking middle-aged man whom Draad introduced as Professor Tovel Jarrasen. The professor stared back at them with sceptical curiosity. Draad gestured out of the rain-streaked window at his back towards the towering bulk of the Ship.

'You know what that is, I take it?' he asked Ian and the Doctor.

'We've picked up the basic facts,' Ian replied. 'Your moon is falling.'

'Yes. By our best estimates it will strike in thirty-three days' time. Monitor: display a current image of the moon.'

'The moon is about to rise over station seven,' a measured voice said.

Another screen lit up to show the night sky over a jagged horizon bathed in a pearly glow that grew stronger by the moment. Suddenly the horns of a crescent moon appeared, rising at incredible speed. Of course, Ian thought, it's moving against the rotation of the planet. In moments a rugged crater-scarred body fully fifty times wider than the full moon of Earth was soaring into the sky.

The camera tracked its progress. Before it had reached a quarter of the way up to the zenith the moon began to redden and dim, then faded into a black silhouette eclipsing the stars.

'It has now passed into Sarath's shadow,' the voice of Monitor said.

'That was relayed from an automatic station on the equator,' Draad explained. 'The moon's so close now that it's no longer visible from these latitudes. Perhaps the fact that the people can't see it any more helps to maintain a sense of normality.'

'It orbits in your equatorial plane?' the Doctor asked.

Unexpectedly Monitor answered: 'The deviation is no more than eleven degrees, Doctor.'

The Doctor blinked. 'Your computer seems to know who we are already,' he observed.

'Monitor is a very sophisticated machine, Doctor,' Draad explained. 'We could not run Arkhaven without him. A duplicate of his mainframe unit has been installed in the Ship. He will be coming with us to aid our colonisation of Mirath.'

'I see.' The Doctor looked into Monitor's camera eye. 'What do you think of such an undertaking, Monitor?'

'I am programmed to serve the city, people and lawful rulers of Arkhaven. If the city state of Arkhaven is transferred to Mirath I will continue to serve it there with the same efficiency.'

The Doctor nodded. 'I see. Well, it is a most remarkable project you are undertaking, Mayor.'

'We have no choice,' Draad said simply, 'considering the alternative...' He faltered as though he could not bring himself to speak further and gestured at Monitor's camera eye. 'Tell them the projections.'

'When the moon strikes it is estimated it will penetrate to a depth of forty kilometres,' Monitor explained. 'The shock wave transmitted through the mantle will open up geological faults across Sarath, releasing lava flows that will cover 65 per cent of the surface. The impact will throw superheated dust and rock of gigatonne magnitudes into the stratosphere, obliterating the sun. When these fall back they will incinerate all remaining organic matter. Life in the oceans, if any still remains, will die as the plankton at the base of the food chain is poisoned. The oxygen will be burnt out of the air by the planet-wide fires and will not be replaced, since insufficient light will reach the surface through the dust-polluted atmosphere to initiate photosynthesis. Sarath will be a sterile world experiencing major earthquakes and volcanic eruptions for an estimated minimum of eight hundred years.'

Ian was silent. Monitor's emotionless catalogue of disaster was chilling. He could think of no suitable response after such an apocalyptic pronouncement. The Doctor was less inhibited.

'You have our sympathy,' he told Draad gravely. 'But I'm afraid we cannot offer any solution to your problem. Even if I had access to the TARDIS I could not carry you all to safety. Nor do I have the means to deflect or destroy your moon before it strikes.'

'I was not expecting miracles,' said Draad. 'But nevertheless you can help us. I have a proposition. We will give you the facilities to make another key for your machine if, in return, you give us your knowledge.'

'Knowledge of what?'

Professor Jarrasen spoke up.

'I am the principal designer of the Ship, Doctor. If your own craft is all that you say then perhaps ours seems very primitive to you. But I assume, as space travellers, that you have at least studied similar devices.'

The Doctor swelled slightly. 'I have a sound working knowledge of atomic rocket technology,' he admitted.

'The Ship is untried and largely untested. The war interfered with much of our research programme. Our practical experience of space travel is limited to the launch of a few unmanned research probes. The normal development process has simply not been possible; consequently there are many details that could be improved. If you could check them over we still have time to make any minor modifications you could suggest.' Jarrasen forced a wan, tired smile. 'You see, I'm not too proud to ask for help. All that matters is that the Ship works and carries us to Mirath safely.'

'Well, Doctor?' Draad asked. 'I think we have a right to seek any help we can get. For the sake of humanity, will you help us?'

'Is it humane that you're going to leave the NC2s behind when you go?' Ian asked accusingly.

Draad pinched the bridge of his nose and his shoulders seemed to sag for a moment. 'Don't you think I would save everybody in Arkhaven, native or not, if I could, Mr. Chesterton? But the passenger capacity of the Ship, plus essential supplies and equipment, was established before the last influx of refugees. We are working up to its safety margin as it is. Don't you agree that it is better to save some than risk losing all in an overloaded vessel?'

'But you are deciding who lives and dies by accident of birth. Natives of Arkhaven get preference over everybody else.'

'And why not?' Draad responded with a little more vigour. 'We conceived the plan and poured time and resources into the project. We persevered even through the war with the Taklarians. Why shouldn't we be the first to reap its benefit? There is only one vessel in the world capable of reaching Mirath and it has fallen to me to choose who will ride in it. Believe me, I didn't ask for such responsibility, but I will stand by my decision.'

Ian said no more. He simply nodded in mute understanding.

'So, Doctor,' Draad asked, 'will you help us?'

The Doctor looked thoughtful. 'Before I answer, there is one question I would like answered.'

'What's that?'

'Why are you illuminating empty buildings and putting dummy drivers into robotically driven cars?'

Consternation showed on the faces of all three Arkavians, but the Doctor glared back at them stubbornly.

'Come now,' the Doctor continued. 'You cannot expect our co-operation while keeping such a thing secret. Just what are you hiding – and why?'

After an uncomfortable pause Draad nodded. 'All right,' he said to his compatriots, 'I'll take the responsibility… and answer to the council if necessary.' He turned back to Ian and the Doctor. 'What I am about to tell you is only known to essential military and government personnel. I must ask you to respect our confidence and to divulge this information to no one outside this office.'

'We can promise nothing until we know the facts, sir,' the Doctor said stoutly. 'Only you can judge whether this revelation is worthy of our discretion.'

Draad sighed. 'Very well. I just hope you will understand. It all began during the war. Spy drones determined the nature of the Ship once full-scale construction began and the Taklarians threatened to destroy Arkhaven unless we agreed to take them with us. But apart from such an option being morally repugnant, we knew the Ship could not carry them as well. Their battlecraft still held several thousand warriors. So they began their attacks. To avoid damaging the Ship they concentrated on the outer suburbs. To maintain public morale we did not dare to divulge the true numbers of casualties. The city council formulated the policy of diverting all available resources to repairing superficial damage as soon as possible.

'Even when there had been considerable loss of life, we tried to make the damaged areas appear populated. Firstly we used soldiers, then simple automatons and automatically controlled vehicles. This also had the effect of deceiving the Taklarian drones, misleading them as to the effectiveness of their attacks. Ruined buildings were patched up and illuminated at night to make them seem occupied, public information screens were kept running, and so on.'

'Wasn't there a blackout?' Ian asked.

Draad looked at him curiously. 'City lights made no difference to the accuracy of the Taklarian weapons. They did not rely on simple optical target-seeking.'

'And a brightly illuminated city was also better for morale,' the Doctor suggested.

'Exactly,' Draad said. 'Anyway, as losses mounted and space became available, the surviving citizens steadily moved inwards from the outlying districts towards the heart of the city. It was, and still is, the safest place to live. People keep to the Inner Zone just to be near the Ship. It's a powerful symbol.

'Luckily Arkhaven is in a relatively stable geological area, so we've had little seismic damage. It's also self-contained. We can fabricate material goods, synthesise food and have ample reserves of power.' Draad hesitated. 'We've heard nothing from outside for half a year. As far as we know, Arkhaven is the last outpost of civilisation on Sarath.'

'But the war's over now,' Ian said. 'Why continue this deception?'

'To make the citizens feel safe,' Draad said bluntly. 'They know there are some deserted areas in the Outer Zone, of course, but not their true extent. They see occasional news reports from outlying districts with automatons in the background to swell the numbers. They are insulated from a desolate world by that band of brightly lit towers. They don't think to wonder whether they are really occupied. Individuals know of family or friends lost, naturally, but only a few of us know the true total.'

'How many did you lose?' Ian asked.

Draad hesitated, apparently too pained to speak. Monitor answered for him.

'Arkhaven had a population of five million one hundred and two thousand before the war, Mr Chesterton,' it said. 'Now there are slightly under eighty thousand registered citizens left.'

Ian felt numb. 'You lost over five million people!'

'We had taken rising casualties for almost four years of war in addition to storm losses,' Lant said. 'Then, near the end, the Taklarians used a new form of chemical weapon on the Outer Zone... it worked only too well.'

'But you can't conceal such a huge loss of life,' Ian persisted. 'People would notice even with your cover-up.'

'Would they, Mr Chesterton?' Draad asked with a humourless smile. 'Tell me, do you live in a city in your world?'

'Yes, London… our capital.'

'What is its population?'

'Well, there are almost eight million in greater London – the centre of the city.'

'Really. Have you counted them personally?'

'Of course not. But there are census statistics…'

'And the census is government controlled?'

'Of course…' Ian faltered for a moment. 'All right, I see what you mean. But I can tell there are tens of thousands of people living and working around me every time I take a walk or travel to work. From that I can estimate the total population of the city.'

'Do you travel down every road to see it is equally busy, or examine every person you pass to know they are real?' Draad asked. 'Do you not actually see most people at a distance or enclosed within vehicles, or simply infer their presence from lights in buildings?'

Ian hesitated.

'I believe the mayor has made his point, Chesterton,' said the Doctor, smiling grimly.

'The people will learn the truth when they reach Mirath,' Draad said. 'But by then it won't matter. We'll have done what was necessary.'

The Doctor glanced at Ian, who nodded.

'Your secret is safe with us,' the Doctor assured Draad. 'Meanwhile, I will be pleased to look over your designs and make any suggestions that seem appropriate.'

On the screen Jarrasen smiled in relief. 'Thank you, Doctor. I'll sort out the details of the areas I'd like your opinion on.'

His image vanished.

'I'd like to go back to the building where we landed,' Ian said. 'To see if there's any news of Barbara.'

'Of course,' said Draad. 'I'll assign Captain Lant as your liaison. He'll take you anywhere you wish. Would you like to visit your granddaughter, Doctor?'

'Thank you, sir,' the Doctor said. 'I was hoping to see her before I start work.'

'I think we can spare you a few hours, gentlemen. Our time may be precious, but we strive to maintain a sense of order and civility. It will be all that sustains us through the last days of the world.'

Half an hour later, Ian and the Doctor stood on the balcony of their comfortable guest apartment in the mayoral residency. They were wearing borrowed dressing gowns while their clothes were undergoing a much needed cleaning by an automated valeting service. The rainstorm had blown itself out, leaving the towering Ship sparkling against a clear sky.

'I feel a bit guilty for having spoken to the mayor like that,' Ian admitted. 'I didn't think what they were up against.'

'Indeed, it's a desperate situation which has brought out both the best and worst in them,' the Doctor proclaimed solemnly. 'Out of the horror of war rises an example of outstanding technical ingenuity, driven by the indomitable will to survive.'

He gestured at the Ship, then lowered his voice: 'Except there was one detail of their story that was inconsistent.'

'What?'

'Think back, Chesterton, and you'll note it. Perhaps it was simply an oversight in the telling, or perhaps... Well, we shall just have to wait and see. But be on your guard!'

Chapter Thirteen
Nightmare

Susan emerged from her self-induced healing trance into what she took to be a very bad dream.

She was in complete darkness and an unpleasant stench of decay assailed her nostrils. Although she was lying flat on her side the surface beneath her seemed to be rippling very slightly. She began to imagine cold damp things pressing against her, clinging to her skin and leaving slimy trails. After some muddled consideration she decided it was probably a side-effect of the hospital drugs, and wished she could wake up.

Then her fingers closed on what felt very much like a ragged strip of cold meat and a rotten apple core.

With a squeal of surprise and revulsion she forced her numbed and stiffened limbs to move, and scrabbled frantically out of the pile of refuse she had been lying in.

She sat upright, swaying slightly. It took determination to breathe the fetid air in deeply, but she needed to force oxygen into her sluggish system. Gradually she felt sensation returning to her limbs and the higher levels of her mind began to function once more. Stay calm, she told herself. This is not a dream, it's real. I must observe and reason before I act. There is no light, so I must use my hands to find out where I am.

She was resting on what felt like a sheet of thick rubber. It was level in front and behind but curved up at the sides. Her fingers reached its edge and were suddenly brushing against a smooth, curving metal wall that seemed to be sliding past her. She followed it up and over her head. It was a closed tube. But why was it moving?

Suddenly the faint ripples passing under her made sense. The tube was not moving, she was. She was on some sort of conveyor belt that fitted seamlessly into a tray in the bottom of the tube, perhaps riding on a thin film of polarised oil.

Her hands, still brushing the tube above her head, slipped momentarily into a void, slapped against a funnel-like metal rim and then continued sliding along the tube wall as before. It had been an opening of some sort in the roof of the tube. Were there others?

She kept her hands in place. A minute later she felt another similar opening, its rim encrusted with slime and caked with shreds of organic matter. The brief contact enabled her to judge that the belt was moving at about walking pace. The openings seemed to be set at regular intervals in the ceiling of the tube. Rubbish chutes perhaps? Was that where the mass of waste she had been lying in had come from? Yes, that was it. She was in an organic waste-handling system that probably ran under the city.

But why? What was she doing here? Where were Grandfather and the others? Her last memories had been of entering a hospital.

For the first time Susan felt herself all over. Her sole garment was a thin disposable gown, now badly stained and beginning to disintegrate in patches. She also discovered several smooth plastic pads, which could only be protective bandaging, adhering to her skin. She shivered involuntarily, suddenly realising how cold and hungry she felt. Well, there was nothing she could do to alleviate either condition at this moment, except to hug her arms about her, so she simply had to ignore them. The chutes were too small for her to climb up even if she could get a grip on their smooth walls. She might as well conserve her strength and let the conveyor carry her along to its destination, presumably some sort of tip or recycling plant. There had to be a way out of there, and hopefully somebody to give her an explanation for her situation. At the moment it seemed as though she was being thrown out with the rest of the rubbish.

A macabre thought suddenly came to her.

She had put herself into a healing trance – a state very close to death. With her metabolism so suppressed perhaps the hospital thought she actually was dead. Perhaps this was how they disposed of bodies in the city. But Grandfather would never have let them do such a thing – unless something had happened to him as well. She clutched her head in despair. This was a nightmare.

Only then did she notice the faint glow beginning to illuminate her surroundings. A pinpoint of light shone out ahead of her, getting brighter by the second. As it did so she became aware of the growing hum of machinery.

The pinpoint became a circle of stark, blue-tinted light and suddenly the tube opened on to a large chamber.

The mouths of a dozen other tubes similar to hers were ringed about its perimeter, their conveyor belts protruding like tongues to hang over the side wall of a great vat that filled the centre of the chamber. From within it came a shrill whirring sound.

Susan leapt over the side of the conveyor belt even as the pile of garbage ahead of her vanished over the edge of the structure.

She climbed unsteadily to her feet and cautiously peered into the vat. Below her an array of whirling blades was reducing the waste to a sludgy pulp that was being sucked noisily out at the bottom, presumably to be taken on to the next stage of the process.

She looked about her. There was no one to be seen. Perhaps the whole plant was automatic and only needed occasional maintenance inspections. But there must still be a door somewhere, she reasoned. She saw a flight of metal stairs running up to a gantry that ringed the chamber wall. That looked promising.

She had to drag herself up the steps with the handrail, realising just how weak her legs were. Healing her injuries had sapped her strength more than she had thought. But her effort was rewarded by the sight of a heavy riveted door. Staggering over to it she grasped its sturdy handle.

It wouldn't move.

She twisted it both ways but it remained absolutely immobile. She kicked and banged on the door, then pressed her ear to it and listened intently for any response. She thought she heard more machine sounds from the other side, but no sign of life. Eventually, exhausted by her struggles, she sank her head against the cold metal of the door panel and slid down on to her knees. The door was either rusted and jammed, or else locked. Either way, unless there was some other way out, she was effectively trapped in the chamber.

An appalling thought struck her. If this world was doomed, as the announcements on the roadside screens had suggested, would anybody ever bother to come down here again?

She felt like giving in to her fear and crying aloud at that point, but knew that she could afford neither the time nor the effort that such a display would cost. Shivering, she feebly wiped a filthy hand across her face and looked about her. Concentrate, she told herself. Perhaps she could find some sort of tool to break the door down.

For the first time she noticed an alcove set a little way round the gantry. Bracing herself against the wall she pulled herself upright and tottered over to it.

On one side of it hung three suits of one-piece plasticised orange coveralls, complete with hoods, overboots and gauntlets. Opposite these was something that resembled an open shower. A mesh drain was set in the floor and a ring of sprinkler heads and control handles was mounted on the wall. For a moment Susan's sluggish mind could not make sense of the arrangement. Then she realised the coveralls were protective oversuits for maintenance workers who had some particularly dirty task to perform. The shower was there to wash the workers down afterwards.

Did it still work?

Hesitantly she twisted the first handle. Rusty water spluttered from the shower heads, gradually running cleaner and faster as the pipes cleared. Susan cupped her hands under the spray and cautiously sipped. The water had an inky tang but at that moment she could not have cared less. She filled her hands again and found the water was growing warm. Somewhere a heating element had cut in.

Twisting the handle further made the water steaming hot. The second handle added liquid soap, which smelled strongly of disinfectant, to the spray. The third handle cut the water and replaced it with a blast of warm air.

Susan looked thoughtfully at the shower and the coveralls, then at the remains of her filthy gown.

Ten minutes later, washed and dried, Susan was pulling on a bright orange coverall. It was far too big for her so she pulled all the fastening strips as tight as she could, folding in excess material. The suit had a lining to make it more comfortable to wear, but because it was designed as an overgarment it was too thin to keep out the damp chill of the recycling chamber. She put a second suit on over the first and fastened it in turn. After a little wriggling and adjusting she began to feel warm for the first time since she had woken up. She was still hungry, but at least she had slaked her thirst and was adequately dressed. Now she could look for some tool to help her break down the door, or some other way out of the chamber...

Her plans were interrupted by a prodigious yawn.

Perhaps she was being too hasty. Even though she felt better she was far from recovered. She simply had to rest before her strength gave out, or she did something foolish because she wasn't thinking clearly.

Wearily she threw the remaining coverall on the floor and curled up on top of it. Worries about her grandfather and Barbara and Ian briefly clouded her thoughts before she felt herself slipping away. How she wished she could wake up in the TARDIS and find it really was all a bad dream.

Chapter Fourteen
Class Barriers

That evening, Ian and the Doctor visited Susan in the City Hospital. She was in a side room of her own in the recovery ward and had not yet gained consciousness. However, the attendant assured them this was quite normal in cases of intense regenerative treatment. To Ian's amazement they apparently expected her to be fully recovered in a few days. Medicine in Arkhaven was clearly highly advanced.

Though he'd already seen her that afternoon, the Doctor's face still showed the depth of his concern. As Ian looked on he bent over Susan and kissed her forehead – a small gesture that revealed more about the gentler side of his nature than the old man usually permitted.

Ian's relief that Susan was making good progress was, however, tempered by his desperate concern for Barbara.

Earlier he had visited Carlson Tower while the Doctor was seeing Susan. Only a quarter of the original building remained standing, rapidly diminishing under the attentions of a swarm of demolition machines. He was properly introduced to Supervisor Curton, who estimated it would take at least another day to finish the job since the rubble in the lowest levels would have to be excavated with additional care. They had scanned the building with various devices but without any positive result. This was not unexpected if, as they suspected, Barbara was in the very heart of the remains.

Ian recalled stories of people being pulled out of buildings destroyed by earthquakes days after they had been given up for dead. In the circumstances he knew it was a slim possibility that the same miracle would be played out here, yet some instinct, however irrational, told him Barbara was alive. He had to act as though that was so because the alternative was too awful to contemplate. Not that this conviction gave him much ease. He knew that it would be at least twenty-four more long hours before he would know for certain – one way or the other.

Meanwhile he wished he had something to occupy himself with. There was nothing he could do on the site itself – the machines did not need his aid to work any faster and he could only get in the way. Helping the Doctor check the plans of the Ship was, of course, a task completely beyond his talents. It seemed there was nothing else to do but wait. Visiting Susan that evening at least helped the time pass.

With Susan still sleeping peacefully, they left the ward. In the corridor outside they hesitated, momentarily unsure of the way out.

'Where's Lant?' asked the Doctor impatiently. 'He's meant to be escorting us.'

'He slipped away a while ago,' Ian said. 'There was somebody he wanted to see, I think. I suppose he has a friend or relative in here.'

At that moment Lant appeared round the corner in the company of an attractive young woman in a staff uniform. They were both laughing at something and clearly had eyes only for each other.

At the sight of the couple the Doctor's impatience seemed to melt away, to be replaced by a look of benevolent amusement.

'Observe, Chesterton, the resilience of the human spirit. Even in such times as these, love is not to be denied.'

'I never suspected you were such a romantic at heart, Doctor.'

'I never deny the power or significance of such an emotion in its proper place, my boy.'

Lant looked up, realised that he and his companion were being watched, made a quick excuse to her and hurriedly joined them looking slightly embarrassed.

'Sorry to keep you waiting, gentlemen.'

'A friend of yours?' Ian inquired mildly.

'Er, Nyra Shardri, intensive care clinician. She monitored Susan's treatment when she was first admitted and advised me on her case this morning. I was just... thanking her for her work.'

'Then you must introduce us so that I can do the same,' the Doctor said, a twinkle in his eye.

Lant flushed slightly. 'Yes, of course, next time we're here, perhaps. This way.'

The spacious mayoral limousine was in front of the hospital. Inside Draad was waiting for them in what was evidently Arkavian evening dress.

'Today was a social day and this is traditionally a night for celebration in Arkhaven,' he explained. 'Everybody, including the mayor and his guests, is expected to appear in public and enjoy themselves for a few hours.'

'Even under these conditions?' Ian wondered.

'Especially under these conditions, Mr Chesterton. We aim to maintain a normal routine in the city until the last minute. That's how we have survived this far without major social disorder. So I hope you will allow me to take you to the Polkatoon. It's our most popular nightspot and serves excellent food.'

'That's very kind,' Ian said, 'but I'm not exactly in a party mood.'

The Doctor gave him a thoughtful glance. 'On the other hand, perhaps this is just what you need to take your mind off things, Chesterton. Worrying yourself into the ground won't help Barbara, you know.'

'Any news of her will be relayed to me the moment it comes in,' Draad assured him. 'Meanwhile, let this serve as a gentle introduction to our society before the more tedious functions you will no doubt be invited to in the coming days.'

Ian was going to protest further, then realised that they might be right. An evening out would help pass the time. He shrugged.

'All right, let's go. But it'll have to be in these clothes. We haven't anything smarter,' he glanced meaningfully at the Doctor. 'Unless we can get the TARDIS open again.'

'I assure you nobody will take offence at your style of dress,' said Draad.

As the car pulled away, Monitor's voice came from a speaker set in a small console behind the driver's seat.

'The item is about to be broadcast on the evening news, Mayor.'

'Thank you, Monitor,' said Draad, switching on a small vision screen.

It showed an image of the same reporter they had seen the previous day. But this time she appeared notably more enthusiastic about what she had to say.

'To return to the main item of news tonight. Within the last hour, the mayor's office announced that a party of four beings from another world landed in Arkhaven yesterday. Here is a further excerpt from their interview with the mayor in which they describe their travels.'

The scene changed to show Ian and the Doctor seated in the mayor's office that morning. From the angle, Ian realised it must have been recorded through Monitor's camera eye. Part of the Doctor's description of the many different life forms they had encountered was replayed, which Ian had to admit made for engrossing viewing. When it was finished the reporter reappeared.

'As you can see the aliens appear externally quite human and speak our language fluently. However, medical reports confirm they are not native to Sarath. Their presence will no doubt revive debate over the so-called "Origin Question", suggesting our ancestors migrated to Sarath many millennia ago from another world system.

'Meanwhile the aliens have agreed to use their superior knowledge of space travel to give technical advice on the final preparations for launching the Ship. The mayor requests that the aliens be treated with respect during their stay with us and not be troubled by idle curiosity seekers...'

Draad turned off the screen to face frowns of disapproval on the faces of Ian and the Doctor.

'You did not mention you would make our arrival so public,' the Doctor said tersely. 'Or that you were recording our conversation.'

'Forgive me, but Monitor records all such meetings automatically,' Draad explained. 'As to the publicity, you must understand that your presence will give the people something else to occupy their minds. Some of the more superstitious may consider your coming as a good omen… or perhaps a challenge to their views. I don't really care as long as it has the desired effect.'

'While also letting them know the Ship will launch fully certified with our blessing,' Ian said.

'Of course,' said Draad. 'The people must have confidence in it. You have come uninvited to our world, but I think you will agree, after our understandable initial misunderstanding, that we have treated you well. Is it so much to ask that you lend your support to maintaining public order?'

The Doctor sighed. 'I suppose we have no choice. Very well, we shall play our part. Can you put on a cheerful face, Chesterton?'

Ian looked at their hosts. 'I'll do my best,' he promised doubtfully.

Arkhaven's Third Avenue, on which the Polkatoon was situated, blazed with light and movement. Neon signs flickered over the entrances of theatres, clubs and amusement halls. The street was full of cars depositing their consignments of pleasure seekers. The buzz and chatter of voices filled the air. For the first time Ian felt the city was truly alive.

The Polkatoon itself was not very different from a high-quality London restaurant club. It even had liveried attendants to open the doors and usher them inside.

Eyes turned as they entered the main saloon and the murmur of conversation momentarily dipped. Evidently news of their arrival had already reached the other diners, who recognised both their host and their non-Arkavian style of dress. But the force of good manners, and Draad's request, evidently prevailed over curiosity and nobody troubled them, though Ian was conscious of many eyes following his every move. He managed a quick smile then hurriedly took his seat and hid behind a menu. The Doctor, however, paused to beam and wave graciously about him, as though bestowing a benediction, before he sat down. Ian found it hard to believe that the old man was not secretly enjoying their new celebrity status.

The Polkatoon's menu lived up to Draad's promise, while a small band provided pleasant background music. At intervals instrumental soloists, singers and a pair of graceful acrobatic dancers performed. Ian and the Doctor made a point of applauding all of them, to the evident appreciation of the staff and patrons. Gradually, perhaps aided by some excellent synthesised wine, Ian started to relax for the first time in days. He began to believe everything would work out all right. Tomorrow they would find Barbara safe and well, then the Doctor would make a new key for the TARDIS and…

'There you are, Draad,' a voice said loudly. 'My father's been looking everywhere for you.'

A perfectly groomed young man in expensive-looking clothes was standing over them. He was wearing an expression of petulant annoyance. At his shoulder were another man and two women of the same type, judging by their dress, while behind them was the Polkatoon's maître d' looking distinctly unhappy.

'He even sent me out on the hunt,' the young man continued, eyeing Ian and the Doctor with mild curiosity. 'He wants to talk to you about these two aliens immediately.'

Draad's face was stony and Ian saw much the same expression on Lant's. Very deliberately, the mayor dabbed his lips with his napkin before replying.

'Do you know what day and hour this is, Vendam?'

'What? Of course I…'

'Then you know I may only be disturbed for an emergency, nothing less. The arrival of these people does not constitute an emergency. Your father may take this matter up in the council tomorrow and not before. Now have the good manners to leave me and my guests in peace.'

The young man gaped at him in amazement. 'How dare you talk to me like that, Functionary!'

'And how dare you give me orders, boy! I am the mayor of Arkhaven and I have more important things on my mind than your fragile feelings. Now, you're causing a scene and disturbing everyone's meal, so why don't you take yourself out of here.'

Lant slid his chair back from the table and let his hand fall lightly on to the butt of his side-arm.

The young man blinked in surprise, hesitated, and then retreated, taking his companions with him. After a minute's urgent discussion among themselves they took a table towards the back of the room and ordered drinks. Meanwhile Draad took a long draught from his own glass. Beneath his outward calm Ian could see he was nervous.

'And who was that unpleasant young man?' the Doctor asked.

'Plaxander Vendam.' Draad said. 'First time I've ever spoken back to him like that, though I've wanted to for years.' He smiled weakly. 'But then this is the season for firsts, is it not?'

'Somebody should probably have done that a long time ago,' said Ian, speaking with a teacher's experience. 'What's so special about his father, then?'

'Lord Vendam is the leader of the Elite families... the last of our aristocracy, since the destruction of the capital and the loss of the royal family. They command a lot of traditional respect. Vendam has a seat on the city council.'

'It seems we do not understand your social system,' the Doctor said. 'Perhaps you'd better explain.'

Draad made a grimace. 'I'm afraid we're divided by class and affiliation. There are the Elite families, the Technical and Service Functionaries, the Church, the Military and the Common Citizens. There is only limited interchange between them.'

'How can the Church be a class?' Ian asked.

'When somebody is accepted into the Church of the Maker as a true believer, not simply a worshipper, they behave as though they are something quite apart from the rest of us.'

'And you do not approve of such commitment?' the Doctor asked.

'Let us say I have my doubts,' said Draad. 'But since the loss of the old capital city made him the most senior churchman on Sarath, Fostel's self-assurance has grown almost beyond measure. Such a degree of certainty makes me uncomfortable.'

'Talking of priests,' said Ian, 'there's one heading this way.'

A dark-robed priest, looking distinctly out of place among the brightly dressed diners, approached their table.

'His Eminence wishes to talk with you,' he said stiffly, and placed a device on the table in front of Draad. It unfolded to reveal a microphone grille and a tiny screen. The image of Bishop Fostel's face appeared on the screen.

'Monitor refused to put my call through, Draad,' Fostel said angrily without any preamble.

'Presumably because he judged it was not an emergency, Bishop,' Draad replied calmly, though his fists were clenched as they rested on the table on either side of the communicator. 'But, now that you have gone to such lengths, why do you wish to speak to me?'

'Because of the aliens, of course! Why was I not informed of their presence sooner? I had to hear it on the public broadcast.'

'That is what the public broadcasts are for,' said Draad.

'What?' Fostel spluttered.

'Public broadcasts are for the dissemination of information and they seem to have served their function in this case,' Draad explained.

'Are you intoxicated?' Fostel asked suspiciously.

'If I am, it is because these few hours are the only time I can allow myself such licence… and you have interrupted me.'

'For good reason…'

'For no reason. The aliens are in my care. They are perfectly friendly and pose no threat to the security of Arkhaven. In addition they are aiding us with the final preparations for the launch; a task which, as you have so often reminded me, is the responsibility of the Functionary class alone since it involves trivial details you do not wish to be concerned with.'

'All your concerns are for material things, Draad,' Fostel retorted. 'What of the aliens' spiritual fitness? They may pollute the minds of our citizens with lies and falsehoods. They must be examined and questioned on matters of doctrine…'

'I have questioned them and I am satisfied they are no more than innocent travellers who chanced to land in Arkhaven. Their spiritual beliefs are a matter for their own consciences. Meanwhile, remember that they are official guests of my office. Unless you want to challenge my authority this close to the exodus and risk the disruption that would create?'

Fostel glared at him but said nothing.

Draad smiled. 'If you'd troubled to check, you would find I sent transcripts of my interview with our new guests to the offices of all members of the council before the first public announcement. Lord Vendam seemed to find time to read his copy, since he contacted me about the matter some while ago. Now, if there is nothing further, good night.'

And he closed the communicator down and waved at the dumbstruck priest to take it away. Those diners close enough to have heard some of the interchange looked at Draad with a curious mixture of surprise and admiration.

'I fear our presence here has caused some friction,' the Doctor said.

'Don't trouble yourself,' Draad said. 'It had to come out sooner or later. With the launch approaching and tension rising it was inevitable.'

'So you stood up to old Fostel at last.'

Plaxander Vendam was beside them once more, smiling condescendingly down at Draad, a drink in his hand. It must have been something quite strong Ian thought, for he already looked slightly glassy-eyed.

Vendam waved his finger from side to side. 'Didn't think you had it in you,' he continued. 'Maybe we should invite you along on our next hunt. Fourteen we caught last night. Think you can do better?'

Ian saw Lant, who had by now half risen from his chair, hesitate at the young man's words. For a moment a puzzled frown replaced the anger on the captain's face.

Vendam stepped back from the table.

'Don't worry, Captain, I'm leaving.' He grinned at Draad without humour. 'But you're still going to regret talking to me like that earlier. Just you wait till my father hears about it.'

And he walked unsteadily away.

Suddenly the jollity of the Polkatoon seemed hollow to Ian. These people were putting on a brave front and trying to maintain a sense of normality until the last minute, but underneath they were fragile and divided. And now their own fate had become inextricably linked with that of the city. Would this last vestige of civilisation hold together long enough? An old saying came into his head:

Eat, drink and be merry... for tomorrow you die.

Chapter Fifteen
The Thing in the Dark

Gelvert woke to find Semanov shaking his shoulder urgently.

'All the lights have gone out in the block around us,' she said.

Gelvert scrambled out of the inner office, now lit only by a pale wedge of light coming through the open door, and went across to where Tressel was crouched, peering over the window sill through the grimy glass. Distant buildings were lit but everything within a few hundred metres of them was dark, including the street lights.

'It happened a few minutes ago,' Tressel said, his voice reduced to a nervous whisper. 'If it was a mains supply failure I would have thought more blocks would have gone out, but the rest of the city looks all right. It seems to have just affected the buildings around us.'

They had decided to lie low during the day, and move only late at night and in the small hours of the morning. At the edge of Penko district, just beyond the zone populated by its disconcerting dummy inhabitants, they had come upon an older section of the city filled with lower-rise buildings. Drawn to the anonymity of commercial premises rather than a private dwelling, they had broken into a small office block. The lower floors had been cleared of furniture, but the third floor and the ones above might have been abandoned only the day before. Cups were set on desks among scattered papers while top coats still hung in lobbies. Only the even layer of dust indicated how much time had passed. Everything suggested the workers had been called away to the shelters and had simply never come back. The building was an ideal place of concealment. A storage tank still held water for the washrooms and, apart from a few dead lumostrips, all the inner-core office lights shone steadily, as they did in the surrounding buildings.

Except that now everything had been plunged into darkness.

Keeping low, Gelvert moved from window to window checking for any sign of activity below. As far as he could tell nothing moved but there were a lot of shadows down there.

Eventually he sat down with his back to the wall and looked into his companions' anxious faces. Why did they have to gape at him like that? Did they expect him to have the answer to everything?

He sighed wearily. 'All right. Things aren't getting maintained around here as they should. This is probably just some accidental power cut.'

'But what if it's the Watch?' Semanov said. 'Maybe they know we're in this area and are trying to flush us out.'

'Turning off the power might make it easier to scan for us,' Tressel added. 'Fewer artificial heat sources to confuse them.'

'That's what we've got our thermal blankets for,' Gelvert snapped. 'Come on… and keep your heads down!'

Back inside the office they had been sleeping in, they gathered up their packs.

'Don't leave anything to show we've been here,' Gelvert said. 'We'll hide in the service unit on the roof in case there's a search. They can't check every corner of every building, and they're not going to scare us into giving ourselves away. Got it?'

Swathed in their blankets they passed through the main lobby and out on to the utility stairway which ran up the back of the building. Light from distant towers shone through the tall windows opening on to the stairwell. They started upwards, ducking low as they crossed each landing.

As they passed the second landing up, a shower of meteors seared across the sky and vanished somewhere over the mountains. They must have posed no threat to the city because the defences did not react, but for a few seconds they lit up the darkness around the building like lightning bolts.

Semanov gasped: 'There's something out there!'

They froze. 'I told you to keep your head down!' Gelvert said.

'I couldn't help it.'

'Well, what was it?'

'A shadow moving along one of the back roads. It was big.'

'A vehicle?'

'I'm not sure – I only got a glimpse.'

'It's the Watch. They're coming for us,' Tressel muttered wretchedly.

'Shut up and keep going,' said Gelvert.

Above the last office level, the head of the stairs ended in a single stout door. Gelvert quickly sprung the lock and they passed through. Slats and louvres in the walls of the enclosure beyond outlined the bulky forms of tanks and air-conditioning equipment.

'Find somewhere to hide yourselves,' Gelvert told Tressel and Semanov as he closed the door behind them. 'And whatever happens, keep quiet!'

They vanished into the darkness. Using the angle of a pipe as a step, Gelvert hauled himself up into the narrow space between the top of a large covered tank and the underside of the roof. He pulled his thermal blanket over himself and lay still, trying to calm his breathing. He was alert but confident. If the Watch was out there targeting this particular building, they'd have made themselves known with lights and loudspeaker demands as soon as they had the place surrounded. If that was going to happen it would have happened by now. Therefore, at the most, they were making a low-key sweep of the whole block and wouldn't have the time or manpower to make a thorough search of every building. All he and his companions had to do was keep their nerve.

Then his straining ears caught a noise from beyond the door. But it was not the sound of service boots.

Something was moving up the stairs with a rustling whisper, getting louder by the second. He concentrated but couldn't make any sense of the sound. The rustling became a rasp and faint staccato patter, then came a soft scrape as something brushed against the door.

Maybe whoever it was would give up when they found the door locked.

They didn't. Instead the door creaked as though force was being slowly but steadily applied to it. That wasn't how you broke down a door, Gelvert thought. What the hell was out there?

With a crack and squeal of torn hinges the door burst open. A moment later a faint red glow suffused the room. Gelvert jammed his knuckles into his mouth to prevent any involuntary sound. His only hope was absolute silence.

From below came a rapid scrabble and clicking, together with a prolonged slither as though a large body was being dragged across the floor. Gelvert's imagination began to race. Improbably, it sounded almost as though the noise was made by some sort of animal. But that was absurd... wasn't it?

A terrible temptation to raise his head over the side of the tank and look down rose within him, yet he knew he dare not move an inch.

The slithering and clicking continued past him but did not diminish. How big could the thing be?

Then the hissing began. It was soft at first but steadily grew louder. Gelvert's tortured mind could make only one association. It was the sound he imagined a giant snake might make.

There came the smack of boots striking concrete at the same moment as Tressel's voice rang out: 'Oh, God no...!'

The hiss became a howling roar as though air was being drawn into monstrous lungs, merging with Tressel's horrified scream.

Then there came a snap, as of huge jaws closing, and Tressel was silenced in mid-cry.

The thing scraped and clicked as it shifted its position. It was hunting them out. The hissing began to grow louder again. Could it smell them?

With a shout of defiance mingled with barely suppressed fear, Semanov burst out from her hiding place. There came the thud of a blow landing heavily. The hiss became a roar. Semanov screamed. There was a metallic clang as a stanchion bar or tool hit the ground. The terrible snap came again, the hissing stopped, and Gelvert knew she was gone.

Now there was only him left.

The thing shuffled and scrabbled, brushing against the fittings in the narrow service space. Gelvert imagined he could hear scales scraping across concrete and metal. The hissing began again.

Two red eyes set half a metre apart rose over the side of the tank.

With a cry of terror Gelvert scrabbled away from them and dropped down the back of the tank. He landed badly, cracking his knee, but he did not notice the pain. His only thought was to get away from the terrible thing that was pursuing him. He scrabbled on all fours through a maze of pipes. For a moment he glimpsed a long body at least a metre across rippling behind the tanks. It was huge. It must still fill the doorway. There was no escape that way.

Then his hand fell on the familiar shape of a bolt set in the wall panelling. Another door!

Gelvert drew the bolt, reached up for the handle that had to be there, twisted and pushed. The stiff hinges resisted for a moment then gave way, causing him to fall through on to the flat roof beyond.

He scrambled to his feet and ran to the edge nearest to him, looking over the low parapet for any sign of an emergency ladder. There had to be some way off the roof.

But there was nothing of the kind visible.

Behind him the thing slithered on to the roof, with a splintering crack as it burst apart the frame of the narrow door.

For the first time Gelvert saw it illuminated by the distant city lights. A black, rippling, tube body supported by many short-clawed legs, baleful red eyes, a long snout. He heard the hissing begin even as an arm-thick tongue extended towards him, flickering with dreadful sensuality, questing to embrace him.

He recoiled from it, choking in horror.

The edge of the parapet caught him in the small of the back.

For a few brief seconds land and sky blurred as the sparkling arc of city lights spun about him. He screamed.

Then came the ground and a final release.

Chapter Sixteen
Questions Without Answers

The morning was still young when Ben Lant rang the bell on the Vendam mansion's imposing front door.

'Captain Lant of the City Watch to see Plaxander Vendam,' he told the servant who answered. 'Official business.'

'Master Plaxander is still sleeping,' he was informed stiffly.

'Well, wake him up,' he replied. 'Tell him he has five minutes before I turn him out of bed myself.'

The mayor's resolute behaviour of the previous night was obviously catching, Ben thought, as he was ushered coldly through to a reception room. They were going to be leaving for a new world soon and taking only what was essential. Meaningless deference to outmoded privilege was something that would be left behind.

Three minutes later the reception room door opened to admit not Plaxander Vendam but his father, still wearing a dressing gown.

Ben gave him the most cursory nod. 'It's your son I want to talk to, Lord Vendam.'

'I know that,' Vendam replied sharply. 'Has this got anything to do with the business in the Polkatoon last night?'

'Only incidentally.'

'Apart from the mayor's incredible behaviour, my son says you threatened him and his companions with your side-arm.'

Ben's eyes widened slightly. 'I can't think where he got that idea from. My gun never left its holster at any time last evening. Your energy might be better spent teaching him how to behave in public. He came close to being arrested for disturbing the peace.'

Vendam flushed. 'How dare you tell me how to raise my son!'

'How dare you let a spoilt brat like that loose in a civilised society?' Ben replied, hardly believing the words that came so easily to his lips but enjoying every syllable.

At that moment Plaxander Vendam entered. He was unshaven and red-eyed. He blinked at the unexpected sight of his father, his face contorted with anger, standing almost nose to nose with Ben.

'I say, what's wrong, Father?'

Vendam senior glanced at him and then back to Ben again. 'I shall be speaking to Commander Pardek about your insolent behaviour at this morning's council,' he warned the captain.

'That is your privilege, sir,' Ben said as he turned away. 'And I will be pleased to repeat everything I have said before any tribunal or court you choose.'

Vendam hesitated at the door, then passed through and slammed it behind him.

Plaxander was gaping at Ben in amazement as though he had never seen anybody talk back to his father before. Perhaps he hadn't. Ben did not allow him to recover his composure.

'Sit down,' he said crisply, and the young man dropped automatically into a chair. Ben seated himself opposite.

'As you can tell, I'm in no mood to take any nonsense, particularly from the likes of you,' he said bluntly. 'Apart from last night there are several outstanding charges I might raise; traffic offences, unruly behaviour, disturbing the peace… I could go on. And you must realise your father won't be able to get you off this time. I don't think rank or title are going to count so much when we get to Mirath, so you might as well start getting used to it.' Plaxander paled a little more. Ben realised he'd pushed him far enough. In slightly easier tones he added: 'But if you answer my questions fully and accurately, perhaps I'll let the rest drop.'

'What do you want to know?' the young man said quickly.

'Last night you boasted about hunting down some escaped NC2s. I want to know everything about it.'

'Why? Your people have never cared in the past… as long as they get them back in fair shape.'

'As the mayor said last night, it's the season for firsts. Just tell me.'

Plaxander told him, recounting the details with growing enthusiasm as he relived the experience. He wouldn't reveal who had tipped him off as to the NC2s' hiding place and Ben did not press the matter, having a fairly good idea already. But otherwise Plaxander gave what seemed to be an accurate account of the chase and captures.

'And you'd caught fourteen NC2s by the time the Watch arrived?'

'Yes.'

'You're sure of the number?'

'Look, we always count them carefully – it's part of the game,' Plaxander said. 'Anyway, your people also counted them into their transporter. It was a full load with all of them inside. Then I heard them say there were three still unaccounted for.'

'Did they search for them?'

'Just around the old warehouse they'd been hiding in. They seemed to think they'd pick them up soon enough.'

There was little more Plaxander could tell him. Finally Ben picked up his cap and rose to leave. Seeing the look of relief on the young man's face, he shook his head.

'I'll give you one piece of advice for free,' he said. 'Never make threats when you're drunk – you may have to justify them when you're sober. I'll see myself out.'

The Doctor sat in a corner of the almost deserted city hall planning department, hunched over a metre-wide panel of white plastic angled like a draughtsman's drawing board. On its surface intricate blueprints sprang into being, which the Doctor then manipulated with an electronic pen. Exploded views of components, circuit diagrams, lists of specifications, chemical, metallurgical and atomic formulae all flashed before his eyes.

On the wall in front of him was one of Monitor's terminals and beside it a screen showing Professor Jarrasen's head and shoulders as he bent over a duplicate imaging board.

'Do you see here?' said the Doctor, tapping his pen and causing a point of light to flash on Jarrasen's board, 'If you alter the timing sequence you will improve the pumping efficiency by, oh, perhaps 11 or 12 per cent.'

'Yes, of course,' said Jarrasen, rapidly sketching in notes and adjustments. 'It's obvious when you point it out.'

Jarrasen's appreciation of the old man's knowledge and powers of concentration had been growing steadily. Occasionally the Doctor would become irritable as he transposed a technical term or made some minor error in his calculations, but it was obvious that he had forgotten more about atomic engineering and spacecraft design than Jarrasen would ever know. How he would love to spend more time with the man; to talk to him in person and even investigate that improbable craft of his, which he still could not quite believe in. But, if the project was to stay within its safety margins, time was the one thing he didn't have.

At last he sat back from his board, massaging the back of his neck.

'Well, you've given me plenty to work on, Doctor. I'll have to get the technicians started on these modifications straight away. Just ask Monitor if you want to link with me again. He can always find me.'

'One moment, Professor. I am curious as to why everything you have asked me to check so far has been concerned solely with the second stage of the Ship. Are you certain the main body will function perfectly?'

Jarrasen smiled. 'It's very simple. The second stage – the landing module – is the unit that's going to do the most work. The main body, despite its size, is really the simpler device. A brute-force lifter and cargo pod. I'm as certain as I can be that it will function correctly, but frankly it's too massive to modify now. It does have the capacity to land on Mirath, but not to take off again, so finding the right landing site is essential. That reconnaissance will be carried out by the Lander. If we don't find a suitable spot it will have to ferry down the colonists and their supplies in several trips. So you see, that's the vehicle that we shall rely on most and which must be as safe as we can make it.'

'I understand now,' the Doctor said. 'Only I had noticed its reaction mass capacity was limited. I would estimate it could only just lift off unaided if it was completely unladen.'

'That's quite correct. The Lander will be refuelled in orbit from the main body as required.'

'Of course. Well, I mustn't detain you any further, Professor.'

After Jarrasen had gone the Doctor stared thoughtfully into space for some minutes. Then he said:'Monitor. What is your estimate of the chances of the Ship launching successfully?'

'Based on the projected performance of the vehicle as specified by Professor Jarrasen, the launch plan has a 96 per cent chance of success.'

'I suppose those are encouraging odds compared to the alternative,' the Doctor admitted.'You know, I'm greatly impressed by the speed with which you have mastered a technology your ancestors must have lost thousands of years ago. It is a remarkable feat to develop such a massive vehicle in such a relatively short time.'

'It is true we are more advanced in other fields, Doctor. Chemistry, cybernetics and medicine have traditionally been fields of special study in Arkhaven.'

'Indeed. The treatment my Susan is receiving is most sophisticated.'

'The war brought about many improvements in medical techniques while also stimulating the development of interceptor missile systems,' Monitor said. 'Prior to that no country on Sarath had reason to develop rocketry or spaceflight technology.'

'Of course,' the Doctor mused. 'Unlike your forebears on Earth, your moon was an insignificant body before its orbit changed. A mere point of light would not fire the imagination as a goal or a stepping stone to other worlds. Other sciences would flourish with disproportionate speed. There would be less incentive to develop space travel.'

'I have observed that the moon is providing us with ample incentive now, Doctor,' said Monitor.

Commander Pardek shifted uneasily in his chair and glanced at his desk clock.

'I can only give you a few minutes, Captain. I'm due at the council meeting shortly.'

'Then I'll be as brief as I can, sir,' said Ben. 'I appreciate my assignment to this squad is only temporary, but I have had to request reports on the search for the escapees each time, rather than being automatically updated.'

'Well, I'm sorry you seem to have been overlooked. Terrel liked to run the squad his way and his men may be less flexible than they could be. I'll have a word with him when he gets back. And I have taken note of your request for additional resources to be diverted to the camp. Now, if that's all…'

'I'm afraid that's not all, sir. I have a query about the number of NC2s that were recaptured the night before last.'

'Well?'

'I was told by Commandant Breen that only six were returned to the camp. However, Plaxander Vendam seems to think he and his friends captured fourteen.'

'Vendam? I wouldn't trust anything that boy says.'

'No, but I assume he can count. Keeping score was all part of the sport for them.'

'Very well. I'll look into the matter.'

'If you could do it immediately, sir. You understand that I must know where I stand with the men under my command, even for just a few days. Especially if they can apparently lose over half of a group of prisoners in a few hours. Sergeant Erindro was in charge. He should be back at headquarters by now. Perhaps if you could have a word with him?'

Pardek checked his clock again, then with evident displeasure picked up the phone.

Erindro came in a few minutes later. When Pardek demanded an explanation for the loss of eight prisoners he looked shamefaced.

'It's sort of embarrassing, sir. One of the transporters broke down on the way back from the scene of the arrest… you know the sort of problems we've been having with maintenance. While the crew were checking it over the NC2s broke out the back and made a bolt for it… I think the rear-cage locking must be faulty as well. Anyway, as they weren't yet booked in and we still had almost half of them, we thought we'd wait a bit before reporting it. We were sure we could pick them up again soon enough.'

'What you're saying is that a whole vanful of prisoners got away because of bad maintenance?' Ben said carefully.

'Yes, sir,' said Erindro.

'But why the hell didn't you tell me?'

'We thought it would look bad for Captain Terrel, seeing as he would have to take the responsibility for not following up on the maintenance.'

'I see. I hope the other transporter was all right.'

'No problem, sir.'

'Well, that explains it. You may have acted out of loyalty, but it was still very stupid. However, any disciplinary action is up to the commander.'

Erindro was curtly dismissed. Pardek said: 'I'm sorry you've been bothered with this, Lant. Anyway, Terrel will be back on duty tomorrow, so you can return to the Wall guard.'

'Actually I'm liaison officer with the aliens, sir. And since the mayor said we were to extend them every courtesy, I'd like to do my best to find the Doctor's missing key.'

'Very well, hunt for your key. But don't waste your time over a few NC2s. They can't do much harm in the Outer Zone. I'm sure they'll turn up sooner or later.'

'I'm sure they will, sir. After all there must be quite a lot of them by now.'

'What do you mean?'

'A good few hundred if Breen's figures are correct.' Before Pardek could respond Ben said: 'But I mustn't keep you from the council any longer. Thank you very much for your help, sir.'

Outside Pardek's office the amiable expression left his face to be replaced by a look of scowling concern. Why was he being lied to?

His phone beeped for attention, and he answered it distractedly. It was one of the regular Outer Zone patrols.

'Captain, I thought I'd call you direct. We've found that runaway you were after.'

* * *

Pardek made his excuses to Draad as he hurried into the council chamber a few minutes late.

For much of the time the various members of Arkhaven's High Council did business with each other remotely, but it was traditional that once every ten days they should gather in person. It was a custom Draad thought they could well do without.

Vendam and Fostel were already seated round the table. An air of expectant tension hung over them, manifesting itself in an uncomfortable protocol-imposed silence. Pardek took his place, completing the assembly and ensuring that all the significant classes of Arkhaven were represented. The Common Citizens would have their say at Low Council. Monitor acted as secretary and keeper of the records.

'I declare this session open,' Draad said.

Fostel and Vendam each tried to speak at once. Vendam won through as he had the louder voice.

'I move that the mayor be asked to explain his inexcusable behaviour of last night,' he said angrily.

For once Fostel nodded in agreement. 'It was a grave insult to the dignity of the Church for a request of its emissary to be so publicly rejected.'

Draad maintained a calm expression in the face of their accusations. When they paused, he said mildly: 'Well, I'm sure I didn't intend to insult either of you … in the same way as I'm sure you did not intend to risk destabilising the city's social balance by disturbing the few hours of relaxation that I permit myself each day.'

Vendam hesitated, still angry, but puzzled by the response.

'How does disturbing you destabilise the social balance, Draad?'

'You must surely appreciate the damage you could have done by making those very public attempts to contact me.'

'What are you talking about?' snapped Fostel.

'The citizens must be reassured that we are in control of the situation… that is one fact we all agree on, is it not?'

'The mayor is quite right,' said Pardek. 'We must keep the people calm.'

'Therefore to show any sign of disunity or lack of co-ordination was the worst thing you could have done,' Draad said. 'And consider the effect on our alien guests. I had to react firmly to reassure them that I was capable of keeping the promises I made to them.' He shrugged helplessly. 'I really had no choice.'

He saw a hint of uncertainty beginning to creep into the faces of Fostel and Vendam, and continued: 'To reiterate: the aliens pose no security threat to Arkhaven. Commander Pardek was informed once their identity was established and since then they have been escorted by a reliable officer of the Watch. They are certainly not going to cause any trouble while one of their number is still lost and the other is receiving hospital treatment. Properly handled, their presence can be used to both divert and reassure the public during the crucial days up until the launch. The elder alien... the Doctor... is giving us invaluable advice on the Ship which may make the difference between success and disaster. Therefore I suggest this is an administrative matter for the Functionary and Technical classes. Of course, you may meet with the aliens and judge for yourselves once they have settled in, but there is nothing to be gained by aggressive questioning or treating them with undue suspicion.'

'What about this craft of theirs... this box thing?' said Vendam. 'I can't believe it's what they claim. Is it dangerous?'

'Whether it is or not, it is safely under guard. If they find the means to open it again we shall be with them. But its impenetrability to any force we have so far applied does indicate a superior science. For the moment I see no reason to doubt their explanation.'

Vendam still looked ill-tempered but seemed willing to let the matter rest. Fostel was less easily satisfied.

'They may not pose a material threat to Arkhaven, but what about spiritually?' he asked, his eyes narrowing. 'They may bring dangerous ideas with them. Already their presence has been linked on the news broadcast with the Origin Question. They cannot be allowed to move freely in public until I have resolved this matter.'

Draad sighed. 'It may come as a surprise to you, Bishop, but the aliens have expressed no desire to undermine our spiritual beliefs. If they wish to worship in the cathedral I'm sure Captain Lant can show them the way. You may talk to them there if you wish. Otherwise, for the next few days at least, they must be left alone if they are to continue serving their purpose.'

Fostel's lips pinched. 'This is a matter of doctrine and morality, therefore Church law takes precedence.'

Draad looked Fostel straight in the eye and said quietly: 'Bishop, this may be a matter of our very survival as a people. I maintain that takes precedence over everything else!'

Ben Lant stood over Gelvert's twisted body.

He would have liked to convince himself that the man looked at peace now, but in truth he looked anything but. Death had frozen a look of utter terror on Gelvert's face.

'Did you find anything on him?' he asked the patrolmen who had alerted him.

'Just a thermal blanket and this.'

One of them handed over Gelvert's pack. Ben emptied it out. There was no sign of the Doctor's key. With a grimace he searched through Gelvert's pockets, also without success.

Ben looked up at the building that Gelvert must have fallen from.

'Find anything up there?'

'We're not sure… perhaps you'd better have a look yourself, sir.'

Once on the roof he saw what they meant.

Just beyond the smashed door of the service enclosure was a curious, long, scrape mark in the pliant waterproofing compound used to sheath the roof panels. On either side of it he could just make out rows of small nicks and pockmarks. What could have left such traces, and had it anything to do with Gelvert's death? Did he fall by chance… or was he pushed?

Ben walked over to the roof parapet and looked down into the street below where Gelvert's body lay, trying to make sense of what he had found. He saw a car arrive containing the forensic examiner. At a time like this they should not be investigating mysterious deaths, he thought bitterly. He looked out over the sprawling city, wondering if it would keep its secrets until the very end of the world.

Ian had spent the morning at the remains of Carlson Tower, pacing restlessly around the command vehicle and watching intently as the machines dismantled the last few floors of the building. Curton would evidently have liked to ply him with questions about space travel and other worlds but, sensitive to Ian's state of mind, he politely refrained.

Then, just after midday, he called Ian into the command vehicle and pointed to one of the screens that relayed images from the robot digging crew. It showed a yellow metal girder frame and a section of mesh protruding from between two slabs of concrete.

'That's the top of the lift cage.'

Ian took a deep breath. 'Any... sign of her?'

'No. I can't detect any sound or find a thermal trace. I'm just moving a grab in to lift that main slab.'

Shovel-like robotic arms reached down into the picture. Metal fingers locked into position. Slowly the slab was raised clear and carried aside. Ian could hardly bear to look but he forced himself to scan the mass of flattened and twisted metal that had been the lift cage, knowing as he did so that nobody could have survived within it.

'I don't see anything. She's not there.'

For a moment he was nonplussed. Had Barbara fallen out of the cage as the tower collapsed? In which case she was still lying under the rubble that still had to be removed and there was no chance she had survived.

While he contemplated this bitter possibility the robot camera had been scanning the scene from all angles. As it passed over the mangled outflung remains of the lift door Ian suddenly pointed.

'What's that?'

Curton brought the camera in for an extreme close-up.

A snag of wool was hanging from a broken strand of door-panel mesh.

'That's the same colour as Barbara's jumper,' Ian said slowly.

'Well, we know she was in the cage,' Curton said.

'Yes, but don't you see… it could only have been torn like that after the damage had been done to the cage! Which means she must have got out before it was completely crushed.'

'Then we keep digging,' said Curton.

Ben wasn't certain why he stopped at the hospital. Perhaps because he wanted somebody outside the Watch to talk to. Even in the brief time he had known her he had found Nyra a good listener and, well, pleasant company. He could always say he was checking on Susan Foreman's progress if he wanted an excuse. The diversion would not interfere with his duty. He knew where the Doctor and Ian were and would be notified at once if they wanted anything.

But as he got out of his car he saw a distinctive black limousine in the sparsely occupied parking zone. As he passed by it he noted the coat of arms of the bishop's office emblazoned on the side. Now what did *he* want here? A sudden thought made Ben quicken his stride.

He heard the raised voices as he entered the recovery ward.

In the side room, two attendants and Nyra Shardri were facing down Fostel and Archdeacon Zeckler. Susan Foreman was awake and huddled in the bed between them looking confused and not a little frightened.

'What's going on here?' Ben demanded sternly.

'The bishop wants to question Miss Foreman about her religious beliefs,' Nyra explained. 'I said she's only just woken up and is still too weak.'

'I see,' said Ben. 'Gentlemen, I must ask you to leave.'

'You cannot order the bishop about as though he was a Common Citizen,' Zeckler snapped. 'This is Church business and no concern of yours.'

Ben realised then how much he disliked Zeckler. He was a mean little man who had risen in the Church through the deaths of better people in the war.

'It is the concern of every citizen, however common,' Ben said. 'We do not bully young girls in their hospital beds, especially when they are guests of the mayor.'

Fostel interjected, sounding oleaginously reasonable.

'I appreciate you are only following orders, Captain. But surely the mayor's instructions only apply to the alien men. This girl is clearly not performing any useful purpose at present, therefore it can do no harm to question her.'

Ben looked at Susan Foreman. Alien or not, to him she simply looked like a frightened young woman, hardly more than a girl. He smiled reassuringly. 'Hello. My name's Ben Lant. I'm a friend of your grandfather and Ian Chesterton.'

She managed to smile back. 'Hello,' she said.

'These men want to talk to you about where you come from and what sort of religion you practise, because they think you might try to subvert our city with dangerous alien beliefs. But I think you'd rather I call your grandfather to let him know you're awake at last.'

Susan regarded the two churchmen with very dark intense eyes and some spirit seemed to flow back into her.

'Do they think I'm going to cause all that trouble from here?' she asked drily, making Ben revise her age upwards a couple of years. 'If it's all the same, I'd rather you called my grandfather, please.'

'There you have it, gentlemen,' Ben said. 'Perhaps you can talk to the young lady when she has fully recovered... and with her grandfather present. But for the time being I'd like you to leave her alone.'

He saw the appalled and disbelieving expressions on their faces and had to admit he secretly found them very satisfying. Zeckler would have argued further but Fostel silenced him, and with bad grace the two departed. Ben knew he was making powerful enemies, but oddly the thought didn't trouble him. The mayor had shown the way and he was glad to follow.

'Now,' he said, turning back to Susan, 'let's put a call through to your grandfather.'

Carlson Tower had been reduced to a few jutting broken pillars of concrete, like a ring of broken teeth. The machines were busy removing the last slabs of rubble from what had been its basement levels. Ian and Curton stood in the middle of the rapidly clearing expanse of concrete floor. Nothing larger than fist-sized fragments remained.

There was no sign whatsoever of Barbara.

Ian looked at Curton in bewilderment. 'How can she have got out?'

'She can't. This building was cordoned off within minutes of the strike. Nobody could have passed through without being checked.'

Ian opened his arms wide in a hopeless gesture. 'Then where is she?'

He began walking about the inside of the enclosure, kicking at chips of concrete and shaking his head. Curton watched him, unable to think of anything to say at that moment.

Suddenly Ian halted. He stamped hard on the ground then went down on his hands and knees and began scraping aside the dust and grit.

'Come here!' he shouted.

'What is it?' Curton asked, running over to him.

'This slab moved. Look: it tilts then falls back into place again. There's a hollow underneath!'

'Let me get a digger over,' Curton said, tapping at the mobile control unit slung over his shoulder.

A large humanoid robot with heavy-duty claws for hands clumped over, grasped the slab and tossed it aside. Below was a rectangular pit half choked with fine rubble that had trickled down into it from above. At Curton's direction the robot began clearing it out. After a few scoops the detritus darkened and turned to heavy mud.

'Of course!' Curton exclaimed. 'It's a feeder to the city drainage system. A few of the older buildings were built right over them.'

'Big enough for Barbara to get through?'

'Yes, possibly.'

The channel passing through the bottom of the pit was exposed and the digger stepped back, its job done.

Ian made ready to clamber down. Curton held him back.

'Wait a minute... it could be unsafe after the pounding it's taken. I'll send a pedacam down first.'

Ian fretted as a small eight-legged robot with a camera and lighting array for a head was brought over. Grasping with its sucker feet it clambered nimbly down the sides of the pit and turned into the drainage channel beneath. Ian peered over Curton's shoulder watching the image the robot relayed to his mobile screen. The machine scurried down and along the culvert until it opened out on to a larger tunnel. Carefully the robot climbed out on to the vertical wall, lifting and twisting its head to scan the whole of the interior.

Ian and Curton both saw the sign scratched into the wall by the robot's feet at the same time.

'She got down there safely,' Ian almost shouted. 'She's telling us which way she went.'

'Yes, but I wish she'd stayed put,' Curton said.

'Well, she must have thought she could get out sooner than we could dig down to her.'

Curton looked worried. 'As we've got closer to Zero Day we've been economising on the maintenance. What with storm damage and a few earth tremors many of the tunnels are pretty unstable. Several access points collapsed. So we sealed off the rest. Your friend won't be able to climb out just anywhere.'

'Then I'll follow her down this shaft. She can't have gone far.'

'Didn't you hear what I said?'

'Yes. I'll take the chance, you don't have to come. All I want is a torch and a map of the tunnels.'

Curton smiled at Ian's determination. 'Well, if you'll just be patient for a couple of minutes I think I can kit you out better than that.' He glanced up at the sky, which was filling with dark clouds. 'I won't be long,' he added, and hurried off.

Ian turned back to contemplate the shaft at his feet. At last the waiting was over. Now he could do something.

Chapter Seventeen
So Close

Barbara woke to find herself lying on the narrow walkway beside the gurgling tunnel stream.

She didn't remember falling asleep. She must have been utterly exhausted. Still, she felt much better for the rest. Her stomach was rumbling for want of food, but she felt unexpectedly alert. Her clothes had dried out completely so she must have slept for some time.

Time.

Suddenly it seemed very important that she should know the time. She snapped on the torch still clasped in her hand and checked her watch. Of course, it had stopped ages ago. She rubbed its wristband and for a moment she felt there was something else she had forgotten. The suspicion of a curious dream flickered on the edge of her consciousness. Then it was gone.

Barbara took a deep breath. What should she do now?

After a minute's thought she decided it might make sense to retrace her steps. She hadn't had any luck finding a way out for herself, but perhaps by now the others had managed to dig down to where she had entered the drains. It would be foolish to keep walking away from them if that were the case. If she got back to find the way was still blocked, she would continue on past that point and try her luck further up the tunnel.

Feeling purposeful once more, she got to her feet and set off.

Dressed in waterproof coveralls and stout boots, Ian strode along the tunnel swinging the beams of his helmet lamp from side to side to make sure he didn't miss any of Barbara's scratched signs. Every couple of minutes he paused and called out her name, then strained his ears over the rush of water for some response apart from echoes.

The pedacam scuttled along in front of him. It hadn't been possible to fit any larger robot down the access shaft, though a team was working on enlarging the hole in case one should be needed. Curton wasn't sure if the robots that were normally used to monitor and repair the drains were still working, but he was making inquiries.

At regular intervals Ian took from his shoulder pack small metal discs sprouting twin telescopic aerials. These devices, as instructed, he stuck to the wall. They were radio booster relays which allowed him to stay in touch with Curton via his helmet radio, despite the growing thickness of earth and rock that separated them. On the surface the engineer was following his progress with a gang of robots, ready to dig Ian out if an emergency arose. Ian hoped they wouldn't be needed but it was raining heavily up above. Sudden intense storms had apparently become more common since the falling moon had begun to alter Sarath's weather patterns. Curton wasn't entirely sure what effect the increased flow was likely to have on the weakened tunnels, but Ian could already see the level rising in the channel by his side. The smaller culverts that discharged into the main tunnel were also running faster, filling the space with a continuous splash of water.

Ian worked his way around a mound of debris that formed a half dam where the roof had partially collapsed, after letting the pedacam scout the way first. The rising stream was already beginning to wash away the lighter material about the base of the fall, he noticed.

Once on the other side the water level was a little lower. He checked the hand-held flat screen Curton had given him which displayed a map of the tunnel system in glowing outlines. Converting from the metric scale he found he had come almost two miles. He looked about him and saw the heartening sight of another of Barbara's signs. She'd certainly made a great effort to find her own way out of here, he thought with admiration. He set another radio relay, checked his position with Curton, then called out Barbara's name once again.

'Barbara...bara...ra!' it echoed away.

'An...an...nn!' came faintly back up the tunnel.

He froze, hardly daring to breathe. Had he imagined it? The noise of the water made it so hard to tell. He called again and cupped his ears.

'Ian... an...an!' came more clearly. It was Barbara's voice!

'Yes! I'm here!' he shouted wildly, and began running along the narrow walkway. The pedacam scuttled on before him, its short legs whirring. In the far distance he saw a bobbing pinpoint of light. As it got closer Barbara's figure began to emerge from the shadows, backlit by scattered reflections from her torch. It was at that moment that he truly realised what it would have cost him never to see her again.

They were no more than twenty yards apart when he heard a sudden rumble behind him.

He spun about to see a wave rolling down the tunnel. The rubble dam had given way, releasing the pent-up water behind it.

'Watch out!' he shouted as he pressed himself flat against the side of the tunnel. The foaming crest rushed past him, washing over the walkway and breaking about his legs. He saw Barbara adopting the same stance. The wave surged past her and for a moment she slithered backwards under its impact. Then it was gone and she found her footing again. He heard her panting with exertion and saw she was trembling, but she managed to call out bravely:

'That was nasty. Too ironic if we got washed away now.'

He started towards her, skidding on the walkway which was still awash.

'Too ironic for words,' he agreed, almost laughing with relief. 'Barbara, you've no idea...'

Without any warning and curiously little noise, a three-yard length of the walkway between them crumbled and slid into the drainage channel.

Even as they both gaped incredulously there came a series of deafening cracks. The side of the tunnel exposed by the collapsed walkway seemed to bulge inwards. Fissures ran up the curving wall. Shards of concrete began to rain down from the roof and plunge into the water, sending up showers of spray.

'Get back, get back!' Ian shouted, waving his arm desperately.

Barbara had the sense not to argue. He saw her turn to run just as the entire roof caved in.

Ian twisted aside, slipped, fell to his knees and scrabbled awkwardly away from the wall of falling concrete. A slab, dislodged from the roof, smashed down on the pedacam as it scuttled along at his heels, flattening it in a brief shower of sparks.

Gradually the sound of falling rock diminished to a soft patter. Thirty yards clear of the fall Ian slumped against the wall, his heart pounding as he raged silently. Curton's voice was shouting from the earphones of his helmet radio but for a moment he ignored it. All he could think of, quite irrationally, was that they had tempted fate by joking about the irony of their situation. How *could* this have happened? They had been so close.

Then reason reasserted itself. At least he knew Barbara was safe. Wearily he acknowledged Curton's call and explained what had happened.

'Is the tunnel completely blocked?' Curton asked.

'Yes.'

'Then you'd better get out of there quickly.'

'No. Send down your machines. We must get Barbara out.'

'Listen. It's still raining heavily. If the tunnel's blocked the water's going to be back up to the ceiling before we can get down there.'

Ian looked down at the swirling water and realised Curton was right. In a few minutes it would submerge the walkway.

'When the pressure builds up enough that plug will blow like the last one,' Curton continued. 'You get back to the Carlson Tower feeder as fast as you can while I open up the next access point downstream. I just hope your friend has the sense not to hang around.'

On the other side of the roof fall, Barbara was reluctantly coming to the same conclusion as Ian. The main channel was being filled by water flowing in from the side culverts, but she could already see small rivulets emerging from higher up the wall of rubble above it. It didn't take much imagination to guess what would happen when it collapsed. She had to get clear and hope Ian could find some way of reaching her further down the tunnel.

She headed back the way she had come, as fast as she could safely go on the newly soaked walkway.

At least Ian knew roughly where she was now, she consoled herself as she stumbled along. And that helmet and overalls he'd been wearing suggested he'd got some help from somewhere… presumably the place that the mechanical dog-thing running along in front of him had come from. Hopefully it meant that when she reached the nearest manhole ladder there would be somebody up there to unseal it this time.

Ian splashed through the water lapping over the edge of the walkway. Still the side culverts gushed with more. Allowing for the gradual fall of the tunnel, the section before the collapse must already be filled to the ceiling. The water would be backing up now, increasing the pressure as it rose. Would the temporary dam last long enough for Barbara to get clear?

He saw lights ahead that marked the mouth of the culvert through which he had entered. Panting for breath he reached the flexible ladder which hung down into the main tunnel. The water was swirling about his ankles as he started to climb.

Then from far down the tunnel he heard a faint booming sound. Even as he peered into the darkness he knew what had happened. The dam had burst.

Barbara heard the roar of water growing in volume like an oncoming express train and knew she would never reach the access shaft in time. If it caught her she would be smashed against the walls by its force even before she had time to drown.

With the terrifying sound filling her ears she looked about desperately for some kind of shelter. A few yards ahead of her on the other side was a smaller branch inlet, a pipe no more than five feet in diameter. She had ignored it during her first journey down the tunnel because it had no walkway. Now it might save her life.

She leapt into the water and splashed across into the mouth of the inlet, fighting the flow of its current. Finding her feet she managed to wade a few yards inside. But even though the pipe was only half-full its flow was too strong... or perhaps now she was too weak. Her feet were sliding over the bottom as she was pushed back towards the main tunnel and certain death. She dropped her torch and grabbed the sides of the pipe, raking her nails into the slime-encrusted walls, slowing her progress for a few vital seconds.

A foaming wall of water thundered through the main tunnel behind her.

Barbara's ears popped as the torrent compressed the air in the pipe like a piston. The water boiled and swelled under her as a part of the cascade exploded into its mouth. She was caught up by a wave that filled the pipe and carried her away into the darkness.

Prince Keldo Arrosthenos sat alone in his conference chamber and allowed himself the luxury of letting his thoughts run free for a few minutes. The end was so close now that he could almost taste victory.

A year ago it had been so very different.

When his flagship had been brought down on the beach just outside Arkhaven's walls, Keldo had expected to die. For three days the fires burnt in the outer hull, fed by exploding fuel and munitions, while he and his men fought to stay alive within the core decks, sustained by bottled air and pressure suits. Out of a crew of over fifteen hundred 132 survived. Only on the fourth day did the fires diminish enough for them to cut their way through to the outside world.

They emerged ready to die fighting gloriously as befitted the last warriors of the Taklarian Empire.

But there were no Arkavians waiting for them, nor did the city batteries blast them to fragments, though they were helpless in their sights. Slowly the ironic truth dawned. The Arkavians believed they had all died in the crash. They had retreated behind their walls again to continue working on their escape Ship.

Keldo's force was safe while the Arkavians did not suspect their presence, but it was intolerable to look upon the brilliantly lit city and know they could do nothing to prevent the Ship launching without them. Even with the element of surprise, they were now too few in number and too ill-equipped to have any possible chance of taking it by direct assault. And no reinforcements would be coming to their aid. Their homeland lay in ruins, pounded by moon storms, the lands they had overrun had degenerated into savage anarchy as the end approached, and now the imperial fleet was destroyed. Though they searched across the radio frequencies they heard no signal of Taklarian origin. They might be the last of their race left alive.

But Keldo refused to accept defeat. It was a year before the moon would strike Sarath. With only a tenth of the original crew to support, the remaining rations could be made to last that long. Keldo consulted with old Thorken Menanius, the fleet scientist. Together they evolved a new plan of action.

They made the wrecked battlecraft habitable again, shielding its remaining operational reactor so their activities could not be detected from the city. They braced and sealed the inner compartments against the surge waves that rolled in from the sea and gradually buried the hulk in the sand even as they washed away the debris of battle.

Once their base was secure they commenced their clandestine assault on Arkhaven.

With improvised tools they began cutting a tunnel from under their craft and along the shoreline towards the city. Progress was painfully slow at first. Weaker sections under the shifting sands first had to be braced with material scavenged from the interior of the battlecraft, then constantly pumped to prevent flooding. Once a meteor strike caused a collapse that killed six men. But the survivors simply repaired the damaged section and continued. Keldo never let them forget that they were Taklarians:

a superior race, the products of a thousand years of selective breeding. To triumph in circumstances where lesser races might succumb was their birthright.

He led by example and inspiration, taking his own turn at the backbreaking and dangerous work at the rock-face. If his men had honoured him before, they revered him now, and would follow him into hell itself if he ordered it. Keldo was counting on that absolute and unquestioning loyalty to sustain them during the final assault.

And so the tunnel progressed, metre by painful metre.

They finally reached the city foundations with forty days to spare.

Now fortune smiled on them. Almost immediately they broke into one of the city's main drainage tunnels. It was an ideal location for their secret bridgehead, essential for the next phase of the operation.

Only in the city did the Taklarians' superior natures put them at a disadvantage. Their size and distinctive physiognomies made it impossible for them to pass among the Arkavians. But they needed to move freely, not only to know the moment the evacuation order was given, but to infiltrate the boarding process of the Ship at the crucial time. Mechanical surveillance methods were inadequate – and potentially disastrous should they be detected. They needed living agents who would not realise they were being used to serve their city's old enemy. Thorken's mind-control technique was the key.

The woman's unexpected discovery of their tunnel mouth, Keldo now saw, was fortuitous. The test had allowed Thorken to prove that the process worked. The woman had been secretly observed while recovering and showed no indication that she recalled what had been done to her. Tonight they would make their first foray out of the tunnels on to the surface, to reconnoitre and begin the search for more like her. They would take single subjects and return them, fully conditioned, in under two hours so they would not be missed. Keldo wanted twenty agents, at least, in place before launch day.

The door tone rang. Keldo came out of his reverie and straightened up. He never allowed the crew to see him as anything less than completely alert at all times.

'Come in,' he said.

An engineer entered, his face grave.

'I regret to report, Sire, that the storm has caused damage to the section of drainage tunnel our shaft connects with. I have had to seal the hatchway to prevent the entire shaft from flooding.'

'How can mere water cause such damage?' Keldo demanded angrily. 'Is that not what the system is designed for?'

'It seems some of the other tunnels have also collapsed, Sire. The flood surges carried a lot of debris. That's what caused the damage.'

Keldo's anger abated slightly and his brow creased in thought. 'That suggests inefficiency. Perhaps the Arkavians are no longer maintaining their drainage system as they should. How long to repair the damage to our tunnel?'

'Many days, Sire. And of course our work may be delayed by the Arkavians' own repairs.'

Keldo brooded for a minute, then said: 'If they are letting their city decay, perhaps they are no longer as watchful as they might be. What is the ground like above the head of our tunnel?

'Loose rock and compacted soil, Sire.'

'Then bypass the tunnel mouth and raise a smaller shaft to one metre below the surface. We may be able to move more boldly than I had planned.'

'It shall be as you command.'

A thought struck Keldo. 'Do you know if our Arkavian female agent got out of the tunnels before the flood?'

'No, Sire.'

Keldo waved his hand dismissively. 'Never mind. We shall find others.'

Chapter Eighteen
The Ship

'You do look terribly tired,' Susan said to Ian, her dark eyes full of concern as she sat propped up in her hospital bed.

'Chesterton has been up most of the night looking for Barbara,' said the Doctor, 'but I persuaded him he needed a break.'

'I'm sure you'll find her,' Susan continued encouragingly. 'After all, you know she's already survived a collapsing building. But I'll understand if you want to get back to the search.'

Ian conjured up a reassuring smile for Susan's benefit. 'Actually there's not much more we can do for the moment. Until the water level drops we can't check the main tunnels properly. Meanwhile, Curton's opening up the most likely access points. There's a chance Barbara reached one of those. If she climbed the ladder into one of the manhole shafts she should be safe... if she can hold on for long enough.'

'She will,' said Susan, placing her small cool hand over his for a moment. 'She's very determined.'

'I'm certain she will have reasoned the same way,' the Doctor said. 'She must have become familiar with the details of the system while she has been down there. It would be the obvious course of action.'

'Yes, of course,' Ian said, privately feeling less confident than he sounded. Had Barbara's luck finally run out?

'And now we must be going, my dear,' the Doctor said to Susan. 'You must get some rest and we have things to do. Since I am giving the Arkavians technical advice, I have requested a tour of their Ship. I want to see this remarkable machine for myself to understand it better.' He glanced at Ian. 'I'm sorry my task is more enjoyable than your own, Chesterton.'

Ian shrugged. 'While you're helping them, I know they'll do their best for Barbara. And it means you'll have the facilities to make a duplicate TARDIS key.'

'I'm sorry I lost my key, Grandfather,' said Susan. 'I must have dropped it when the tower collapsed.'

The Doctor smiled. 'I think it's excusable in the circumstances, my dear. Never mind. I have ample time to make another one. Meanwhile you concentrate on getting well. However advanced the treatment you have received, there is no substitute for proper rest.'

'I have been resting... though I did have a strange dream. I thought I was lost somewhere cold... dark and damp. It was very odd.'

'Well, try to think of something more cheerful,' the Doctor said dismissively. 'At least the mayor assures me you will not be getting any more visits from over-zealous priests.'

Fostel sat in the private study of his palace gazing morosely out of the window. Through it he could see both the cathedral and the Ship.

And the simple fact was that the Ship overshadowed the cathedral. To be brutally honest it dwarfed it. The Ship might be necessary but it was not right that it was so vast and, yes, he had to admit it, so magnificent and overwhelming. But what was worse, the Church could not take the credit for it. Functionaries and Technicians had been responsible and as a result they had gained hugely in prestige.

This had forced a bitter about-turn upon the Church. After years of denying Professor Jarrasen the funds he needed for his foolish rocket research, through the council, it had been humiliatingly obliged to turn to him for its very salvation. Jarrasen had become something of a hero among the people, which in turn increased the standing of his class, boosting its self-confidence. Now this self-confidence had evidently grown to such proportions that the mayor felt strong enough to openly defy Fostel himself.

The people were beginning to think that cold calculations and impersonal metal were going to save them, not prayer. The proportion of committed Believers was falling alarmingly. It was not surprising. How could the Church rival as massive a symbol of salvation as the Ship?

When they reached Mirath, would the Church be able to maintain its position of influence? That the old Elite families had fared no better against the rise of the Functionaries was little comfort. He did not want the company of Vendam and his kind if their classes, traditional pillars of society, dwindled into irrelevance on the new world.

Then had come the final insult. The mayor had welcomed aliens into the city without so much as consulting him. That was clearly a violation of Church prerogative. If he was to maintain any sort of following he had to act, even if it was... clandestine. Still, the truth would be allowed to filter through to the Believers to reassure them that the Church had stood firm.

He would consult with Zeckler. The archdeacon was not a likeable person but his single-minded devotion was unquestionable and Fostel knew he could trust him to carry out his orders to the letter. Perhaps that was what they all needed now to restore their faith.

A show of old-fashioned fundamental religious principle.

'Why do you need to take such precautions inside the city?' the Doctor asked. 'Surely nobody would wish to interfere with work on the Ship.'

Lant's car was passing the high security fence that ran around the entire launching site, enclosing not only the Ship and its gantry but the storehouses and workshops that serviced them.

Lant made a wry face. 'You'll see in a minute, Doctor.'

On either side of the main gate, in addition to a standard checkpoint guardroom, were two temporary huts rather like those in the NC2 camp.

As the regular guard stepped forward to check their passes, men emerged from the huts. One was a dark-robed priest, the other a young, smartly dressed man. Each was carrying an electronic notepad on which they recorded the registration number of the car and details of its occupants. Both glared at the Doctor with varying degrees of suspicion and resentment, evidently recognising him from the public broadcasts.

'Why are you taking this alien on to the Ship?' the priest demanded of Lant angrily, pushing his face up to the open window. 'We don't know if his kind can be trusted.' Lant ignored him.

'Will he be coming with us?' the well-dressed man asked from the other side of the car. 'We can't spare the room and I won't be giving up my place for him.'

'I can assure you I have no intention of usurping anyone's place,' the Doctor said sharply.

'Do you recognise the will of the Maker?' asked the priest. He was wearing a token marked with a series of concentric circles on a chain about his neck. Now he thrust it forward intimidatingly.

'I know nothing of your god,' the Doctor snapped back.

The sentry waved them on and they passed through the second set of gates.

'Sorry about that, but now you see how it is,' Lant said. 'The Church and the Elite can't be trusted to keep to their baggage allowances and they're always accusing each other of trying to smuggle extra stuff on board with the general cargo. To keep the peace we have to let them check everything that goes in or out of the launch site. That's why we have the fence and the security. We have to keep track ourselves to stop them making false claims. A waste of time and manpower, but there it is.'

'I presume that was why the mayor was hesitant about letting me view the Ship... knowing my presence might cause more animosity.'

'Probably. This is one place where we *must* keep to schedule, so the engineers' wishes come first around here. I'm going to be working myself on Launch Day, stewarding the people on board. I'm not sure what you'll be able to see. They're still loading the last of the cargo, and the flight crew are running through simulations in the control cabin of the Lander. If they're busy we can't disturb them.'

'I had hoped to meet Professor Jarrasen in person,' said the Doctor. 'So far I have only conversed with him over a video link.'

'Well, he should be here if anywhere.'

The car drew up beside the gantry and they got out.

The Doctor craned his neck to look up at the vast latticework structure set immovably into a massive concrete apron. Around its base, transporters were unloading modular containers on to large cargo lifts. A maze of pipes and lift shafts ran up through the gantry to the service arms and bridges that reached out to the silver skyscraper of the Ship. From where they stood they looked up into the multiple array of hexagonal exhaust nozzles protruding from its tail, each the size of a small house. A huge pit had been excavated in the ground beneath the nozzles. The Doctor walked over to the guardrail that ringed it and peered down.

'Why excavate such a large blast pit?' the Doctor asked. 'The Ship will only be lifting off once, and surely it hardly matters what damage it does to the surrounding buildings since by then the city will be empty.'

'Apparently Professor Jarrasen calculated that the backwash might damage the Ship's support legs. Vent shafts from the bottom of the pit radiate out in all directions and come up just inside the perimeter fence.'

'Ah, of course.'

They turned back to the gantry.

'Where do you want to start?' Lant asked.

'At the lowest level possible and work upwards.'

'Well, the engines themselves are sealed off now the atomic fuel elements have been installed. Nothing but service robots can get near them. The lowest accessible decks are the cargo holds.'

'Then I will be pleased to see them. I have an interest in fine engineering wherever I come across it.'

Lant looked at him doubtfully. 'Your technology is obviously far more advanced than ours. This can hardly interest you, surely.'

The Doctor's eyes sparkled. 'On the contrary, Captain. I believe this Ship will prove to be the most remarkable vessel of its kind I have ever encountered.'

* * *

Susan blinked up at the dimly blue-lit ceiling in confusion. She had been dreaming she was in a warm bed. Then, gradually, it all came flooding back to her: the conveyors, the recycling plant... the locked door.

She sat up stiffly. At least her double layer of coveralls had kept her warm, and while she slept her body had had a chance to finish healing.

She drank some cold water from the shower and tested the door again. It was still immovable and still nobody responded to her pounding and shouting. She searched the chamber carefully but found no tool with which the door could be forced. That left the garbage conveyors as the only means of escape. She had been dumped on to the conveyor somehow, so logically there should be a way back out. Unfortunately it was impossible to turn the belts off, so to make any progress she would have to run against their motion – without a chance to rest or any idea how far she would have to go. If only the standard rubbish chutes she had encountered were not so narrow.

Rubbish.

She sniffed the air. It was quite fresh despite all the waste being continually passed through the chamber. This meant it was replaced rapidly, which suggested a high-volume venting system. She chided herself for not having thought of this earlier, though she knew she had been too tired.

Now that she was looking she found the vent grilles easily enough. One was set low down at ground level, while the other was positioned high up in the opposite corner of the chamber, above the walkway.

She tested the lower grille and felt a steady draught of cool air emerging from it. Obviously fresh air entered at the bottom of the chamber and was drawn out from the top. Assuming the system force-vented air on the exhaust side, the bottom grille was the one she needed to open.

Except that it was secured in place by four heavy recessed screws that were quite impossible to turn by hand – and she had no tools.

It took a couple of agonised minutes before she thought of using the edge of one of the coverall buckles. After some straining she managed to release the screws and drop the grille to the floor. The square metal tunnel beyond was just large enough to take her.

With a last look round the reprocessing chamber Susan took a deep breath and climbed into the shaft.

The Doctor really did want to see *everything* in the Ship, Ben soon discovered.

In the cargo decks he pottered along rows of modularised pods and cartons already secured for flight. He stamped on floor plates and tapped the great structural girders that ran up inside the hull. In machinery spaces he examined tanks of water and oxygen, pumping systems and air-purifying equipment. On the passenger levels he studied intently the row upon row of couches that were stacked three deep, filling each deck from floor to ceiling.

'To make the take-off easier, everybody but essential crew will be anaesthetised beforehand,' Ben explained. 'Then they'll use light sedation throughout the flight. That will keep the demands on the life support systems down to a minimum and prevent people moving around too much. With eighty thousand on board it's going to be pretty cramped in here otherwise.'

Eventually they reached a set of double bulkheads and airlocks leading into the landing module.

Once again the Doctor subjected every accessible part of the vessel to close study, tapping and prodding and occasionally muttering: 'Really... most remarkable,' to himself.

They reached an upper bay crowded with banks of electronic processor units. A familiar green-ringed camera eye stared out of a console.

'Ah, Monitor,' said the Doctor. 'Yes, of course. This is where your duplicate mainframe unit has been installed.'

'That is correct, Doctor,' Monitor replied. 'While landlines connect the ship to the city communications net, I can operate from here as well as any other terminal.'

'Can we visit the control cabin or are they in the middle of another simulation?' Ben asked.

'One moment, Captain Lant, I will check,' Monitor said. In a half a minute he answered: 'You may enter.'

They climbed up to the cabin and its crew of six. Captain Warvon greeted them and introduced the Doctor to his co-pilot, navigator and flight engineers.

'You can imagine we have been very keen to meet you and your companions, Doctor,' Warvon said enthusiastically. 'As we understand it, you've done in reality what we've only done in simulations.'

'I admit I have not piloted this class of craft recently,' said the Doctor modestly. 'However, if you feel you can benefit from my practical experience I will be only too glad to help. I imagine it is the landing on Mirath that is troubling you.'

Warvon looked relieved. 'It is. Putting a vessel of this size down safely on largely unknown terrain, with unpredictable meteorology, is going to be no small task.'

'No indeed. How many variables have you programmed into your simulation?'

The conversation became technical and Ben felt excluded. Fortunately it was interrupted when Professor Jarrasen's face appeared on one of the bridge screens.

'I'm sorry I could not meet you in person, Doctor,' Jarrasen said, 'but I was called away at the last minute. I hope Captain Warvon has been explaining everything to you.'

'He has, thank you. I must congratulate you, Professor. A most extraordinary feat of engineering, considering the limited time you have to master the technology. You must be very proud of it.'

Jarrasen grimaced. 'After so many years of frustration, I'm not sure I have that much pride left in me, Doctor. All that time my research was starved of funds because the Elite said it was a waste of money and the Church thought building rockets might offend God. But when the emergency came and they realised a rocket was their only means of escape they were quick enough to support the project.' He chuckled mirthlessly. 'Then they were surprised to learn how long it would take to design and build a working ship capable of reaching Mirath. But we did it anyway. Not just for ourselves but to show them that we would be saved by scientists and engineers, not empty prayers or meaningless titles.'

Ben sympathised with the sentiment but felt uncomfortable at its expostulation before a stranger. The bridge crew, however, seemed to thoroughly approve of Jarrasen's passionate speech.

The Doctor simply looked about the flight deck nodding slowly to himself.

Barbara was scrabbling her way through a cleft choked with mud and rock. She was sobbing with the effort even as she fought back the utter terror that threatened to engulf her... the fear that at any moment the earth would collapse and she would be buried alive, to die in this darkness. If only she hadn't been forced to drop her faithful torch.

When the surge of water had finally subsided and deposited her, coughing and gasping for breath, in ankle-deep water she had no idea of how far she had been carried along the pipe. Worse, she knew she had been tumbled over several times in the process and had completely lost her sense of direction. Which way led back to the main tunnel?

The water about her was now motionless. Presumably the increased flow had been caused by a rainstorm. If that had passed, the flow would subside, but wouldn't there still be some movement of water? Unless the tunnel behind her had blocked again. Or did she mean in front of her?

After what seemed an endless period of indecision she had simply guessed. Forcing herself to her feet, she had begun her painfully slow progress, bent half double with one hand outstretched ahead of her in the blackness.

After another timeless interval she had become so exhausted she had to rest, sitting with her back braced against the curve of the pipe and her legs in the water. Incredibly, she actually fell asleep in this position.

She had woken shivering and deathly cold, not knowing how long she had slept, but certain that she could not survive much longer in soaking wet clothes without food or warmth. The only way to warm up was to move.

Shortly afterwards, sand and gravel had begun to crunch under her feet, then pebbles and small rocks. Finally she stumbled over a mound of earth and rock. Feeling about in it she came across a section of curved, hard plastic half-buried in the pile. The pipe had cracked and caved in.

The discovery had almost broken her spirit. She knew she could not return the way she had come. In desperation she had reached up over the top of the mound to see if she could possibly pass over it. Her hand stretched further upwards than she had expected. There was a slight gap between a sloping wall of compacted earth and the mound of debris that filled the pipe. She blinked. After so long in total darkness her eyes had become very sensitive and she thought she could see a ghostly glimmer of light filtering down from above.

She began to climb the mound. It was loose and she had to claw frantically just to prevent herself sliding down again. Stones embedded in the wall of hard earth scraped her back. There was hardly any room to move, but the light was growing stronger! A glimmer became a hard-edged chink at some indeterminate distance above her.

That was all that kept her going, lifting one hand above the other, kicking and pushing with her feet, hugging the earth to stop herself losing the precious ground she had gained.

And suddenly there was open air and the fading light of day about her.

She flopped forward on to hard, level ground and lay still.

It was evening before the Doctor returned to the apartment in the mayor's residency. Ian was just coming out of the bathroom, his hair wet from the shower. A glance at his face told the Doctor there was no news of Barbara.

'We've no idea what's happened to her,' Ian explained, sitting down heavily on the side of a bed and feeling almost as baffled as he was anxious. 'If she'd simply been... washed away, then there are gratings and traps designed to catch rubbish and anything that might block the system. But there's no trace of her. They're checking along the smaller branches now... but there are miles of them. Many of the tunnels are cracking up. She might have been caught by another cave-in. It's been hours since I saw her. Even if she's still alive, I don't know how much longer she can last.'

The Doctor shook his head in sympathy. 'You look completely exhausted, Chesterton.'

'That's what Curton said,' Ian admitted. 'He had to take a break as well. An assistant is running the search.'

'You need some fresh air. Come out on to the balcony. The night's quite fine.'

Blinking wearily, Ian scuffed over to the balcony window and stepped out. Beyond, the twinkling lights of the city were growing brighter as the last flush of daylight was leaching from the sky. Before them stood the Ship, brilliantly illuminated by a ring of searchlights. Red warning lights picked out the darker mass of the gantry by its side.

The Doctor lowered his voice to a barely audible whisper, but the edge of urgency in his tone was unmistakable.

'I don't want to add to your worries, Chesterton, but there is something you must know.'

'What?'

'It's about the Ship. I've had a chance to examine it closely today and talk to its crew.' He suddenly sounded affronted. 'They must think I am incapable of elementary mental arithmetic or cannot estimate dimensions and masses accurately by eye.'

'Come to the point, Doctor.'

The Doctor told him. When he had finished, Ian shook his head in disbelief.

'But why... and what can we do about it?'

'Nothing... until we learn where the real truth lies!'

Chapter Nineteen
Lost and Found

'I hear you got a visit from the Watch this morning, Plax,' said Orm Herstwell.

Plaxander Vendam lifted his head from his contemplation of the depths of his drink to glower angrily at Herstwell. 'What about it?'

Herstwell smiled languidly. 'Nothing… except that it was the same Captain Lant who faced you down in the Polkatoon last night. I hope you put him in his place… this time.'

The chatter in the lounge of the Sentinel Club faded as its occupants sensed the increase in tension.

'How do you know Lant came to see me?' Plax demanded.

'Oh, I have my sources in the Watch who know how I appreciate certain juicy titbits now and again. Well, did you?'

'Did I what?'

'Put him in his place.'

'It's none of your business.'

A mocking howl arose from the onlookers. Plax flushed.

Herstwell smirked at his discomfiture. 'I think Captain Lant has got you frightened.'

'I'm not frightened of anything!' Plax retorted.

'Not even of the Creeper?'

'What?' Plax exclaimed. There were a few other puzzled murmurs.

'You must have heard the stories,' Herstwell said. 'The thing they say lives in the Outer Zone? Well, Lant has been checking the files about it and from the maps he's copied it looks like tonight he's going to take a look for himself. And my contact has told me his proposed route.' He fixed his eyes on Plax. 'Think you're up to meeting him out there? A brick through his windshield, maybe? That'll teach him… and prove you aren't afraid.'

Plax looked at the ring of expectant faces about him and knew he had no choice.

'All right… I'll do it,' he said.

Ian had snatched a couple of hours' sleep, then dressed to go out again. Before leaving he had another whispered conference with the Doctor on the balcony.

'But why ever would they do such a thing?' Ian asked once again.

'I'm not sure,' the Doctor said. 'But you realise the chaos that will ensue when the truth comes out. This is why we must be sure we can leave here as soon as possible. I'm going to start work on the duplicate key tonight. The laboratory they promised is ready and Jarrasen has enough advice from me to be going on with for now.'

'You were going to visit Susan again tonight.'

'Well, maybe later. I must make a start. We may not have as much time as we thought.'

Ian nodded. 'By the way, do you think Lant's in on it? I hope not, he seems a decent type.'

'We cannot be sure. Remember, he was part of the deception over the true population of the city.'

'Surely that was understandable in the circumstances?'

'And so may this be, but we cannot afford to take any chances. Now you had better go... and good luck.'

Ian was mildly surprised to find Lant himself waiting outside.

'I've got business in the Outer Zone myself,' the captain explained. 'I got a map of the drainage tunnels from Curton's crew and it seems we want to cover much the same ground. This way we can check two branches at the same time.'

'Thanks,' said Ian, getting into Lant's car. As they pulled away he asked: 'Are you looking for somebody as well?'

'Somebody... or something.'

'What?'

'I'm not sure... but I think I'll know it when I see it.'

Barbara woke shivering and numb with cold.

Very slowly she turned her head and saw the ragged hole in the ground beside her. It wasn't a dream, she really was free of those interminable tunnels at long last.

The realisation failed to cheer her. She no longer seemed to have the energy or willpower to move any further. That last effort had totally drained her reserves.

Rest for a minute, she told herself, gather your strength.

She was lying in a grassy courtyard overlooked by three- and four-storey buildings. Their lower floors were dark but several upper windows glowed with light.

Where there was light there must be people, Barbara thought, and tried to call out. But her voice came out as a feeble croak. She licked her lips and tried again. 'Help me... please.'

She lay there panting, waiting for a response. In the far distance she thought she could hear the soft hum of one of the city cars, but there was no sound from the surrounding buildings.

'Help... anybody,' she shouted again. 'Ian... Ian... please hear me!'

Her cries gave way to a fit of coughing. Where was everybody? If she lay here all night would she be alive in the morning? Fear and anger lifted her to her knees, where she remained, swaying dangerously. 'Ian... please help me!'

Then she heard the footsteps.

A shapeless figure in a bright orange coverall appeared through an archway in the corner of the courtyard. It gaped at her for a moment, then ran across and knelt by her side.

'Barbara?' it said in an incredulous voice.

It was Susan.

The column of gyrocars circled about and came to a stop. Their occupants climbed out and looked about them.

They were on a patch of waste ground bordered by automated factory units. A two-storey burnt-out building, a relic of the war, stood forlornly amid the weeds and piles of rubble. It was the sort of place they usually came to when they were hunting NC2s.

'Here we are, Plax,' said Herstwell, throwing an arm over his companion's shoulder and patting him heartily, then turning him about so he could take in the landscape. 'Lant will be coming through in about an hour's time. You'd better find a good spot.'

Plax shook himself free.

'I don't want to get into any trouble this close to the exodus.'

'Lant really has got to you, hasn't he?' Herstwell said with a sneer.

'No... I just don't want to do anything stupid,' Plax protested.

'What are you worried about?' one of the others asked. 'I thought your father could fix anything.'

There was nothing Plax could say. He was trapped in this stupid challenge now.

'Try up there,' Herstwell said, pointing to an external flight of stairs that led to the ruined building's first floor. 'We'll park the cars somewhere out of sight.'

Plax tramped up the rickety stairs and cautiously peered into what remained of an upper room. The floor didn't look too sound, but there was plenty of cover. If he...

A horn sounded from below and he looked out to see the cars rolling away... all the cars!

Herstwell called up out of the side window of Plax's own car: 'I don't actually know if Lant's coming precisely this way or not.' He held up his hand. 'By the way, I've got your phone. You can walk home if you haven't the nerve to stay, otherwise we'll pick you up here tomorrow morning. Give my regards to the Creeper if you meet it.'

Plax tore down the stairs to the ground but by that time the cars were just a cluster of vanishing tail lights.

He cursed under his breath for being taken in by Herstwell. When he saw him again he'd... but that would have to wait. First, he had to endure an uncomfortable night.

Suddenly he laughed.

There was an easy solution to the whole thing. He had his money card. He would simply pay some local to put him up for the night, then return here to be picked up in the morning.

It took him fifteen minutes to walk to the edge of the industrial park and find a small street of shops and private houses with tiny front gardens. He opened the gate to the nearest house showing lights, strode up to the door and knocked. After a minute he knocked again impatiently. There was no sound from within. He tried another house in the row with no better luck.

What was the matter with them all?

He realised he'd never been alone in the Outer Zone before. Even on hunts he'd never been out of earshot of the idling hum of his gyrocar. Now he noticed how very quiet it was. Somewhere in the distance traffic purred along a thoroughfare, but this whole street seemed absolutely still. Surely there should be some noise. Didn't the people here play music or watch the vidi shows or anything?

Anxiously he worked his way along the street banging on doors at random. There was no response. It was as though the whole district had been abandoned. But if so, why was it still lit?

He suddenly found himself wishing he'd never boasted about the hunts or made those stupid threats to the mayor. Then Lant wouldn't have called round and he wouldn't be stuck out here.

All right, he'd just have to find some other sort of shelter. If the houses were all abandoned he could simply break into one of them and…

The street lights flickered and went off.

For a moment Plax stood stock still. Then he began to edge slowly over to the nearest of the illuminated houses.

The building lights down that side of the street went off.

His nerve failing, he turned in the other direction.

The rest of the street was plunged into darkness and he stumbled to a halt, reaching out to find a wall before he ran into it. The only light now was from the skyglow that hung over the city.

And then he heard a noise.

It was a faint rasping, clicking sound and it was growing steadily closer.

With Barbara's arm slung across her shoulder, Susan guided her through the doorway of a small café. It was dimly lit but deserted. She sat Barbara down, pulled a dusty tablecloth off the nearest table and draped it over her friend's trembling shoulders.

Susan looked about her intently. There was a dispensing machine mounted on one wall advertising a selection of

161

prepacked drinks and sweet and savoury snacks. Determinedly, Susan picked up a chair and smashed its front panel so she could reach inside. She pulled out a handful of chocolate bars and several airtight plastic tubes of fruit drink. She unwrapped a bar, sniffed it cautiously, then helped Barbara guide it into her mouth. Then she wolfed down a bar herself.

Fifteen minutes of gorging on chocolate and fruit juice brought the colour back to Barbara's cheeks. Meanwhile Susan used more tablecloths to dry her and clean the worst of the mud from her clothes. Finally Barbara wiped her mouth and, sounding more like her usual self, said: 'Thanks. I really needed that. I haven't eaten since we got here.'

'I haven't either,' Susan admitted, starting on another chocolate bar, 'but I think I've spent longer sleeping than you have… and at least I managed to stay dry.'

'How did you get here? And where did you find those clothes?'

Susan told her story.

'…so after clambering up airshafts for what seemed like hours I eventually came out of an intake vent in a sort of deserted industrial site. I was wandering around trying to decide which way to go when I heard you calling Ian's name. Do you know where he is? And Grandfather?'

'I did see Ian briefly… but that was hours ago.'

Barbara then summarised her own harrowing adventures to which Susan listened with wide-eyed interest and appropriate sympathy.

When she finished Susan said: 'At least what happened to you makes sense. But how did I get on to that rubbish conveyor?' She looked at one of the minor dressings on the back of her hand and scratched it. It peeled away easily to reveal perfectly healed skin beneath. 'Why treat me then throw me away with the rubbish… unless they thought I was dead.'

'But Ian and the Doctor would never have allowed that,' Barbara said firmly. 'And I know Ian was all right when I saw him… he had a sort of miner's helmet on and that robot thing with him, so he must have found help.'

'Then where is it? Where *is* everybody?' Susan asked. 'This place must have been deserted for months. And nobody's gone past since we've been here. I thought the city felt odd from the start.'

Barbara rubbed her watchstrap absently. 'We must get back to the city centre. I think that rocket is very important.'

'But won't Ian be searching in this area if he's followed the line of the drainage tunnels?'

'He might be miles away. If we get back outside maybe we can find him.' Barbara stood up rather shakily, pulling her improvised blanket about her like a cape.

Susan looked at her doubtfully. 'Shouldn't you rest more first?'

'No, I'm feeling much better. Maybe we can stop a car when we come to a main road.'

'They didn't take much notice of us before.'

'Well, we can find a telephone box and call the emergency services.' Barbara blinked. 'Shouldn't there be a phone in here? Maybe it's still working.'

'I shouldn't think so,' Susan said. 'In advanced societies everybody has their own pocket phones.'

'What, everybody?'

'Well, I suppose there might be a few public booths left.'

'Then let's find one. Wait a minute.' She picked up a sauce dispenser from a side table, then they went out on to the street. Barbara used it to write another symbol on the large café window, then stepped back to admire the result. 'There. Just in case Ian does come this way.'

They looked about them. The rows of lighted buildings devoid of any sign of life or movement were unsettling, and the two women automatically edged a little closer to each other.

'If we can get on to some open ground we should be able to see that giant rocket,' Barbara said. 'That'll give us something to aim for.'

Fortunately they didn't have far to go. From the end of the street they saw the dark expanse of a small park and walked along to it. Its grass and shrubs were overgrown, but from its centre they could see the spire of the rocket between the trees.

They were deciding which way led most directly towards the Ship when the lights around the park went out.

They stood very still. The park was ringed by the silhouettes of darkened buildings and the shadows among the trees and bushes were inky black.

'Was there anything in front of us?' Barbara asked.

'I don't think so.'

'Then hold my hand and we'll go forward carefully. We'll be all right when we reach the street.'

They had hardly gone ten yards when Susan started at a slight sound. 'What was that?'

'Probably a bird.'

But then the sound came again and this time Barbara heard it as well. Some large body was moving through the grass. The two girls clung together as a rustling whisper grew steadily louder. But its source was impossible to place in the darkness and they hesitated for a few brief seconds, unsure of which way to run. The sound was coming from all around them.

Two glowing red eyes blinked out of the darkness and they heard a terrible anticipatory hiss of indrawn breath.

With barely stifled screams they turned from the dreadful sight and ran, only to collide with a pulsating leathery barrel of a body that lay across their path. As they recoiled from this new horror there was a heavy swish and smack, like the crack of a huge whip. Barbara screamed and Susan had the impression of her struggling form being dragged across the grass towards the eyes. There was a howling rush of air, a snap and she was gone.

Before Susan could take in what had happened the eyes blinked into being again and glided towards her. With a whipcrack the thing's tongue lashed out, caught her round the waist and jerked her off her feet. The hiss became a roar as huge jaws opened. The tongue contracted and, kicking and screaming, Susan was sucked into a monstrous slimy gullet.

Ian was shining his torch down the tenth manhole they had uncovered when Lant's phone rang.

Lant listened intently for a minute then rang off.

'I asked to be informed of anything unusual in this area,' he said quickly. 'Well, there have just been two unexplained power failures close together.'

'What does it mean?'

'I've no idea, but I'm going to take a look. Coming?'

It occurred to Ian that the incident might just have something to do with Barbara. If it didn't he could come back later. 'Yes, I'll come.'

Lant's driver sent the car hurtling through the deserted streets, squealing round corners, towards the location of the latest power failure. Ian saw the captain checking his side-arm.

'You think there might be something dangerous out there?'

'Maybe. I've been examining the records today. Over the last year or so there have been some odd sightings in the Outer Zone and a few people have gone missing.'

'Including NC2s?'

'Perhaps.'

They slowed slightly as they entered the target area. The lights were still out but Lant's car had independently steerable spotlights mounted on its roof. They trained them up each street as they passed.

Suddenly Lant's driver called out: 'Something there, sir!' At the same time he whisked the car about and sent it racing down a side road.

Ian had a momentary impression of a black hulking form crossing the far end of the road.

They turned in the direction it had gone and again Ian glimpsed something in the distance but could not make out any details. Whatever it was, it was moving very fast.

'Can't you call up a helicopter or something?' Ian said, bracing himself as they raced along in pursuit.

'I want to see what we're dealing with first before I involve anyone else,' Lant said.

The chase wound through twisting side roads. Slowly they began to close the gap between them and their quarry. But the thing, whatever it was, remained impenetrably black and shapeless, almost like a racing shadow.

'What is it?' Ian exclaimed. 'A car... or an animal?'

'We'll find out soon enough,' said Lant, consulting the glowing map screen he held in his hand. 'That turn leads to a dead end.'

They screeched around the corner in time to see the shadow vanish round the next bend.

'Got it!' said Lant.

Hardly five seconds later they turned the same bend. In front of them their headlights illuminated a three-sided yard formed by the blank, high back-walls of adjacent buildings.

It was absolutely empty.

The car stopped and they got out, staring about them in disbelief.

'Well, it can't just have vanished,' Ian said. 'Could it fly, do you think?'

'Then why didn't it do so earlier? No. There's a trick to it and I'm going to find out what.'

But even as he started forward his pocket phone rang. He listened for a moment and his face set. He rang off and looked at Ian.

'It's your friend, Susan. She's been kidnapped.'

Chapter Twenty
Investigation

'I went down to check on Susan while I was on my break from intensive care,' Nyra Shardri explained to the intent group of people gathered in Mayor Draad's office. 'Well, she was my patient and she is something of a celebrity. While I was there a man came in who said he was from City Hall… he showed us his government pass before we even asked to see it, so we had no reason to doubt him. He said that they were holding a surprise function in honour of our visitors and wondered if Susan would be well enough to attend.

'Susan wanted to go, so the ward supervisor and I checked her latest tests and decided it would be all right for a few hours, as long as she didn't get too tired. She got dressed and we saw her driven off in a car that looked just like the official ones. And that was the last we saw of her.

'A couple of hours later, just when we were wondering when she would be coming back, the Doctor arrived. Then we realised what had happened.' Nyra looked at the Doctor. 'I'm so sorry.'

'Needless to say my office did not send any car, neither was there any special function planned,' Draad said heavily.

Ben thought he looked desperately tired. He must have enough worries without the kidnapping of his guests.

'I do not doubt it, Mayor,' said the Doctor. 'But who is responsible? What about those men who tried to talk to her the other day… Bishop Fostel and his archdeacon? Would they commit such a crime just to question Susan about her religious beliefs?'

Ben said: 'It is possible, Mayor. Fostel made it very clear he considered it his right to question Miss Foreman. He was certainly angry enough when I stopped him. But I didn't suspect he'd try anything as bold as this.'

'Maybe you underestimated his determination,' said Ian.

'Fostel was holding services throughout the evening,' said Draad, 'and they were broadcast live. He could not have been personally involved.'

'Then perhaps it was somebody acting for him,' said the Doctor testily. 'Who else in Arkhaven would have any cause to kidnap Susan? We understand something of the tension that exists between you, but he does seem the most likely suspect. He must be questioned at once.'

'I would need a very good reason for disturbing Fostel in the small hours of the morning,' Draad said. 'You must realise that I simply cannot make such an accusation without absolute proof... perhaps not even then. He's turned my own argument against me. For the sake of the city, even if Fostel is responsible, I cannot risk the disruption such a revelation would cause. Meanwhile he can save face in the eyes of his followers by getting away with this little victory.'

'What you are saying is that you cannot move openly against him?' the Doctor asked.

'Yes, Doctor. A full investigation has already been initiated, but it will be low profile. You understand we do not want this news to get out just yet.'

'So you're saying that the investigation won't target Fostel specifically?'

'No.'

'But we have no idea what he intends to do with Susan when he's finished with her.'

'I'm sorry, Doctor.'

'Then I cannot continue to advise you on the Ship,' the Doctor replied bluntly.

'I understand,' Draad said sadly. 'All I can do is repeat that, officially, my hands are tied.'

Ian caught the subtle nuance in Draad's words. 'And unofficially? Suppose we find your proof. Better yet find Susan. Will you turn a blind eye?'

'I cannot let... excuse me, aliens take our law into their own hands.'

'We do not intend a rampage through your city,' said the Doctor. 'We would want Captain Lant's help anyway... if he's agreeable. He can ensure we do not overstep reasonable bounds. If we simply take Susan back from Fostel with the minimum of fuss, he can hardly make a public complaint, can he?'

'I'm willing if you give the word, Mayor,' Ben said.

Nyra said quickly: 'I want to help as well, Mr Mayor. Susan is not fully recovered. Even if she's not been harmed physically, this sort of mental trauma may cause problems. I should be there to give medical assistance if required.'

Ben gave her a quick nod of approval and she flashed a warm smile back.

The mayor looked at them thoughtfully. 'Would you need to involve anybody else?' he asked Ben.

'Just my driver and a couple of men from the Wallguard I can trust.'

'All right. If the rest of you would withdraw I must speak to Captain Lant alone.'

When the doors closed Draad said: 'I wanted to speak to you anyway, Captain. I understand you've been spending some time in the Outer Zone. I assigned you as escort to our guests and to see if you could find the Doctor's missing key. Neither of these duties should involve chasing after ghosts. Yes, I've heard about your researches.'

'The lead I was following was connected with the deceased NC2 who stole the Doctor's key,' Ben explained. 'As for ghosts, I did see something unusual in the zone while I was helping Chesterton search for his friend, but we had to break off our investigation when your call came through.'

'What did you see?'

'I'm not sure, sir. I wouldn't like to commit myself until I've investigated further.'

'Well, the safe recovery of Miss Foreman takes precedence over everything else for now.'

'Yes, Mayor.'

'You appreciate, if it emerges the Church is responsible, the situation must be handled with the utmost delicacy. The minimum of disturbance and nothing public.'

'I understand, sir. But if it comes to a choice between Miss Foreman's safety and that of her captors, what should I do?'

Draad looked at him levelly

'Then, Captain, I should expect you to uphold the law.'

Ben emerged to find the others waiting for him somewhat impatiently.

Making calls on his pocket phone as he went, he led the way to a small conference room. They seated themselves at the long table in front of a multi-screen display wall.

'The mayor has instructed Monitor to give us unlimited and unrestricted access to all criminal files and public databases from here,' Ben explained. 'All the information that is available to the regular force is at our disposal.'

Several screens lit up on the wall displaying maps and strings of data updates. Ben scanned them rapidly.

'Apparently the regulars have just found the fake limousine the kidnappers used to take Susan from the hospital.' He saw the others look hopeful and added quickly: 'No trace of Susan, I'm afraid. The car was abandoned here.' A point on the map of the city centre lit up. 'It'll be examined but it looks as if any bio-traces were very thoroughly flushed.'

'How was the car found so quickly?' Ian asked.

'We have traffic cameras monitoring and recording all the main Inner Zone roads and junctions. The system caught the car after it left the hospital until it entered a blind spot and never came out.'

'A "blind spot"?' Ian asked.

'Somewhere outside traffic-camera range… underpasses, minor junctions shielded by intervening buildings, small off-road parking bays, that sort of thing.'

'So Susan was transferred to some other vehicle, probably before the car was abandoned,' the Doctor said.

'Probably, but they wouldn't be stupid enough to make the transfer where they could be seen. The car passed through three other blind spots before it got there. The switch could have taken place at any one of them. Tracking down and eliminating all the vehicles that also passed through those points at about the same time could take days.'

'No doubt that is the procedure the regular investigation will follow,' said the Doctor dismissively. 'However, we start with the assumption that this Fostel was responsible. If that is so, where might he have taken her?'

'Not to his own residence or the cathedral,' Ben said. 'That would be too blatant even for him. The home of a Believer perhaps, or some commercial building. The Church does own a number of properties around the city.'

'Can we see them?'

Monitor displayed a map of the Inner Zone with Church properties highlighted in red. Apart from the cathedral, the bishop's palace and two other churches, there were over twenty lesser buildings.

'It'll still take too long to check them all,' Ian said. 'That's assuming he hasn't had Susan taken to the Outer Zone.'

'Fostel stays close to the Ship like everybody else,' Ben said. 'Besides, he's on the council and knows any unauthorised vehicle leaving the centre would stand out among the dummy cars.'

'Dummy cars?' Nyra asked.

She didn't know about the deception, Ben realised. 'I'll explain later,' he promised.

'Let us stay with the possible locations we have for the moment,' said the Doctor. 'If our suspicions are correct we can perhaps reason backwards. Is there any correlation between vehicles observed close to any of these specific places and vehicles that intersected the path of the bogus car in any of the blind spots you mentioned?'

Ben's respect for the old man's intellect rose another notch. 'Yes, of course!'

'As confirmation, the same vehicle may have been seen leaving the same location prior to the time of the kidnapping as well as returning there after the transfer,' the Doctor added.

'Monitor: run an index scan according to the pattern the Doctor suggested. If you have no positive index match go for closest vehicle-type match.'

'There is a light goods transporter that fulfils these requirements, Captain,' Monitor replied promptly. 'It was recorded entering the junction of Eleventh Avenue and orbital four thirty-five minutes before Susan Foreman was abducted. It left the junction three minutes after the car presumed to be carrying Miss Foreman passed through. From this junction there is access to a parking bay that is not currently covered by traffic surveillance cameras.'

'Based on average traffic flow and the observed times of the limousine either side of the junction, was there time for it to have entered the bay?' Ben asked.

'There is a discrepancy of one minute and fifteen seconds between the observed travel time and average projected time over the same distance,' Monitor said.

'That sounds promising. Who owns the vehicle?'

The details flashed up on a screen and Ben read them off.

'The owner is a declared Believer. He used to run a health club in a building on the edge of the Inner Zone that's leased from the Church. The club closed almost a year ago.'

'That has to be it,' said Ian. 'How quickly can we get there?'

'We've got a few preparations to make first,' said Ben. 'Don't worry, I'm sure nothing further will happen to Susan for now. After taking all this trouble Fostel is going to want to question her personally. Just in case he tries to slip out of his palace in the middle of the night we'll have a watch put on it, but I'd guess he won't move until the morning at the earliest. We'll have Susan safely out of there before he arrives.'

The Doctor contained his evident impatience and concern with a visible effort and merely nodded. He glanced across at an equally silent Ian.

'I'm sorry, Chesterton. This interferes with your search for Barbara.'

'Curton's crew are still on the job,' Ian said lightly. 'I'll get back to it once we find Susan.'

Ben looked at him curiously. He'd spoken quickly and easily, though his face was lined with worry. Was Ian privately losing hope of finding Barbara alive?

Chapter Twenty-One
'...You Are Nothing'

The cage, just high enough to allow Barbara to sit upright, pitched and swayed crazily, throwing her from side to side.

As she clung grimly to the padded bars she swallowed hard once again, partly to fight down growing motion sickness, but also in an attempt to make her ears pop. They had not recovered from the vacuum effect that had sucked her along the monstrous, improbable hose-pipe and dropped her into this dimly red-lit space. Apart from the mechanism for aligning the end of the hose with the sliding doors on the roofs of a row of cages, the rest of the interior was quite featureless.

With a sudden painful click the pressure in her ears equalised and she could hear properly again.

'I'm Plaxander Vendam!' a man was shouting from a cage further along the row. 'My father's Lord Vendam! When he hears about this...' the voice faded uncertainly for a moment, then: 'Orm? If this is one of your tricks it's gone far enough!'

Barbara couldn't see much of him through the intervening bars, but he sounded frightened beneath his angry words. She was surprised to find that, now the initial shock had worn off, she herself felt puzzlement at her predicament rather than fear. She'd had so many brushes with death over the last few days that perhaps she was learning to take the consequences in her stride.

There was a groan from the next cage. Through the bars she could just make out Susan trying to sit up.

'Oh... that was awful,' Susan said weakly. 'I thought it was a gigantic snake... I saw it eat you!'

'It was those two "eyes" that made us think of snakes, together with the hissing,' Barbara said. 'Maybe that was the idea. It was just a glorified vacuum-cleaner built into some sort of vehicle. Are your ears all right?'

'Just about. Who's that shouting?'

'I don't know. We haven't had time for introductions. Hello?' she called out to the man.

He ceased his angry demands and peered through the bars at them. Barbara saw wild eyes set in a young face.

'Who are you?' he demanded. 'Do you know who's responsible for this?'

'Sorry, we're just as much in the dark as you are. We're strangers in this city.'

'NC2s!' he said dismissively.

'What are NC2s?'

He looked at them more intently, his anger diminishing slightly. 'You're not the two alien women? The space travellers? I thought one of you was in the hospital.'

Susan and Barbara exchanged puzzled glances, and Susan said: 'I think I was, briefly. How do you know about us?'

'They broadcast an interview with your companions.'

'They did? They're both all right?' Susan asked anxiously.

'Better than we are apparently,' Plax said bitterly. 'When I find out who's responsible for this…'

At that moment the swaying motion ceased abruptly as the vehicle carrying them came to a sudden halt. Immediately it was replaced by a sinking sensation which lasted for a few seconds and ended with a slight jar. Then the vehicle began to move forward again, but this time at a moderate speed and without the apparent twists and turns that had gone before.

'While we're stuck in here anyway,' Barbara said to Plax, 'perhaps you could tell us what's going on in your city? Then we might be able to work out who's responsible for this.'

'Starting with that huge rocket,' Susan added.

Curiosity replaced Plax's bluster. 'You really don't know about the Ship, do you? It's going to take us to Mirath…'

He gave a concise account of the situation in Arkhaven and a more grudging explanation of his own presence. This knowledge, however, did not help to explain their current circumstances and they could only speculate about what lay ahead. They examined their surroundings once again but the cages remained depressingly secure.

Plax kept saying: 'Don't worry. They'll soon let us go when they find out who I am.' Almost as an afterthought he added: 'I don't suppose the mayor will let anything happen to you either.'

Barbara thought he was speaking more for his own reassurance than theirs. Her ears popped again. 'Did you feel that?' she asked Susan.

'Yes. I think we must be climbing very slowly.'

After half an hour of steady travel their speed slackened, the vehicle made a few gentle turns and then stopped. A hatch at the end of the compartment opened, flooding it with harsh artificial light. The doors of their cages slid back and a voice said:

'Come out of there. Don't try anything... we're armed.'

Stiffly they climbed out of their cages and walked over to the hatch. Against the dazzle of light they could just make out a flight of metal steps leading downwards. Cautiously they descended and stepped on to dry, hard-beaten gravel.

They were in a large cave lit by strings of artificial lights. One end was open to the night sky while the mouths of half a dozen smaller tunnels ringed its walls. Three men carrying what looked like snub-nosed machine guns stood waiting for them. They wore grey one-piece uniforms without any visible markings or insignia.

'Move,' said one of the three, indicating the way with a twitch of his gun barrel.

Plax opened his mouth as though to protest, but with an evident effort contained himself. As they moved in the direction indicated, Barbara looked back at the machine that had brought them there.

Its roughly teardrop-shaped body was covered in some material so completely matt-black that it was hard to make out any details even under the cave lights. She could only just identify the hose 'snake' concertinaed along its roof, its head

177

projecting forward over the heavy rounded prow of the vehicle and making its outline even more bizarre.

They passed along a side tunnel and then into a small alcove fitted out like an office. Within it a middle-aged man, dressed in another of the featureless grey uniforms, was seated behind a desk. His tired eyes flicked over them briefly as they entered but then turned back to his desk, almost as though he preferred not to look at them.

'If you obey orders and work well you'll have decent food and quarters,' he said without any preamble. 'If you slack or cause any trouble you'll lose your rations. If you try to escape you'll probably die. The only way out is guarded and you'll find any other route impassable.'

He spoke mechanically, as though reciting familiar but distasteful phrases.

'What is this place?' Susan asked. 'Why have you brought us here?'

'That's not your concern,' he said flatly. 'If you want things to be easy, you don't ask any questions.'

'But you've no right to treat us like this,' Barbara said.

The tired eyes flicked across her once again. 'Right? Maybe not but that's how it is. Be sensible and make it easy on yourselves.' He handed them numbered metal tags hanging on thin chains. 'These are your work numbers. You'll need them to get rations.'

Plax, who had been listening to the exchanges with evident growing disbelief, could finally contain himself no longer.

'What is this nonsense? You can't make me another number. Do you know who I am?' He took a step forward and thumped the desk. 'My name is…'

A guard drove the butt of his gun into his stomach. Plax doubled up and dropped to the ground, gasping for breath. The man behind the desk looked down at him wearily.

'Here you are nothing – just another worker, no more, no less. You're fined one meal for speaking out of turn.'

The man looked at the others dispassionately.

'I advise you all to get some sleep if you can. You'll start work as soon as it gets light.'

He nodded to the guards.

'Now take them away.'

Chapter Twenty-Two
Inquisition

Fostel dressed in his full ceremonial robes. He felt the occasion justified it. In the absence of his usual attendant, Zeckler assisted.

'There was no trouble taking her?' the bishop asked.

'No, my lord,' Zeckler said. 'We were able to gag her before she realised anything was wrong and the transfer was made without incident. We took all precautions against being followed here.'

'Good. We must not be disturbed until we have determined the truth. It cannot be mere coincidence that these aliens have arrived here at this critical time.'

'I have given the matter considerable thought, my lord. Have they been sent to test or mislead us? To sabotage the Ship, perhaps? Are they demons in human form? There are descriptions of such things in the holy scripts.'

Even Fostel found Zeckler's literalism was sometimes hard to accommodate – but if he were right...

'Perhaps tonight we shall find out,' he said.

The surroundings were hardly suitable for such an occasion, Fostel thought, but in these times one had to make do.

The girl was tied to a chair positioned in the middle of what had been the health club's gymnasium. Exercise bars and frames were still fixed to the walls.

Fostel sat down in the cheap moulded chair at the desk, which was set with lights arranged to shine in the girl's face, and gestured to one of the acolytes to remove her gag and blindfold.

She blinked at them, obviously frightened. Well, she only had herself to blame, Fostel thought. She should have co-operated in the hospital.

'You are here to be judged in the court of the Supreme Maker,' he told her. 'You will answer all questions fully and accurately... or else suffer the consequences.'

She fought to keep her voice steady.

'What questions? Why have you kidnapped me?'

'To show the faithful that aliens are not above the divine authority of the Church. To determine your true natures… and whether you are fit to participate in the salvation of our race.'

'You must be feeling very insecure,' she retorted with unexpected spirit. 'Does your Supreme Maker usually have to resort to kidnapping?'

'You will not question the will of the Maker,' he said, 'or use His name irreverently.'

'I'm not questioning your deity, just the actions of his servants.'

'Hold your tongue, girl,' snapped Zeckler.

'I can't answer your questions and hold my tongue at the same time,' she retorted quickly. 'Unless you're overruling what your bishop just told me.'

'Stop playing foolish games with us,' Fostel warned her.

'Would it make any difference in the end? You're determined to do whatever you want anyway. But you won't get away with it. The authorities will guess you're responsible. Wherever this place is they'll find me sooner or later.'

'I'm sure the mayor will suspect me,' Fostel agreed, 'but he cannot prove anything, and without proof he can take no action. No doubt my residence is being watched even now because they think I returned there after midnight service. In fact it was a Believer who bears a close enough resemblance to me in the dark to serve as my double. I can return by similar means. So you see, I will not be personally connected with anything that happens here this night. But you are wrong when you say your answers will not make any difference to your fate.'

'You really mean you'll simply let me go if I tell you what you want to know?'

'If we are satisfied with your answers.'

'And what's to stop me telling everybody what you did afterwards?'

'I have no doubt the mayor will advise against any such action. He cannot risk disturbing the peace this close to the exodus.'

'But we're not any threat to you. We came here by accident. My Grandfather's even helping with your Ship!'

'We cannot accept alien knowledge if it is false, or corrupts our people and diverts their attention from the One Path.'

'But we're not trying to convert your people to other beliefs,' she said. Then she frowned. 'You want to claim all the credit for getting everybody to Mirath safely, don't you? That's what all this is really about.'

Zeckler stepped forward, clasped a handful of her hair in his fist and pulled her head backwards until she stared up into his cold narrow eyes.

'You will not speak to His Reverence in that accusing tone again. You are here to answer questions, not ask them. Do you understand, alien?'

'I understand,' she gasped.

Zeckler released her hair slowly, in the process letting his hand slide across her shoulder, Fostel noted. She flinched away from his touch.

'Your grandfather talked of a plurality of worlds inhabited by many different beings, but nothing of their spiritual nature,' Fostel said. 'Do they all acknowledge the Supreme Maker?'

The girl licked her dry lips and said carefully: 'There are many different beliefs about supernatural creators… probably as many as there are races in the universe.'

'But they must hold one truth in common to explain their existence, their origins.'

'No, and that's the truth. I don't know anything about any Supreme Maker, only science and reason. Many races use science to explain their origins and how they evolved into what they are.' She added quickly: 'But science cannot prove or disprove whether such a being as your Supreme Maker actually exists.'

'Then you worship science,' Zeckler interjected contemptuously.

'Science isn't a religion, it's just a way of finding out the truth about how things work.'

'It is an evil if it denies the One Truth!' Fostel said.

'If you believe so,' she agreed hastily. 'Maybe you're right... I can't tell.'

'Then tell us what your science says of our origins, girl,' Fostel demanded.

'Well... from the instrument readings in our ship, my grandfather thinks your ancestors came here thousands of years ago from Earth.'

'What is Earth?' Fostel asked suspiciously.

'Earth is the homeworld of your species. It was the starting point for many voyages of exploration and colonisation that reached out across the galaxy. There must have been some disaster after landing here on Sarath that left your ancestors without technology or records of where you came from. In the struggle to survive, knowledge of your past was lost or turned into legends. It's not that unusual. I've been to other worlds where this has happened.'

'Is this Earth known as the holy world?' Fostel asked.

'I don't know what you mean.'

'Is it not revered?'

'It's the planet on which humanity evolved. Otherwise it's perfectly ordinary.'

'How can you know that, alien?' Zeckler said.

'Well, I've lived there for a while.'

'Liar!' said Zeckler. 'An alien would never be permitted to walk the Holy Land... or are you a demon under your deceiving skin?'

'That's stupid... I'm not a demon!' she said. 'And I can't change the facts. Earth is just a planet like this one.'

'Then you are saying we are merely the descendants of travellers from some mundane world?' Fostel asked.

'Well... yes. What's wrong with that?'

'It is blasphemy,' Zeckler said. 'Sarath was populated directly by beings created in the Maker's own lands: the Blessed Fields, Edran, Matherarth. Sarath was created in their image.'

'Edran?' she repeated. 'No, don't you see what's happened? The words have become distorted over the years. Edran is Eden... and Matherarth might mean Mother Earth. That's how people

184

sometimes referred to it...' She trailed off as she saw the expressions on their faces.

'We cannot let these lies spread, my lord,' said Zeckler. 'If the people believe we are not the chosen ones, but are merely one mundane race among millions, the Church will fall. Especially with the Ship about to embark upon the very kind of voyage this alien claims our ancestors made.'

Fostel nodded slowly. 'I agree. Besides, she has condemned herself as a blasphemous unbeliever.'

'I've told you the truth!' Susan shouted, but they ignored her.

'Put her to the ancient test, my lord,' said Zeckler, his voice suddenly sounding hungry. 'We have the means here. Let the Maker decide her fate.'

Dare they? Fostel wondered. Then chided himself for the doubting thought. The years had made him soft. If he and Zeckler truly believed in the Maker they dared anything. Now was the time to make a stand.

'Let it be so,' he said.

The Believer stationed inside the rear entrance of the former health club paced back and forth stoically. The draughty corridor was a gloomy place to stand guard. He would have liked to witness the trial of the alien woman for himself, but his duty had been personally assigned by Archdeacon Zeckler. The guard held the Maker's talisman he wore about his neck, while silently reciting the precepts of obedience, and consoled himself with the knowledge that he served the holy purpose even in this humble station.

There was a scratching from the other side of the door that opened on to the backyard. There was that cat again.

The first time he had heard it he thought it was a rat, but then he had made out the husky purring. There were many such creatures roaming about Arkhaven; survivors of wartime raids in which their owners had died.

Now the cat was getting impatient and yowling indignantly. It began scratching more fiercely at the door. Why didn't it go away? Maybe it recalled being fed here at some time in the past. If it didn't stop they would be able to hear it inside. It might disturb the bishop.

Hastily he drew back the bolts, pulled the door open and peered out into the yard, swinging his boot back in preparation for a kick.

'Get out of here, you little…'

There was no cat.

He never saw the figure flattened beside the door, or the hand that chopped down with trained precision on the back of his neck.

They piled silently into the corridor, dragging the limp form of the unconscious guard back in with them. Six dark-clothed figures with their faces half-masked by bulky night-sight goggles. Ian, the last inside, closed the door on the deceptive lights of the city. Through his goggles he could still see the interior clearly, as though it was lit by a grainy-green radiance.

Lant and his two colleagues from the Watch were in the lead, each carrying drawn handweapons. They were followed by the Doctor and Nyra Shardri, who was clutching a medical bag. Ian brought up the rear armed with an official issue watchman's baton. They did not exchange a word. Plans of the building drawn from the city archives had already indicated the most likely places where Susan might be held.

They padded along to their first objective: a ground floor storeroom. Lant tested the door, found it unlocked and silently swung it open. He checked inside then closed it again and shook his head. They continued on. Ten paces down the corridor, Nyra suddenly held up her hand.

'Listen,' she hissed.

They strained their ears and heard the murmur of distant voices.

They followed the sounds through a door into a deserted changing room lined with dusty metal lockers. At the other end of the room reflected light shone through an open archway. They padded over to it, the voices getting louder all the time. The archway was the inner one of an offset pair connected by a short passage. Beyond the second Ian could just see a narrow strip of tiled floor.

'... judgement of the Supreme Maker be carried out,' they heard an echoing voice intoning solemnly. It sounded like Fostel's. 'We consign you to His mercy...'

Lant dropped to his hands and knees, wriggled forward and snatched a glance into the room beyond. Ian saw him start momentarily as though in surprise. Then he sprang to his feet and darted through the archway, the rest of them following at his heels.

The chamber beyond enclosed a medium-sized swimming pool, stained and grimy about the edges and filled with slightly murky water. Stacks of plastic moulded chairs and small tables were scattered about the poolside, as though the space was being used for temporary storage. On the other side of the pool stood Bishop Fostel, dressed in the same ornate robes and chains of office that Ian and the Doctor had seen him wearing on the broadcast the day they had arrived. Beside him was a man in only slightly less magnificent dress. Forming a semicircle about them were half a dozen figures in hooded white robes. What looked like a small diving board had been extended from the poolside out over the water. Balanced on the end of it, gagged and bound hand and foot, was Susan.

'I am Captain Lant of the City Watch,' Lant called out. 'I hereby arrest you on charges of kidnapping and false imprisonment.'

His gun was pointing directly at Fostel. On either side of him his grim-faced fellow watchmen covered the rest of the group.

For a moment the strange tableau opposite remained frozen in surprise. Susan twisted her head around to face them, her wide eyes showing starkly against her pale face, and she tried to say something that was muffled by her gag. Ian, the Doctor and Nyra started around the pool towards her.

'You would not dare pull that trigger, Captain,' Fostel said, recovering his composure.

'Don't count on it,' Lant said coldly.

'This is the Maker's will,' Fostel replied simply. 'It cannot be denied.'

As they rounded the end of the pool Ian saw that a cord ran from Fostel's hand down to the supports of the board on which Susan lay.

'He's holding something!' he shouted to Lant. 'Tell him to...'

The double doors on the far side of the room burst open and two men appeared holding handguns.

The watchmen fired by reflex, dropping one of the intruders where he stood. But the distraction allowed the ceremonial party to scatter behind the stacked chairs, the acolytes drawing guns from the folds of their robes. As Fostel threw himself to one side he tugged the cord.

The board flipped upwards and Susan dropped into the water with a small splash and vanished beneath the surface.

For an instant Ian stood frozen in horror. Than he flung his baton aside and made to dive in after her.

A fusillade of shots from the white-robes acolytes kicked spray up into his face and chips flew from the tiled edging of the pool. A flying fragment stung his cheek, driving him back to the shelter of a pile of tables beside the Doctor and Nyra. The three watchmen were also taking cover. Gunfire criss-crossed the pool. But Fostel's side had more weapons... enough to keep all Susan's rescuers pinned down until it was too late.

'Lant!' Ian shouted. 'Give me some cover!'

But Lant had evidently already assessed the situation. 'Take out the lights!' he ordered.

The watchmen's guns lifted and burred in rapid-fire mode. The luminescent panels in the ceiling shattered. Wiring sparked and crackled. In a few seconds the pool room was plunged into darkness, except for the faint city glow filtering through a row of high fanlights. Fostel's unprepared followers were left shooting blind. Ian sprinted forward and dived headfirst into the pool.

He swam rapidly down through the murky water until he touched the bottom, then began working his way along, swinging his arms out wide as he tried to find Susan.

The water was like a dark opalescent mist around him. The sounds of battle above took on a muffled tinny quality. He heard

188

a distant crash and rattle, then the louder splash and rush of bubbles as something else entered the water. The seals around his goggles, which were not designed to be waterproof, were leaking. In a few seconds he would be effectively blind.

Then his hand brushed something. He clasped a pair of bound ankles that jerked feebly at his touch. In a second he had a grip around Susan's waist and kicked upwards.

They broke surface in the middle of the pool, stray bullets smacking the water about them. He lifted Susan's chin up, felt for the broad strip of tape covering her mouth and ripped it free, leaving her coughing and gasping for breath. Ian was disorientated, trying to see through goggles half-full of water while supporting Susan. Then his ears cleared and he heard the Doctor's voice calling out urgently: 'Over here, Chesterton, this way!'

He struck out towards the sound and in a few seconds touched the side of the pool where the Doctor and Nyra were kneeling. Ian boosted Susan up into their arms then began to lift himself out of the water. There was a crack of gunfire. Tiles exploded into fragments at Ian's side and he felt the rush of a bullet past his forehead. At the same moment Susan jerked violently and gave a cry of pain.

The Doctor and Nyra slithered away from the pool edge as Ian heaved himself out of the water, dragging Susan with them. There was a dark stain spreading rapidly down the left side of her jumper.

'Let's get out of here!' Lant shouted from further round the pool.

As the Doctor was tearing the tape from Susan's wrists and ankles, Nyra pulled up the girl's jumper and sprayed foam from a small aerosol applicator over the wound. In seconds the foam set into a rubber-like pad.

'All right,' Nyra said.

Ian gathered Susan in his arms and they stumbled towards the archway through which they had entered, while the watchmen kept up a barrage of covering fire. They retraced their steps through the changing room and down the corridor to the back entrance. Lant had his pocket phone out.

'Come and get us,' he ordered.

As they ran out into the backyard a large jeep tore down the narrow service road and screeched to a halt, its doors swinging open to receive them. Carefully lifting Susan on to the back seat they scrambled in after her.

'City Hospital as fast as you can!' Lant directed.

The engine hummed with power and they sped off into the night.

When the last echoes had died away and he was certain the watchmen had departed, Archdeacon Zeckler shouted loudly from behind his sheltering stack of chairs: 'Lights! We must have light.'

Somebody felt their way along the wall until they reached the door to the corridor and flung it open. A fan of light shone in and sparkled across the surface of the pool. Zeckler cautiously stood up and looked about him, still dazed by the sudden turn of events. A guard and two of the acolytes were lying motionless on the ground. A third was resting against the wall clutching his bloodstained leg.

'The bishop? Where's the bishop?' Zeckler demanded. 'Did they take him? Bring torches!'

There was no sign of Fostel around the poolside or in the adjoining rooms. Several minutes passed before one of the acolytes thought to shine his torch into the pool itself.

Chapter Twenty-Three
Skin Deep

The jeep drew up outside the City Hospital as the sky began to turn grey with pre-dawn light. A trolley and two attendants were already waiting for them, alerted by a radio call from Nyra.

Susan was transferred on to the trolley and taken through the accident unit entrance. Nyra had given her a localised painkilling injection during the journey and she had recovered sufficiently to relate her experiences remarkably calmly as they went inside. Ian smiled in relief as well as wonderment at her constitution.

'It was like a medieval trial by water,' she explained, clutching her grandfather's hand as she was wheeled along. 'According to the bishop if I sank and drowned his Supreme Maker had granted me the absolution of a natural death. If I somehow managed to float I was obviously under the influence of an evil force and would have to be disposed of in some other way. When I went under I just tried to hold my breath as long as I could... and hope.' She looked at Ian. 'Thank you.'

'Yes, Chesterton,' the Doctor said gruffly. 'Thank you once again.'

'Well, if everything's under control here, I'll just report in to the mayor,' Lant said, taking out his pocket phone and stepping back outside.

Nyra Shardri, who had been conferring in low tones with one of the attendants, returned to them.

'I'm afraid we've had a minor system breakdown. There are no treatment tanks available right now. It's nothing to worry about, but Susan will have to wait on the support trolley until one is ready.'

Ian gestured at the empty room with its array of gleaming equipment. 'What's all this for then? Can't you use it? You said her wound wasn't that serious.'

Nyra looked slightly uncomfortable. 'I could, in an emergency, but we usually leave surgery to the autosystems nowadays.'

'I doubt if you'll be able to maintain this level of automation on Mirath,' the Doctor said. 'You must learn to reduce your dependency on machines at some point.'

Ian suspected the Doctor was testing Nyra. The clinician looked at them uncertainly for a moment, then seemed to come to a decision.

'You're quite right. I'm perfectly capable of this sort of work... if that's all right by you?' she asked Susan.

Susan smiled reassuringly. 'I'm sure you'll do fine.'

Nyra called over an attendant to assist her.

In a minute Susan was lying on her side on a treatment table, covered by a silvery blanket with a window over the wound. A sterile field enveloped the operating area so there was no need for masks or gowns. The Doctor and Ian were able to watch from close by.

Nyra pulled down a probe mounted on an extensible arm and held it over the injury. An image appeared on a screen at the head of the table.

'The scan shows no deep internal damage,' she said to Susan. 'The coagulating agent in the temporary dressing has limited the blood loss so you won't need a transfusion. Luckily the bullet passed right through. You've got a couple of broken ribs and some lacerated muscles. Nothing I can't fix. In an hour you'll be as good as new.'

She sounded more confident now, Ian thought; even pleased with herself.

Using another aerosol applicator she sprayed a release agent over the temporary dressing and it fell away easily, revealing the blood-caked wound underneath. Nyra took up a swab and a suction device and began to remove the clotted matter.

'I'll just clean this up first, then I can rebuild those ribs and...'

She faltered and Ian saw her face go pale. She took a step back from the table, dropping the suction tool which swung loosely on its hose hissing loudly.

'Oh... good grief,' she said faintly.

'Is there a problem?' the Doctor demanded, striding quickly to Nyra's side.

Susan was trying to twist about to look up at them. 'What's wrong?' she asked, her voice catching.

Ian saw incredulity and then utter dismay flicker across the Doctor's face. Ian moved forward, clasped Susan's hand in reassurance, then nerved himself to look closely at the gaping wound in her side.

A flap of skin had been torn open by the passage of the bullet, exposing her ribs. But where there should have been white bone there was only buckled silvery metal and plastic.

Chapter Twenty-Four
The Plateau

The lights in the cave that housed the workers' barracks flickered on, illuminating tiers of metal-frame bunk beds filled with sleeping figures. A speaker came to life, blaring out the shrill of a bell. The figures stirred wearily, groaning and coughing. A voice replaced the bell: 'First meal in fifteen minutes. First meal in fifteen minutes.'

Barbara and Susan blinked the sleep from their eyes and gave each other slightly forced smiles of reassurance. They had been so tired from their exertions of the previous day that they had slept even in these new and disturbing surroundings.

Around them women were climbing stiffly from their bunks. They appeared thoroughly downcast, hardly sparing the newcomers a glance as they tramped wearily through to the adjoining washroom. Barbara and Susan wearily followed their example.

On their return they saw Plaxander Vendam through the double partition grille that separated the women's section of the dormitory from the men's. He looked lost and afraid. When he saw them he gave them a half-hearted wave, then dropped his hand as though embarrassed.

Sets of barred doors slid back automatically, opening on to a short tunnel. They filed down it into another cave laid out with plain tables and benches. It was a communal dining hall with space for about two hundred people. They gathered up plastic utensils, cups and trays moulded with depressions for food. As each worker put their numbered tag in a slot in the wall a hopper dispensed a portion of vegetable stew, a hunk of bread and a slice of hard cheese on to their trays. It was not especially appetising but Barbara and Susan were too hungry to care and started chewing on the bread before they even started to look for space at a table.

When Plax put his tag in the machine it only gave him a measure of water. He looked bemused and began thumping its scarred metal panels angrily. Others in the queue behind him pushed him aside.

'You've been docked a meal... don't waste your time, boy,' a man told him impatiently. Plax rounded on him, losing his temper.

'How dare you speak to me like that. Do you know who I am? I'm...'

Barbara and Susan quickly intervened, pulling him aside.

'Don't be stupid,' Barbara said. 'Sit down quietly and have some of ours.'

They found spaces at a table in a corner of the room and sat Plax between them. He sank his head in his hands. Barbara exchanged rueful glances with Susan. On top of all their other concerns they had somehow become responsible for the young man. They fed him bread soaked in stew until he managed to look shamefacedly at them.

'I've never had to take... charity before,' he said.

'There's a first time for everything,' Susan said encouragingly. 'You'll be all right.'

Barbara said: 'This is all new to us as well, but we have survived worse things. Be patient, look, listen and learn. It's the only way we're going to get out of here. I know our friends will be looking for us and from what you've said so will your father. So we must watch out for them, or for anything else that might help us. But meanwhile don't start unnecessary fights, understand?'

Plaxander nodded. 'Yes... and thank you.'

They had hardly finished eating when the speakers came on again: 'You will report for work assignments!'

They disposed of their trays and utensils down a larger slot in the food machine and filed down another tunnel to a solid, much heavier door.

It slid back revealing a long, cold cave open to the outside air at its far end. They could see the sky flushing from grey to dawn-pink. Looking down on them from gantries that circled the walls were a dozen grey guards, the first they had seen so far that morning.

Hanging on wall racks were one-piece coveralls, overboots and thick gloves, which the workers began to put on. Numbers matching those on their tags were stencilled on the backs of the coveralls. Barbara, Susan and Plax found their respective sets of workwear and pulled them on gratefully, for their breath was steaming in the bitterly cold air. Beyond the racks of clothes were stacked picks, crowbars, shovels and simple two-wheeled hand barrows.

A grey man carrying a clipboard addressed them from above.

'Form into five teams of thirty,' he commanded. 'Each team to take ten barrows, five picks, fifteen shovels. First three teams out will board the transporters.'

The workers milled around obeying their orders, and Susan, Barbara and Plax eventually found themselves in the fourth team. The girls took up shovels while the young man gingerly chose a pick, looking as though he had never held one before in his life.

In their teams they marched through the cave mouth into the open air.

They were standing on gentle slopes that rose at one end of a plateau that Barbara guessed was perhaps eight miles long by five wide. Around them jagged peaks capped with snow thrust up into a sky filled with ragged clouds, edged with gold by the still invisible rising sun. Purple shadows cloaked the frosted plateau floor which stretched away, level and even like a dry lakebed, to distant foothills.

'What's that?' asked Susan.

Two dark parallel lines ran from a point not far below them in a die-straight line along the length of the plateau floor, until they were lost in the shadows of its far rim. Between them was a streak of silver that mirrored the lightening sky.

Under the watchful eyes of the grey guards they marched along a well-worn path that wound down the hillside in a series of switchbacks. As they descended and the light grew brighter they saw that the valley floor was not quite as smooth as it had at first seemed. It was pockmarked by craters of all sizes, making it look like a stretch of moonscape.

'Meteor craters,' Susan said. 'This place must have been hit by meteor storms. Like the city.'

'It looks as though a lot of them get through,' Barbara observed. 'Isn't it defended in the same way?'

Plax spoke up, seeming to lift himself from his dejection for the first time. 'Anywhere within a hundred kilometres of the city you'd see the defences working. They must want to keep this place secret.'

The parallel lines resolved themselves into steep-sided earth embankments fifteen to twenty feet high. The silver streak between them was obscured as they reached ground level, but they could now see that the embankments merged into the hillside. The ground had been cut back between them to form the mouth of a tunnel which was closed by towering aircraft-hangar-sized double doors.

Three balloon-tyred trucks were waiting with wide flatbed trailers in tow. The first three teams loaded their tools and themselves on to them and were driven out across the plateau. The fourth team was marched away in the same direction.

At regular intervals they passed narrow slots in the embankment, just wide enough for a man to pass through, but could not make out any details of what lay beyond. After half a mile they came to a place where the embankment wall had partly collapsed. There was a fresh meteor crater a hundred yards away and the shock and ejected material from this had clearly done the damage. The team was set to clearing the loose debris and rebuilding the embankment.

A relay of barrows was arranged. Susan and Barbara shovelled loose material into them while Plax used his pick, rather inexpertly, to break up larger rocks so they could be more easily handled.

After an hour the sun had lifted high enough to burn off the last of the cold mist and they were all sweating. Plax was getting blisters for the first time in his life. Now they could see that the embankments on the far side of the plateau did not stop at the edge of the level ground. Keeping to the same line they ascended in a gentle curve up through the foothills, and vanished in the glare of the rising sun somewhere amongst the high peaks.

'But what's it for?' Plax muttered for the fifth time.

'I wish I knew,' Barbara admitted. She stopped digging for a minute, straightened her back and wiped her brow. 'We could ask… but these people don't seem to be very forthcoming.'

'Maybe they're too frightened of the guards,' Susan suggested.

As if to prove her wrong the man pushing one of the barrows they were loading said: 'You three are new, aren't you?'

'Yes,' said Barbara, looking about furtively and lowering her voice. 'Who are you?'

'I'm Tressel, this is Semanov,' he went on, nodding at the woman handling the barrow next to him.

Barbara introduced Susan, Plax and herself.

'Don't worry about the guards,' Tressel continued. 'As long as we keep working they don't care if we talk.'

'They almost act as though we're not here,' Barbara said, making a show of her shovelling.

'We were only brought here a few days ago, but other workers who've been here over a year say they've always acted that way… when you can get them to talk, that is. Most seem to have given up.' He and Semanov took up the handles of their full barrows and started off towards the embankment. 'Speak to you again next time round.'

When they returned, Barbara said: 'The guards almost seem guilty, as though they'd rather we weren't here.'

'They should feel guilty about making people work like this,' Plax interjected with feeling. 'Even NC2s don't deserve this sort of treatment.'

'But why don't they use machines?' Susan asked. 'They'd be much more efficient.'

'There's some wrecked earth-moving equipment up near the caves,' Semanov said. 'They lost it in a bad storm and couldn't replace it. Slave labour was the next best thing.'

'By kidnapping citizens with that ridiculous machine?' Plax asked.

'I think it's an old disguised security enforcement vehicle,' said Tressel. 'The suction device was meant to pick out targeted individuals from a crowd or occupied buildings.'

'But who's using it?' Plax asked. 'Is this place run by the government or a private faction?'

Tressel looked uncomfortable. 'We've been wondering about that. I used to work for the government myself... but I've found out recently how little I knew about Arkhaven. We don't know and nor does anybody else we've asked.'

Susan said: 'We guess these walls are meant to protect whatever's between them from the fragments thrown up when a meteor hits, but what is it?'

'See for yourself,' Semanov said. 'Take over our barrows for this trip. As long as we keep working they don't care who's doing what.'

Susan kept her shovel while Barbara and Plax exchanged their tools for the loaded barrows. They followed the wheeltracks up the side of the embankment to the top of the section being rebuilt. They took their time tipping and pounding the rubble into place while they looked down the other side.

Barbara estimated that the walls of the two embankments were sixty or seventy feet apart. A flat-bottomed trough perhaps thirty feet wide and lined with gleaming sheet metal had been sunk in the ground between them. It might have been designed to channel water, except that it was quite dry. Running along both sides of the trough, and standing almost ten feet above it, was a peculiar kind of fence. It was formed out of massive stanchions, obviously set deep into the ground and braced from the outside by angled struts. Heavy cables could be seen rising out of the ground at regular intervals and running up to the fence's single wide rail. On the inside face of the rail above each stanchion was mounted an ovoid coil of heavy copper-coloured wire over three feet long. Both the trough and fences ran in an unbroken line along the entire length of the embankments.

'What's it for?' Plax wondered.

Susan was frowning. 'I don't know... but it must be important.'

Suddenly the futility of their situation seemed to weigh down on Barbara. She fingered her watchstrap irritably. An image of the Arkavians' great escape rocket came into her mind. The Ship, Plax called it. Yes, it was vitally important that she got to the Ship… but she didn't know why.

Chapter Twenty-Five
Flesh and Blood

Lord Vendam was initially disappointed, rather than concerned, when he learned at breakfast that Plax had not been home at all that night. He assumed he must have stayed over at a friend's house.

Captain Lant's visit the previous day had strained relations between father and son. Vendam had never been happy about Plax's involvement in the so-called 'hunts'. There was the matter of Outer Zone security, of course, although the deception they maintained there should be capable of standing up to temporary intrusions of the sort the hunts entailed. It was more the element of risk involved in the chases. He recalled friends of his own youth who had come to grief while racing fast cars, and Plax was his only heir… and the last living reminder of his beloved late wife. The boy had definitely grown wilder after she had died, but Vendam had refrained from ordering him to stop because he believed a young man should learn by experience as far as possible. He also had a shrewd idea how far such a ban would diminish Plax's standing among his peers… and there were few enough of them left in Arkhaven.

But now that the hunts had caused a watchman to come to the house to question Plax like some common criminal, it was a different matter. The Vendam family had certain standards to uphold, after all. The previous day he had told Plax of his change of mind.

'I don't want you to take part in any more of these hunts of yours.'

He should have realised it was not the right time to lay down the law. Lant's disrespectful treatment of him had clearly reduced his authority in Plax's eyes. The boy was still young enough to find that hard to accept. His pride was wounded and he had to strike out against something.

'Why shouldn't I?' Plax had retorted indignantly. 'Chasing a few escaped NC2s doesn't do any harm. The Watch are after them anyway.'

'That is their job. It's not seemly to be too closely involved with either them or with escaped criminals. Let's just say I would rather you did not go into the Outer Zone again.'

But Plax would not let the matter rest. 'Why not? We don't bother anybody. The people keep out of our way.'

'Plax, don't argue, just do as I say for once. It's for your own good.'

Plax's mouth set in a stubborn line. 'I think I'm old enough to know what's good for me,' he had said, and stormed out of the house.

It was after breakfast when Orm Herstwell called, wanting to know if Plax had come home yet. When he learnt he had not, he reluctantly admitted the challenge he and his friends had set him.

'We returned to the same spot early this morning,' Herstwell explained, 'but Plax wasn't there. At first we thought he was getting back at us but, after a while, when he still didn't appear we began to wonder if he'd had some sort of accident. We searched the area pretty thoroughly but there was no sign of him. In fact there was no sign of anybody. The whole area seems deserted. Has something happened out there, sir?'

'Never mind about that,' Vendam said quickly. 'You and your friends are not to leave the Inner Zone again, do you understand me?'

'But what about Plax, sir? We feel responsible. We'd like to help find him.'

'I'll take care of Plax,' Vendam assured him.

After Herstwell had gone Vendam sat for several minutes staring bleakly into space. What had happened to Plax? Some of the buildings out there were dangerously fragile. Perhaps he had gone inside one for shelter and a floor had given way. There were any number of possibilities. And even if he was safe, he could not wander around for long without realising the truth. There could be serious repercussions if the actions of his own son and others of his class exposed the deception. Even if the discovery was successfully suppressed the incident would dangerously strengthen the hands of the mayor and the Church, to the detriment of the Elite families.

Therefore he couldn't call the Watch in to help... at least not for a few hours.

But he couldn't leave Plax out there either. When all was said and done, he was still his son and his responsibility.

He picked up the house phone.

'Meeks... have my car made ready... No, I wish to drive myself.'

'You are not Susan, you're an android, a simulacrum, an impostor!' the Doctor said. 'What have you done with my Susan?'

As she had for the past half hour, the thing that looked like Susan Foreman sat huddled in a chair hugging her arms about her, face pale and incredulous, eyes red-rimmed, cheeks tear-streaked. Despite knowing the truth, incredible as it was, all Ian could think was how very frightened she looked.

'Please stop it!' she begged. 'Grandfather, don't say those things. You know who I am!'

Nyra Shardri held up a sheaf of print-outs from her medical scanners. She had recovered from her initial shock and was almost as angry as the Doctor. She had been badly deceived and now one of her patients was missing.

'You look like Susan, and something inside you fools the automatic scanners, all right,' she said. 'But the biopsy probes I made prove what you are: flesh grown over a gellfibre musculature and magnoalloy skeleton, with synthetic internal organs and a block of crystal micro-circuitry for a brain.'

'But when was the switch made?' Ian wondered.

'Susan wasn't like that when she came in here,' Nyra said, 'I saw that with my own eyes. And she was under continuous observation since then... except for the kidnapping.' She glared at the android again. 'Is that when you were substituted?'

'I don't know!' the android said desperately.

'Could the bishop be responsible?' the Doctor asked Lant.

'I don't see the Church using technology like this,' Lant said. 'I didn't even know this sort of thing was possible. If it *was* them, then that ceremony we interrupted was staged and we were meant to get her... this fake... back.' He frowned. 'Then they spoilt everything by wounding her. Was that just an accident, or does it mean they didn't know what she was either?' He rubbed his eyes. 'Sorry. It's been a long night and this is getting beyond me.'

'It must know the truth,' the Doctor said, glaring balefully at the android. 'And it will tell us.'

'Doctor!' Ian said sharply. 'I know you're afraid for Susan... the real Susan, but you're frightening it... her. I don't think she knows. Maybe as far as she's concerned she is Susan. If she's a machine, couldn't she have been programmed to believe it, or something? Well?'

With a visible effort the Doctor restrained himself and instead sat down heavily, resting his head in his hands. He suddenly looked very old.

In the weary silence the android Susan appeared to take in a deep breath and steady herself. She looked at the Doctor with sad longing, then reached out for the print-outs Nyra was still holding so accusingly.

'Please,' she said.

Nyra handed them over with grimace of distaste. The android examined them carefully. After a minute Ian saw her shudder but keep reading. When she was finished she closed her eyes tightly and Ian wondered if she was crying. Could a machine really cry?

Without warning she sprang to her feet, spun round and punched the wall behind her with all her strength, crying out not in pain but from inner anguish. They looked on in shocked silence. Slowly she withdrew her fist from the indentation it had made in the wall panel and looked at her bleeding knuckles expressionlessly. Then she turned to the ring of grim faces surrounding her, her gaze finally settling upon Ian.

'I remember being on Earth in 1963. I was a pupil at Coal Hill School and I gave you such problems in science classes... Then you and Barbara followed me back to Totter's yard. That's right, isn't it?'

Ian nodded. The android looked at the Doctor, who reluctantly met her eyes.

'You were so angry with them for prying, Grandfather...' she faltered '...Doctor. In fact you were quite rude. I recall every detail. But if I search deep enough I don't think those things happened to me... but I can only tell because I know the truth about what I am. It takes an effort to look that hard. If I stop... then I am Susan and this is a nightmare.'

The Doctor said: 'Why were you given Susan's memories? Who was responsible?'

'I don't know,' the android said wretchedly. 'I really don't know!'

Ian stepped forward and took her hand. It felt perfectly normal. 'I believe you,' he said. He looked round at the others. 'Let's stop blaming her for something she can't do anything about.'

'All right,' said Lant. 'But what am I going to tell the mayor? I've already said we'd recovered Susan safely. Now how do I explain this?'

Archdeacon Zeckler looked down on Fostel's body as it lay in a closed side-chapel in the cathedral.

It had been moved with indecent haste from the health club, before a larger force of watchmen descended upon them. Now, standing among the solemn candles and sweet smell of incense, Zeckler realised the burden of guardianship had passed to him. He gave a silent prayer up to the Maker that he might make the right decisions. Only a handful of the brethren knew what had happened for the moment, but in a few hours he would have to make some sort of public announcement. He must decide how to reveal the circumstances to the greatest benefit of the Church.

Of course, the bishop's demise had, technically, been accidental. He had fallen into the pool in the darkness and confusion and, with tragic irony, had been dragged to the bottom by the weight of his own robes. But Zeckler knew that in the Maker's eyes the watchmen and the aliens, and even the mayor, were responsible, though it would be difficult to prove this to the unenlightened citizens. It was almost regrettable that the late bishop did not bear the mark of violence. A bullet wound from a watchman's gun, now that could have been turned to good purpose.

Zeckler hesitated. Was this divine inspiration?

It was not too late to add such a detail to the remains to reinforce the greater fundamental truth. He was sure Fostel would understand. After all, what was left of him was now only an empty shell of flesh and blood.

Chapter Twenty-Six
Tidal Stress

From the day of the asteroid impact, fissures had been extending through the core of the falling moon.

Every time its irregular mass passed close to Sarath the tidal force acting across its one hundred and fifty kilometre width opened the cracks a little further, as the opposite sides of the moon tried to orbit at slightly different velocities. In addition to the gravitational stress, there was the interaction between Sarath's magnetic field and the ferrous lodes within the moon's core. Even as this force slowed the moon's forward motion, the lodes twisted and flexed against the rock around them. Myriad cracks met and merged and sheer planes formed. Deep within the moon, rock grated against rock through fractured strata whose combined surface area would have measured many tens of kilometres square. Inexorably friction generated heat.

As the moon spiralled ever closer to Sarath the stress force at its heart multiplied. Unable to radiate away into space, the gathering pool of heat around the fracture zones began to melt the surrounding rock.

Magma chambers formed and sent questing roots back up through fissures towards the surface. Steadily the pressure of the molten rock rose until it could no longer be contained.

Chapter Twenty-Seven
Rift

'You shouldn't have allowed Lant to play the hero,' Commander Pardek told Draad angrily.

'I was trying to avoid taking any official action against Fostel,' Draad snapped. 'You know I couldn't move without proof. We never expected that the bishop's men would be armed.'

Both men were tired and short-tempered. They had little enough sleep at the best of times and this last night had been worse than usual.

'Yes, and if we'd had a proper team in there we could have had him for holding illegal weapons,' Pardek replied with barely concealed disgust. 'As it is, by the time my squad got there the place had been cleaned out of anything incriminating. The weapons are probably stored all over the city by now. We know one of their cars delivered something to the cathedral, but they got it inside before we could intercept them. Do we risk making a search?'

Draad shook his head. 'The Watch has never set foot in the cathedral on official business since it was consecrated, far less searched it. I want to keep the Believers off-balance, not provoke an all-out confrontation.'

'But we can't let them keep unlicensed weapons.'

'We may have to. At least we know they exist now.'

'Your pardon, Mayor,' Monitor interrupted, 'but standing orders require that I inform you immediately about any changes in the condition of the moon. Observations from our remaining automatic equatorial stations show rapid changes on its surface.'

'Let's see them,' Draad said.

Wall screens lit up to show the scarred body of the moon seen from three different camera positions. One view was intermittently obscured by wisps of drifting cloud, but the others were clear enough. They showed a cluster of half a dozen flickering red points of light on the moon's limb. Even as Pardek and Draad studied them they grew more intense and new spots sprang up about them. In minutes they were forming into crooked lines that radiated outwards across the moon's surface.

'Volcanoes?'

'Apparently so, Mayor,' Monitor confirmed.

'But where did they come from… and why are they appearing now?'

'Internal heat may have been generated by cumulative stresses within the moon's interior. They are erupting along pre-existing fault lines, which would provide points of least resistance to subterranean magma pressure.'

The flickering volcanic vents were being obscured by dark clouds of ejected material. About them the normally sharp surface features were being blurred as though by a rolling fog. In its last days the moon was gaining a temporary atmosphere of dust and vaporised rock. Occasionally it was lit from below by ruddy glows and blue-white electrostatic discharges.

'Will these eruptions affect our projections for Zero Day?' Pardek asked anxiously.

'Not at their present magnitude, Commander,' Monitor said. 'Any net thrust the volcanoes impart to the moon will not alter its trajectory to an appreciable extent in the time remaining. Ejected material that reaches us will add negligibly to the residue from the primary event still impacting Sarath. The Ship's intended escape trajectory should carry it clear of any fresh matter in orbit.'

'Good,' Draad said. 'Continue close observation just in case.'

'As you request, Mayor.'

Draad and Pardek resumed their deliberations. They were wondering if Fostel could be reasoned with privately when Monitor interrupted once again.

'Mayor. An unscheduled live broadcast is being made from the cathedral.'

'What? Put it on.'

Archdeacon Zeckler's grave features filled the screen.

'Fellow Believers, citizens of Arkhaven,' he said. 'It is my sad duty to inform you that Bishop Fostel is dead. He was tragically killed during the early hours of this morning while conducting a special ceremony in the private premises of some of his closest followers.'

The camera cut away to a shot of Fostel laid out in splendid robes before an altar. The camera moved in closer to show his face and the red-stained bullet-hole in his chest.

'There will be a special service of remembrance at the cathedral at midday,' Zeckler continued. 'Meanwhile we demand that those involved with this foul crime be brought to justice immediately. They are Captain Benadik Lant of the City Watch, two as yet unidentified watchmen and the aliens known as the Doctor, Ian Chesterton and Susan Foreman. If, by the end of the service, those named have not been taken into custody, then I call on all Believers, and others who hold truth and justice in high regard, to march on City Hall and demand an explanation from the mayor himself.

'Go with the blessing of the Maker upon you.'

The screen blanked.

Draad was cursing under his breath: '…damn the man! Even after he's dead he still causes trouble.'

Pardek shrugged. 'Do you suppose Lant actually killed him? He didn't mention specific casualties.'

'It doesn't matter how Fostel died or who did it,' said Draad. 'Zeckler's going to tear the city apart with a rabble-rousing speech like that. The fool!'

'Listen, Mayor, I've got to follow this up now the accusation's been made. I must bring Lant and the others in if only for their own safety. If some of those fanatics get to them first, well, you can guess what might happen.'

'I know… but I'm not going to hand them over to Church justice just like that. Especially Lant. Despite everything he's a good man.'

'Yes, he is,' Pardek agreed. 'But maybe too honest for his own good? That is why we kept him off the list, after all. Will it make any difference in the end?'

Even as Draad slowly shook his head, Monitor interrupted sharply: 'I am now detecting major gravimetric changes on the moon.'

They turned back to the wall screens in time to see fountains of fire boil up through the clouds enshrouding the moon. They rose in seemingly graceful slow motion, sending showers of sparks out into space. Draad blinked. Sparks? To appear as sparks on this scale the smallest point of light would have to be the size of a tower block. The fire fountains merged into a solid jagged line that cut across the moon's surface, curving about the rim. On another screen he saw the crooked tendril of fire creep inexorably on round the moon. Then, appearing over the moon's limb, came a second line of incandescent fountains.

The two rifts met and merged, encircling the moon in a ring of fire. The ring became a chasm which gaped wider and deeper by the minute.

Then came a blaze of light rising from the very heart of the chasm.

An almost perfect halo of flaring rock and dust was flung out into space, expanding in apparent lazy slow-motion.

'The core of the moon has exploded,' Monitor announced.

Draad and Pardek stared in horrified fascination as, with ponderous majesty, the two segments of the moon began to drift apart.

'Internal pressure and gravitational stress has split the moon into two bodies of unequal size, the larger approximately twice the mass of the smaller,' Monitor continued unemotionally. 'In addition there are numerous secondary fragments of magnitude one kilometre and over. I am calculating the modified orbital dynamics of the new bodies now.'

Silently Draad crossed to his drinks cabinet and poured two glasses of a strong mixture he rarely touched. With his back to Pardek he took a pill from his pocket dispenser and swallowed it, then returned to the desk with the drinks.

'First approximation,' Monitor said. 'The larger body has been raised to a higher orbit by the force of the separation. It will not strike Sarath for at least sixty days. Secondary fragments will begin impacting within one hour. Significant atmospheric and seismic disturbances of progressively increasing intensity can be expected. The lesser body will strike Sarath in approximately eight hours' time. The effects of the impact on the biosphere and planetary crust will be only 15 per cent less than that projected for the original body, since its angle of impact will be slightly greater. Possibility of survival for life on Sarath remains negligible.

'Today is Zero Day. I am awaiting further instructions.'

Pardek downed the remaining contents of his glass in one gulp, then looked at Draad. Like Monitor he was waiting for an answer.

Draad forced himself to take a more measured swallow of his drink. He felt curiously detached. Though no event had ever been so completely planned for in Arkhaven's history, now that it was upon him he could not believe it. All he knew for certain was that the next few hours would be both wonderful and terrible. One history would end and another begin... or everything would be lost.

It was almost by reflex that he cleared his throat and said: 'Monitor: initiate Operation Exodus immediately.'

Chapter Twenty-Eight
Exodus

The same message flashed over every public screen, house vidi and pocket phone in the city. The text scrolled up the screens in a continuous loop even as Monitor's measured tones provided a verbal accompaniment.

'ATTENTION ALL CITIZENS OF ARKHAVEN. This is an important announcement from the Mayor's Office. Today is Zero Day. Operation Exodus will begin immediately. Please cease all other activities and make your way to the launch site in an orderly manner, taking with you only your permitted item of baggage for personal effects. There is no need to hurry. The City is in no immediate danger and the Ship will not launch for a minimum of three hours. This is not an exercise.

'Message repeats: 'ATTENTION ALL CITIZENS...'

There was a metallic snap. Susan straightened up and examined the blade of her battered shovel, twisting a sliver of bent metal free.

'We'll wear these things out if we keep digging right up to the end,' she said.

'We can't stay here that long,' Barbara snapped. 'We must get back to the city.'

Susan gave her friend a curious look. 'I know, but we have to think of a way first.' She frowned thoughtfully at the piece of metal in her hand.

'All of you: down tools!' the guards began shouting. 'Leave them where they are! Back to base! Move it!'

The workers toiling along the embankments looked up in surprise, disconcerted by the sudden change in routine. There was a slow clatter of picks and shovels and a shuffle of feet as they formed up into their work teams. At another word of command they started back at a half-walk, half-trot.

'Do you think there's a storm coming?' Plax asked.

'They would tell us if there was,' said Semanov. 'There would only be a two- or three-minute warning. No time to get back to the cave so we shelter in the ditch. This is different.'

Two trucks pulling trailers raced past them towards the teams working further along the embankment.

'I think this is it,' Tressel said, panting with the effort of keeping up.

'What do you mean?' Barbara asked.

'The exodus… it must have begun!'

Those who heard him stumbled and broke step. The guards shouted at them to keep together.

'I thought there was still a month to go,' Susan said.

'How can we find out for certain?' Barbara asked. 'I must know for certain!'

Susan looked at her in surprise. There was a very strange look about Barbara's eyes. 'Are you feeling all right?'

But Barbara didn't seem to hear. She was looking about her with quick, darting movements of her head while her hands were clenching and unclenching nervously.

They reached the foot of the winding path that led to the cave complex and started climbing up it. Guards on the ledge under the cliffs above them shouted to them to hurry. Looking back across the plateau floor they saw rising clouds of dust as the trucks raced back with the first three work teams.

'Something's stirred them up,' said Plax. 'If it is the exodus, do we just let them lock us up and leave us?'

'Be quiet!' Barbara said, with such startling ferocity that Susan and Plax were shocked into momentary silence.

They were passing the mouth of the cave they had been taken to when they arrived at the complex. Echoing faintly from within they heard an unemotional voice saying:

'…and the Ship will not launch for a minimum of three hours. This is not an exercise. Message repeats…'

Barbara's eyes glazed. She pulled off her wristwatch, turned it over and pressed her nail hard into a groove in the base plate.

Susan gaped at her in astonishment. 'What did you do? What's the matter with you?'

Barbara blinked and shook her head, looking foolishly at the watch still clasped in her hands. 'I don't know... I had to do it. I've got to get to the Ship. Yes, I've got to get to the Ship!'

By now they had been herded through to the end of the equipment cave. The heavy door leading to the barracks stood open before them. Some workers, inured by routine, had stopped to remove their boots and coveralls and hang them up. They were being harangued by impatient guards. The end of the cave began to choke with milling figures.

Heedless of Susan's cries to stop, Barbara began trying to claw her way back to the entrance of the cave, through the crowd of workers. With desperate strength she pushed a man out of her way. He tripped and pulled somebody else down with him as he fell. Voices were raised, blows exchanged and suddenly a scuffle began with Barbara in the middle. The guards waded in, swinging their guns menacingly.

Barbara dragged herself out of the struggling throng and stumbled awkwardly towards them, her eyes wild with blind determination. A guard shouted a warning but she took no notice. As she tried to push past him he reversed his gun and jabbed with the stock. It cracked against her forehead and she dropped to the ground.

Commandant Breen was in his office in the NC2 camp when the warning came through. After a shocked moment he recovered himself and remembered his duty. He sent a call out for the senior guards to see him at once, then took the packet of sealed orders from his safe. TO BE OPENED ONLY ON RECEIPT OF OPERATION EXODUS ALERT was stamped in large letters on the outside.

He tore the envelope open and unfolded the single sheet of paper within.

When the senior guards arrived he was still sitting at his desk, his normally florid features ashen.

'It's Zero Day,' he said in a dry voice. 'Withdraw the guards quietly, seal all the internal gates. Be ready to move out in ten minutes.' He silenced their sudden babble of questions with a sharp gesture. 'Just do it!' he snapped. 'The sooner we start the sooner we get to the Ship.'

Once they had left he got up and put on his coat. There was nothing else in the office that he valued. In fact he wanted no mementoes of the camp whatsoever. Memory would be a heavy enough burden to carry with him.

He took one more look at the paper lying on his desk. He didn't want to touch it again. It would be the only time he had ever failed to carry out orders. He supposed technically it was dereliction of duty, but this wasn't a war. He was no murderer. And besides, who would ever know?

As he stepped to the door he heard shouting from outside.

'Are you positive it's her signal?' Keldo asked Thorken. 'We are still many days from the projected impact date. We reasoned the Arkavians would not be ready to launch until close to the end.'

'The signal was faint but unmistakable, My Prince,' the old scientist said. 'She must have survived the flood in the tunnels and is now obeying her instructions.'

'Could it have been transmitted by accident?'

'Not by the agent. Her conditioning makes it impossible for her to send the signal unless she is certain the evacuation of the city has begun. Perhaps something has happened to make them accelerate their plans.'

Keldo brooded for a moment, then said: 'We cannot risk ignoring the warning.' He opened the ship's speaker circuit.

'This is Keldo. The time has come, my warriors. Prepare for battle!'

In the hospital they were still trying to come to terms with Zeckler's incredible announcement when the alert came through. From the treatment room they could hear Monitor's message repeating over the public screen in the waiting area.

'I thought you still had thirty days left?' Ian said to Lant.

For a moment Lant appeared to have lost his customary composure. Then he put a call through on his phone and listened for a minute.

'There's been a massive volcanic eruption on the moon,' he reported. 'It's split in two. One part is going to hit us in about eight hours, but smaller fragments will start impacting from one hour onwards.'

Ian looked in dismay at the Doctor. 'Eight hours. Not time enough to make a new key for the TARDIS, I suppose?'

'No, Chesterton,' said the Doctor grimly, 'not nearly time enough.'

'Come to the Ship,' said Lant. 'I'm sure the mayor will agree to you joining us after the help you've given. At least you'll have the same chance as we will.'

'And me?' the android Susan said in a small voice.

As they hesitated the Doctor said firmly: 'My Susan is in this city somewhere. I will search to the last minute to find her. She may even still have her TARDIS key.'

Ian saw the look of determination in his face and didn't try to argue, though he was aware of how slim their chances were. He had to stand by the old man. 'All right, but where do we start?'

'That health club... it's the only lead we have.'

Lant was looking troubled. 'I can give you a car, but I'm afraid you'll have to go alone. I've got to let my driver go and get to the Ship myself.'

'And I've got to help evacuate the remaining patients,' Nyra said.

'But we may need your help,' Ian said. 'You know the city. Besides, don't you want to find out who made the android and why? Hasn't that got security implications?'

Even as Lant considered this, his phone rang. He listened for a minute, then said: 'Right, we'll be there as soon as we can.' He rang off and turned back to Ian and the Doctor with a very curious expression. 'That was Curton. He thinks he's found where your friend Barbara left the drainage system. Now he says she might be with somebody who has the initial "S" in their name.'

'S!' the Doctor exclaimed.

Ian felt a momentary dizziness, coupled with a surge of wild hope that he'd thought he'd never feel again. He was dimly aware of Lant exchanging a glance and nod with Nyra, then checking his watch. 'In the circumstances we'll give you an hour.'

Vendam received the exodus alert over his car screen, as he quartered the empty streets around the rendezvous point Herstwell had described.

He stopped for a moment to put a call through to his house. He ordered his servants to make their way to the Ship with his own and Plax's personal baggage, and assured them that he would be with them before take-off. He knew that, as first among the Elite families, he should be there at the Ship in person to see them safely on board but he could not abandon Plax. He realised with stark suddenness how alone he was. Nobody else would spare the time to help him search now, as the last hours ticked by.

He had to think! He couldn't continue driving up and down at random. If Plax had left the area where would he go? If he'd headed towards the city centre he'd have turned up by now. And even Plax would have called home when the alert sounded.

But where else was there in the other direction but the wall... and the NC2 camp! Yes, considering Plax's interest in its occupants, he might have gone there out of sheer devilry. Or perhaps a patrol had found him. If he couldn't give a proper account of himself they might have taken him there directly as a suspected escapee.

Vendam tried to put through a call to the camp but got no answer. Was the phone system already failing? He couldn't take the chance. He swung the big car around and sped off.

As Zeckler oversaw the hasty packing of the most precious of the church relics into their prepared carrying cases, his mind worked furiously.

He had prayed for guidance and had received this blow instead. If he had only been granted a few more days to establish his authority. Unless this was a test of his fitness? Yes. Somehow, he must make the best of the situation.

There would be no midday service now. All the people, even the Believers, would only have one thing on their minds. But Fostel's demise must not be wasted. Very well, if they would not come to him, he must go to them. There would be one powerful symbol of the old world that the people would carry in their thoughts as they boarded the Ship.

From his office window Draad could see the stream of cars start to arrive at the launch-site gates. He could also see the tiny dots of those who lived close enough to walk, merging with each other until they looked like columns of ants. Capsules were stopping every half-minute at the nearest tube station and disgorging their quota to swell the growing throng. He hoped the Watch would be able to keep order. He didn't want any panic. The people must board the Ship and take their places calmly.

'All executive orders of phase one have been carried out, Mayor,' Monitor said. 'The rest of the building has been evacuated. Your car is waiting for you.'

'Thank you, Monitor. Commence phase two. Transfer all command circuits and relays to the Ship. Close down all non-essential terminals.'

'Command executed, Mayor.'

The wall screens went blank. The green ring about Monitor's camera eye faded to darkness.

Draad picked up his small bag of personal effects, the same as everyone else carried, and took one last look around.

There was so much else he had planned to do… all irrelevant now. Perhaps it was better this way. Thirty days of anxiety and potential intrigue wiped away at a stroke. Still, he would like to have had time to talk to the Doctor about the stars again.

He left his office for the last time and did not look back.

Keldo looked down upon his men assembled in the flagship's cavernous hold, its crumpled walls and floors canted like those in the rest of the vessel. Many still carried half-healed scars of the crash, but they were unbowed and ready to fight. He felt fierce pride swell within him.

'Fellow Taklarians. Today we are done with hiding, with skulking in darkness. Today we return to the light!'

They cheered, waving their weapons in the air.

'We may be the last of our race, but we are warriors and carry the tradition and glory that was ours within us. And I promise you we will be mighty again, when we rebuild our empire on a new world.

'Even now the Arkavian ship is preparing for launch. All attention will be focused on embarking their people. After a year of inaction their military will be lax and we shall have the advantage of surprise. They think we are dead... soon we shall show them how wrong they are! We shall make our way to the surface, take whatever transport we need and make for the launching site. There, at the prime moment, we shall attack. Our objective is the ship's control centre. Once that is in our hands they dare not use unlimited force against us. They will have to launch as planned.

'Once en route to Mirath we shall demand sufficient Arkavian women be made available for our purposes. I know the prospect of mating with members of an inferior race is repugnant, but the progeny will at least be half Taklarian and will be brought up in the Taklarian way on Mirath. Inheriting superior genetic stock they will survive the rigours of the new world better than the Arkavians. In a few generations they will be the only race on Mirath!

'Remember, we may be outnumbered but we are Taklarian warriors! We shall conquer and we shall prevail!'

They cheered wildly and stamped their feet. Keldo strode to the mouth of the tunnel that led to the city.

'Now follow me to victory!'

Chapter Twenty-Nine
The Will to Live

As Vendam drove along the last stretch of road leading up to the NC2 camp he glimpsed shabby figures running across the wasteland towards the city. But such was his preoccupation over Plax that the significance of what he saw did not register in his mind. It was only when he turned a curve of the road as it wound between hillocks of rubble and had to brake sharply that he understood.

An angry mob, perhaps fifty strong, filled the road in front of him. Before he could reverse more people appeared, swarming over the mounds of rubble and surrounding the car, beating on its sides with their fists. There was a terrible animal-like howl of voices:

'Stop it! Don't let him get away!'

Before Vendam could lock the doors they were torn open and rough hands pulled him from his seat. He lashed out desperately, trying to defend himself, but there were too many of them. He fell to the ground under a rain of blows. A kick from a heavy boot caught him in the ribs while another struck his temple.

Dimly he was aware of his attackers climbing into his car, fighting among themselves for space. With half a dozen more clinging to its sides it turned around and headed back towards the city, with the rest of the mob running along in its wake.

Then everything faded into blackness.

Half a dozen Taklarians broke through the thin shell of earth that had been left over the head of the new tunnel, swinging their guns to cover the comrades emerging behind them. Assault teams sprinted across the open ground and burst into the adjacent buildings, breaking down the outer doors with single kicks of their heavy boots. They swarmed upstairs and pounded along corridors, kicking open inner doors as they went, ready to silence any opposition. In a few minutes the reports came back to Keldo.

'The buildings are empty, Prince. From the looks of them they've been abandoned for some time.'

'It is as we hoped. To the nearest roadway. We must find transport.'

The Taklarians passed through the ground level of one of the deserted buildings, moving very quietly for such large men, until they came to a row of grimy windows set in an outer wall. They looked out on to an empty street with four cars parked along its length. There was no sign of any pedestrian traffic.

'Better this was done at night, but we have no choice so we shall be bold,' Keldo told his personal squad. 'After me. Each try a car.'

He found a door in the wall, checked that they were unobserved and led his men across the pavement.

The nearest car was unlocked. He forced his bulk into the driver's seat, and after a moment's fumbling with the unfamiliar controls, activated the main power-feed. The instrument panel remained dark. The car's power cell was dead. Cursing under his breath he hauled himself out of his seat. The others were doing the same, shaking their heads. All four cars without power? Keldo ran his fingers over the car's roof-shell, leaving metallic streaks in the layer of fine dark dust that adhered to its surface. His eyes darted up and down the street, noting for the first time broken windows in the building opposite. Then a faint hum came to his ears.

'Vehicle approaching, Prince!'

'Stop it as it passes.'

They crouched behind the parked cars until the vehicle was almost upon them then sprang in front of it, guns levelled menacingly. It screeched to a halt, the driver staring fixedly ahead of him as though frozen with shock. Before he could move Keldo reached the door, tore it open, grasped the man by the neck... and found himself holding a legless dummy in his hand.

The rest of the squad gaped at him, guns drooping carelessly, astonishment for a moment overcoming even their inbred discipline. Keldo looked incredulously at the limp mannequin and then at the street about him, trying to assess anew the quality of the silence and stillness that enveloped it. Then he tossed the dummy aside and signalled to the rest of his force. They swarmed out of the building on to the street.

'There is something wrong here. Spread out. Stop all moving vehicles. We must get to the Ship with all speed.'

Lant pulled up beside Curton's battered truck and they all got out. Ian and the Doctor hurried forward eagerly while the Susan android followed quietly along at the rear.

The engineer led them off the road and through an archway to an enclosed courtyard.

'This is almost the last branch we checked,' he explained. 'A pipe camera came on a blockage but managed to get past it to find this.'

There was a sunken depression in the ground with a muddy hole in the middle. Several palm prints showed clearly in the soft earth. Ian touched them. They were narrower and smaller than his own hand.

'There's more,' said Curton, leading them out of the courtyard and down a narrow passageway. 'Before I called you I had a look round, thinking I might find your friend nearby.'

They emerged on to a small street of shops. Curton led the way along to a spot outside a small café and pointed to the window. Daubed on it in red sauce was the symbol B+S–>.

'A vending machine's been broken into, there are a lot of sweet-bar wrappers scattered about and you can see where two people sat down for a while.'

Ian held out his hand to Curton. 'Thanks for keeping up the search,' he said simply.

'Well, you didn't give up while we were excavating the tower, and it seems your friend doesn't quit either,' Curton said. 'I could hardly do any less.'

'You'd better be getting along to the Ship now,' Lant suggested. 'We'll take over here.'

'I'll hang around for a bit longer if you don't mind,' Curton said. 'I'd like to see my last job finished. I've got my case with me and no family to worry about.'

'As you like,' said Lant. 'We'll bring the cars round,' he told the others. 'Stay here.'

Lant and Curton hurried off. Nyra was peering in at the café front while the android stood a few paces away in withdrawn silence.

Ian turned eagerly to the Doctor. 'Could Barbara and Susan really have met up somehow?'

'It seems likely. Who else would she identify simply with one initial?'

'They can't have gone too far. As long as Barbara's left more signs...'

The implications of what he was saying struck him like a physical blow. His shoulders sagged. He said quietly: 'It doesn't matter if we find them or not, does it? When this planet is destroyed we'll all die. It's hopeless.'

'Have courage, Chesterton,' the Doctor said. 'All may not be lost quite yet. Let us find Susan and Barbara first, then... well, we shall have to see.'

Lant and Curton returned with the cars. They climbed in and headed in the direction indicated by Barbara's arrow.

After a minute Ian said: 'Wasn't it somewhere near here where those power cuts happened last night, and we chased that thing?'

'You're right,' Lant agreed. He swung the car round a corner and headed towards a belt of trees. 'The second blackout was centred around this park.'

'There may be a connection between Barbara and Susan and the blackout,' said the Doctor. 'This thing you followed; can you show me where you lost it?'

Lant handed over his electronic map pad.

'It's marked... and we're down there.'

228

The Doctor mused over the image for a moment, then adjusted the controls to show a smaller-scale view of the entire city. 'Have there been many of these unexplained blackouts in the same area?' he asked.

'A few,' Lant admitted.

'Any associated with unexplained disappearances?'

'As it happens there was a blackout in the area where we found the dead NC2 who we thought might have your key. You can see where it's marked.'

'Yes… all in the same quadrant of the city.' Ian heard the Doctor mutter to himself for a moment, then say aloud: 'Yes, I think we should make for the place where you lost your mysterious quarry.'

'Shouldn't we search this area first?' Ian asked.

'No, trust me, Chesterton.'

'We haven't much time,' said Lant.

'Then drive faster, Captain,' the Doctor said.

They tore along deserted streets, passing only a few robot-driven vehicles with their dummy drivers. Presumably they would continue their meaningless travels until the end came, Ian thought morbidly.

As they approached a junction Lant braked suddenly, throwing them against their seat belts and almost causing Curton to run into them.

A mixed column of cars and goods vehicles was speeding across the road ahead of them. They were packed with shabbily dressed people, a few clinging desperately to the sides of their transports.

'NC2s!' Lant said angrily. 'They must have broken out of the camp.' He punched a number into his phone. 'Launch Security, this is Lant. There are about a hundred escaped NC2s heading in your direction parallel with Fourteenth Avenue. They may be trying to board the Ship.' He rang off and immediately entered another number, but there was no response. 'The camp doesn't answer,' he said. 'Sorry, but I'll have to check it out. I promise this won't take longer than necessary.'

He pulled away and turned in the direction from which the NC2s had come.

As Draad got out of his car he saw Pardek with the Watch guards at the base of the gantry, checking the queues of people lining up before the elevators. Good, the commander was making his presence public. Draad stepped forward, assessing the mood as he went. A few children were crying, more from confusion than genuine fear, and every face was drawn to some degree, but in the circumstances people were remarkably calm. Perhaps the premature alert had prevented anticipatory panic building up among the ordinary citizens.

As long as they didn't start wondering why there were so few of them. No, they only had eyes for those remaining between them and the doors of the elevators. The ground was level so they couldn't see far enough to judge total numbers, or know how many had gone before them. Once they were in the subdivided compartments in the Ship they would be in no position to make a count.

Draad waved to them reassuringly as he passed.

'Just checking my seat's been reserved,' he called out lightly. 'Remember, I'll be wanting your votes in the first elections we hold on Mirath.'

There were a few nervous laughs and scattered applause.

'Lant just called in,' Pardek said in a low voice as Draad reached his side. 'Some NC2s have escaped and are heading this way.'

Still smiling broadly for his audience Draad said: 'Damn. Breen must have made a mistake. Where is he?'

'He hasn't arrived yet.'

'I wanted the NC2s taken full care of. They mustn't interrupt the boarding procedure.'

'We know the direction they're coming from. I'll send a squad straight out from the Ship to intercept them. I doubt the NC2s will have any weapons.'

Draad sighed. 'All right, do it.'

There was a commotion from the direction of the gates and a rising babble of voices.

Zeckler appeared, marching slowly up between the waiting columns of citizens at the head of some sort of procession. Behind him came acolytes holding church banners. Following them were four priests carrying something shoulder-high between them. As they passed many of those in the crowd bowed their heads.

The procession reached the base of the gantry and Zeckler directed them to set their burden down. It was a litter bearing the body of Bishop Fostel, dressed in gold and white robes and with his staff of office beside him. The bright red stain soaking through the fabric over his heart was even more prominent than it had been on the broadcast. Zeckler turned to the people and raised his hands.

'We have brought the mortal remains of Bishop Fostel here so you may pay your last respects as you board the Ship, knowing that he is with you in spirit. His killers must also pass by him and know they will not escape divine justice.'

He stepped over to Draad and Pardek and said quietly: 'I want the aliens and Captain Lant.'

'Well, you can't have them,' said Pardek. 'They're still out in the city.'

'When they arrive you will hand them over. Unless you want to be denounced in front of the bishop's body.'

'This is not the time or place for playing games, Zeckler,' Draad said angrily.

'Exactly, Mayor. I'm sure you'll see reason. Let the aliens take the blame if you want to save Lant… that's my only concession. But they must be revealed for what they are.'

Aloud he announced: 'In the Maker's name I will bless this ship. If you have faith we shall have a safe voyage to the new world.'

He started off towards the nearest landing nacelle, carrying a cup of holy water and an aspergillum, leaving a couple of priests standing vigil over Fostel's litter.

'Let him go,' Draad told Pardek. 'When the first tremors start arriving they'll get inside quickly enough. You deal with the NC2s, but don't take too long. I'll check inside.'

He rode the reserved elevator up to the first passenger deck and walked across the gantry bridge into the Ship. Inside people were being checked off and shown to their bunks. Attendants were helping to strap them in and put on their breathing masks. In a few moments the passengers were slipping away into a gentle sleep. The atmosphere was calm and surprisingly quiet, the growing ranks of somnambulists lending a sense of peace to the scene. For a moment Draad felt a little of the burden lift from his shoulders. Perhaps it wasn't going to be as bad as he had thought. Then he saw the small form of a sleeping child and had to turn away quickly.

Resolutely he began to make his way up to the Lander's control deck.

Lant pulled up beside the body lying on the rubble at the side of the road and the others scrambled out of the cars. Nyra knelt beside the man, unfolding her medical kit. The gravel under his head was stained dark with blood.

'It's Lord Vendam!' Lant exclaimed, staring at the pale bruised face. 'What's he doing out here?'

There was no answer, of course. Nyra checked Vendam over before they moved him, and diagnosed cracked ribs and possible concussion. Under her direction they lifted him carefully into the back of Curton's car, and she climbed in with him.

They saw more bodies, both NC2s and guards, in the camp's outer compound as they drove in through the open gates. The ground was littered with pieces of stone and brick. Lant drew his side-arm before getting out. Ian and the Doctor followed him cautiously. The inner gates leading to the prisoners' compound were hanging open on twisted hinges.

Lant knelt beside one of the uniformed figures lying face down on the ground and turned its head.

'It's Breen,' he said simply.'Looks like he was battered to death. What in hell happened here?'

'Your prisoners simply wanted the same chance at life you had,' Ian said bitterly.

Lant looked sickened. 'I'd better report this over the secure channel. Curton,' he called out, 'stay in the car with Nyra. Keep your doors locked.'

Cautiously he led them into the guard block and through to Breen's office. A few drawers had been pulled open and their contents scattered on the floor, but otherwise it seemed largely untouched. The desk terminal had a spray of torn cables dangling from its socket. Lant was about to turn away when his eyes dropped to a sheet of paper lying on the desk. He picked it up and read it in silence, then looked at them despairingly.

'Before you ask, I didn't know about any of this. These are orders to Breen to add poison to the camp's water supply. He was meant to wait an hour for it to take effect before leaving. The prisoners must have realised what he was doing and rioted.'

'Or he could not bring himself to carry out such an order,' the Doctor said. 'He was under considerable strain and perhaps no longer had it in him to kill people in cold blood.'

'Obviously this was intended as the most humane solution,' Lant said.

'The NC2s might disagree with you there,' Ian said harshly.'But for luck the Doctor and I might still have been with them.'

'I didn't say I approved,' Lant retorted.

Curton's car horn sounded. They dashed outside. There was a crowd of perhaps thirty NC2s shuffling uncertainly out of the huts in the inner compound and up to the broken gates. A few were older people, the majority younger women and children.

Lant holstered his gun and walked towards them holding his hands up reassuringly.

'It's all right,' he called out.'We're not going to hurt you. I just want to know what happened here.'

They shuffled anxiously, not wanting to meet his eye. Ian realised they had stopped short of the threshold to the gates as though frightened to cross over the invisible line. How long had they been prisoners, he wondered in disgust.

'I promise none of you will be blamed for anything,' Lant said. 'I just want to know the truth.'

Finally one of the younger women spoke up, her voice trembling.

'The men knew something was going on. They'd been planning to make a break when the evacuation sounded. Some of them had made a lever from scrap metal and broke open the gates. Others threw rocks when the guards tried to stop them. They kept hitting the guards until they eventually stopped moving. The first ones out took the guards' cars, the rest went on foot. They didn't hang around in case more soldiers came.' She looked at Lant fearfully. 'We hid... we didn't have anything to do with it.'

'I believe you,' Lant said.

The Doctor moved up to his side and said quietly: 'Find the keys to the camp stores. It will keep them occupied.'

Lant nodded, recovered a bunch of keys from Breen's body and held them out to the nervous crowd. 'Here, take what you want from the stores.'

They looked at him in disbelief as though suspecting some sort of trick. Unexpectedly the Susan android stepped forward and took the keys from Lant's hand.

'Do you know where the stores are?' she asked the women. 'Good, show me.'

She led the pitiful group away.

'We must do something for these people,' Ian said.

'There's nothing we can do,' Lant said bluntly. 'There's no room for them on the Ship, you know that.' He checked his watch. 'We'll examine the place where we lost that thing the other night, but we haven't much time left. If we don't find any trace of your companions we'll have to get back.'

Nyra and Curton joined them.

'Vendam is as comfortable as I can make him,' Nyra said. 'I think he'll be all right when he wakes up, but we must get him back to the Ship quickly so that they can strap his ribs properly before launch.'

Ian looked at the Doctor and saw his lips pursed grimly. They were running out of time. He must say something soon.

Lant's pocket phone beeped. He put it to his ear, but they could all hear the desperate words issuing from the tiny speaker.

'Emergency... all Watch personnel to the launch site immediately... the Ship is under attack!'

Chapter Thirty
The Taking of the Ship

Keldo tried not to allow himself to be overawed by the sheer towering mass of the Ship, but secretly he had to admit the Arkavians had built it well. It was magnificent; an inspiring symbol of hope that he would see served a noble purpose.

His men were concealed on the fourth floor of an otherwise deserted multi-level car park overlooking one side of the launch site. They had reached the location with surprising ease. The few vehicles they had passed had paid them no attention. But then how could the Arkavians possibly suspect that their old enemy, long thought dead, was driving through their own city so openly?

Through binoculars, Keldo observed the ranks of abandoned vehicles surrounding the site, and the last snaking columns of people filing into the elevators at the base of the gantry. He and his men couldn't wait much longer, but the guards stationed about the base of the gantry could still cause them fatal delay. Without a team of conditioned agents inside the Ship, as he had planned, the assault would have to be timed exactly. There had been no further signal from the conditioned woman, so they could not count on her support during the attack. Still, she had served her primary purpose.

Then came a flurry of unexpected activity down on the launching site. Uniformed men were moving away from the gantry and climbing into half a dozen military vehicles. In moments the small column had driven out of the gates and sped away, leaving only a handful of guards behind.

Why had they sent out a squad now? Was it a trap? Had they somehow detected the presence of his force?

'Be alert,' Keldo warned his troops, 'the enemy may be trying to get behind us.'

For some minutes there was no change, except that the columns waiting to ascend the gantry elevators dwindled rapidly.

They would have to move soon. Then came the sound of distant gunfire from the direction the convoy had taken. For a second Keldo could make no sense of it, then he grinned in fierce delight. The undisciplined rabble were fighting among themselves!

'Go!' he commanded, climbing into his car.

His little fleet rolled down the ramps and out on to the street. They drove up to the nearest gateway at moderate speed, doing nothing to arouse the suspicions of the guards. Their caution was hardly necessary. The guards were only half watching them, their attention diverted by the sporadic echoes of gunfire.

Keldo's car slowed as it came alongside the gatehouse and the guard reluctantly tore his attention away from the distant conflict to his check-pad. Keldo lowered the side window. As their eyes met he saw the guard's frown turn to incredulity.

He shot him through the heart with a single round from his pistol, even as his driver did the same to a guard on the other side. The two shots were muffled, contained largely within the car, and the sound did not carry far. Still at the same steady pace, Keldo's convoy drove on through the gateway and down the clear track between the ranks of parked cars. As they approached the launch site, the Ship and its gantry seemed to swell until they filled the sky.

The convoy drew up in an orderly manner ten metres from the row of elevators. The last few people filing into them hardly looked round. Some kind of religious ceremony seemed to be taking place. Men in priestly robes stood by a body resting on a litter, while another more gaudily dressed holy man was shaking water over the stanchions beside the elevators. What purpose this served Keldo neither knew nor cared.

'Go,' he said, over his command link.

They climbed out of their cars as one and started forward with their long rifles levelled. The guards by the elevator doors looked up. Keldo revelled in their expressions of disbelief as they saw their supposedly dead enemies marching towards them. The Taklarians were able to take three more strides before the guards recovered sufficiently to reach for their holstered side-arms.

'Now!' Keldo shouted, and the guards fell in a hail of automatic fire.

'Taklars!' somebody screamed.

Keldo's men ran forward to secure the elevator cages, trampling over people who, panic-stricken, had thrown themselves to the ground, and brushing aside those still standing. Keldo found the litter in his path. One of the priests guarding the body flung out his arms as though trying to ward him off.

'No! You must not...'

Keldo knocked him aside and kicked over the litter so that the body rolled in the dirt.

'Nobody tells a prince of Taklar what he may not do!' Keldo shouted exultantly.

The holy man who had been scattering water was standing before him, defiantly holding up a circular amulet he wore on a chain about his neck. There was a wild look in the man's eyes.

'In the name of the Maker, I denounce you! Stand back, heathen, or else you will be consumed by His terrible fire...'

Keldo shot him in the chest, the force of the blast lifting him off his feet and sending him sprawling backwards. He lay twitching slightly, eyes staring up at the sky. To Keldo's mild surprise he still clasped his amulet. Faint words bubbled up with the froth of blood about his lips.

'Maker... receive the soul of your servant...'

Keldo shot him again and he lay still. On an impulse he tore the amulet from the man's bloody hands, snapping the chain, then strode on to the elevators. They had secured five of them with their cages on the ground. All the guards were dead and the remaining evacuees were a cowering, confused rabble who posed no immediate threat.

'Thorken... stay by me!' Keldo commanded.

They crammed as many men as they could into each cage, leaving the rest to follow when they sent the cages back down. Keldo punched the topmost button on the control panel. He had to reach the command decks before the Arkavians had time to seal them off.

The cage creaked and rattled upwards with what seemed like agonising slowness.

Halfway up the Ship they passed the lowest of the retractable bridges that spanned the gap between the gantry and the gleaming hull. The large hatch at the far end, obviously intended for loading cargo, was closed. Good, they would need all the supplies they could carry with them to settle Mirath. The first of the bridges leading to smaller passenger hatches went by and he saw the occupants of the last elevator to ascend ahead of them, running across it. Keldo peered upwards impatiently. Three more hatches, then a gap, then the highest bridges of all that connected with the capsule at the summit of the ship. That was where the control room would be.

Then, as they came opposite the last of the passenger access levels, the elevator stopped.

Keldo pounded on the upper buttons of the control panel until the panel began to crack, but the elevator cage would not move.

'Prince... stop,' said Thorken. 'Access to the higher levels may be restricted... we may need a code or key to go further.'

'We have no time for such things!' Keldo snarled impatiently. He tore open the cage doors and started across the bridge, his men pounding along at his heels.

There was a crackle of gunfire from the hatch at the end of the bridge and one of his men fell with a choking cry. The rest returned fire, bullets flashing off the hull around the hatchway. Slowly the hatch began to swing closed.

With a roar Keldo threw himself forward and into the narrowing gap between the hatch and its frame, thrusting his arm and shoulder through so that he could fire at the figure standing by the controls on the other side. The man fell even as Keldo forced his bulk inside and slapped his hand over the controls, hitting buttons until the hatch halted and then began to swing open again. His men piled through after him.

They were in the Ship.

'Two of you guard this hatchway,' Keldo said. 'The rest come with me.'

Keldo kicked open a door leading to an inner compartment opposite the hatch, gun swinging round to cover the space beyond, expecting to meet further resistance. Instead he saw only rows of tiered couches with masked and sleeping forms lying upon them.

'They have sedated the passengers for flight,' Thorken said.

'If every deck is like this, we shall only have the crew to deal with,' said Keldo. 'Forward!'

They slipped between the tiers of beds until they came to the central core. Here a stairway circled around the small lift shaft that seemed to run the length of the ship. Not trusting the mechanism, Keldo started up the stairs.

They climbed through six decks until they reached a closed hatchway set in the bulkhead that divided the nose section from the rest of the ship. Thorken directed the positioning of a cutting charge on the hatch and they moved a deck down before triggering it. With a crack and billow of smoke a neat disc of metal was blown out of the hatch and fell down the stairs. A second hatch was dealt with in the same way and the Taklarians climbed into the upper capsule.

All was silent. There was no sign of the crew and the tiers of bunks in the passenger levels were empty even of sleepers.

'Why do they waste these spaces?' Thorken wondered.

They climbed on until the stairs ended before a locked hatchway. A sign read: CONTROL ROOM – AUTHORISED PERSONNEL ONLY.

'We should not use force on this as we did on the others, Prince,' Thorken cautioned. 'We may damage vital controls on the other side.'

A call came through on Keldo's communicator:

'Men are stationed on each level as planned, Prince. There is little resistance. Most passengers are sleeping. The enemy column that left earlier has returned but we are holding them off easily. We have the Ship!'

The men with Keldo cheered wildly.

Keldo hammered on the intercom panel beside the hatch.

'This is Prince Keldo Arrosthenos of the Taklarian Empire. We control the rest of the ship. If you do not open this door your people below will suffer. Do you understand? Can you hear me in there?'

After a few seconds the intercom screen came to life revealing the careworn face of a middle-aged man. 'I can hear you,' he said.

'Who are you?' Keldo demanded.

'Brantus Draad, Mayor of Arkhaven.'

'Then you can order this door opened.'

'Why should I, if you're going to kill us all anyway?'

'Not if you serve us well. We have need of your kind.'

'To live as your slaves. I don't think so.'

'You have no choice. My men control this ship.'

'Yes, I know. I've seen them on the monitors,' Draad said.

'Then you can see they have your people at their mercy. Open this door or I will order them to kill a hundred as an example.' He held up the bloody amulet. 'They will die as your holy man died.'

To Keldo's amazement Draad began to laugh. It was a tired, chillingly bitter laugh without humour; simply an acknowledgement of the perversity of fate. It made Keldo shiver.

'Poor Zeckler,' Draad said. 'I almost feel sorry for him. But he should have boarded earlier instead of performing his blessings. Then he'd have been asleep by now and wouldn't know anything about this. That was the plan, you know.'

There was something wrong, Keldo realised. The man was not reacting as he should. Out of sight of the intercom camera, Keldo gestured to his men. A soldier began laying a cutting-charge strip around the control room door.

'If you don't care for your priest there are others aboard who you must care for,' Keldo said.

'Care for?' said Draad. 'Oh, yes, there are thousands aboard that I care for. But the most I could do for them was to see their last hours were filled with hope… and that they wouldn't feel any pain at the end.' Draad looked to one side as though consulting another screen. 'I see your men have killed the last of our watchmen and are now all on board. That always was something you Taklarians were good at, killing.'

'We fight to survive. The strong destroy the weak. That is as it has always been.'

'Not any more, I hope,' said Draad. 'Where have you come from, as a matter of interest?'

'The battlecraft on the shore. You could have destroyed us at any time if you had thought to search it properly.'

Draad sighed. 'I should have had it broken up and removed, but there was so much rebuilding to do in the city. And the Church and the Elite said it made a fitting monument to our victory. Too late now.'

The soldier stood back, detonator held ready.

'Yes, you inferior races are always making such errors,' Keldo agreed. 'Such as this one!'

He snapped his fingers. The soldier pressed the detonator and the door blew in.

Keldo charged into the control room through the billowing smoke. His gun swung over banked instrument panels studded with switches; across screens and flashing lights and empty acceleration couches with safety straps hanging loosely down their sides. Draad's face looked out from a screen over the engineer's console.

'Are you satisfied?' he said. 'The Ship is all yours now.'

'Where are your crew hiding?' Keldo raged.

Thorken was pulling at his sleeve. 'My Prince, I think we should leave.'

'No, please don't go,' Draad said. 'Your being here makes it just a little easier to do what I must.'

'What do you mean?' Keldo demanded, feeling the cold touch of true fear for the first, and last, time in his life.

'This,' said Draad simply.

Chapter Thirty-One
Last Chance

A golden fireball enveloped the Ship's landing module, blossoming like an evanescent sunflower over the jagged city skyline. A string of explosions tore down the silver skyscraper hull, peeling back the plating and exposing the ribs of the ship to the air. Slowly the naked skeleton folded in upon itself, crumpling and fragmenting, melting away in blazing shards. As it fell a vast billow of grey smoke laced with red and yellow fire rose to meet it, rolling upwards to lick at the base of the clouds.

Even on the outskirts of the city the ground trembled with the impact of its collapse, the vibrations racing through the earth ahead of airborne sound.

The Ship was gone and where it had stood was now a blazing column of fire that licked hungrily about the girders of the launch tower.

For long seconds the tower seemed untouched by the destruction of the Ship, its broken stubs of gantries and bridges still reaching out as though to embrace the space its lost companion had occupied. Then it began to twist and buckle. With awful majesty it toppled over and vanished below the skyline. A fresh upwelling of smoke and flame erupted as it joined the pyre which consumed the last hope of Arkhaven.

The pocket phone dropped from Lant's numbed grasp as he stared at the rising smoke cloud. He had been asking for more information, uncertain whether he should abandon his companions to obey the desperate call for help. There had been no response to his call. Now there was nobody left to answer him.

Curton said: 'Oh, God no.' Nyra covered her eyes.

The Susan android and some of the NC2s emerged from the storeroom to stare at the scene in disbelief. A huge pall of smoke rolled upwards from the heart of the city where Ship and tower had stood in undisputed dominance for years. The sound of their destruction finally reached the camp; the thunderous roar of multiple explosions followed by the agonising groan and shriek of thousands of tonnes of falling tortured metal.

Then it was past and fading into a prolonged rumble.

Some of the children began to cry.

The Doctor turned to the still-shocked Arkavians and suddenly he seemed to swell with purpose.

'The Ship is gone now and there is nothing you can do about it,' he said with almost cruel emphasis. 'You must contain your questions, and your grief for those who died, for later. There is still a slim chance for us all, but only if we act quickly.'

Nyra was shaking her head woodenly, her eyes bleak with despair. 'There's no chance... no hope. Without the Ship it's all over!'

'No, there is still hope,' the Doctor said, glancing at Ian. 'Because the Ship could never have flown!'

He had the Arkavians' absolute and undivided attention now. They gaped at him incredulously, as though he was suddenly speaking nonsense.

'What do you mean?' Lant said.

'The Ship was a monstrous deception. It did not have sufficient power to lift itself one inch off this planet. I cannot go into the details now, but I beg you to trust me. Consider that if I am wrong you have nothing to lose. Well?'

There was a masterful edge to his words that could not be denied. Curton nodded slowly. Nyra rubbed her eyes and tried to stifle her sobs of despair. With an obvious effort of will Lant met the Doctor's gaze squarely.

'All right... what do we do?'

'We go to the place where you lost track of the thing you chased. If there is any way out it will be there.'

'Doctor,' said the android Susan, standing before the nervous crowd of NC2s. 'We can't leave these people here. If there's a chance we must try to save them too.'

For a moment Ian thought the Doctor was going to argue. Then he inclined his head slightly.

'You are right. They deserve the same chance as we have.' He turned to Lant. 'Take Mr Curton and Miss Shardri with you, drive into the city and find additional transport. Commandeer some of those dummy cars if you must, but bring back enough vehicles to carry these people. Quickly.'

The three climbed into Lant's car and sped off towards the city. They seemed relieved to have a job to do; to distract their thoughts from the destruction of the Ship. The Doctor addressed the NC2s.

'Divide up the provisions into bundles you can easily carry. If you can find more clothes put them on. Use anything in the camp you need. This... young woman will help you.'

Galvanised by the Doctor's words the NC2s began to move with a sense of purpose for the first time. They laid out blankets and plastic bedding-sheets and began piling goods from the storeroom on to them.

Suddenly Ian felt the ground tremble, and staggered slightly. A few of the children began crying again.

'Earth tremor,' said the Doctor. 'Shock waves generated by minor fragments from the moon's break-up striking the equatorial zone. We can expect worse to come.'

Lant and the others returned after only fifteen minutes with two low-slung six-wheeled light trucks.

'They were in a factory yard,' Lant explained. 'Power cells still half-charged.'

Two older NC2s who could drive the vehicles were found and the rest climbed on board. Once again Nyra rode in the back of Curton's car to watch Vendam, who was showing signs of regaining consciousness. The Susan android climbed in with her, while Ian and the Doctor rode with Lant. The little convoy swung about and drove out of the camp.

Over the tops of the distant towers they could see fresh columns of smoke rising from spreading fires to join the central pall, shrouding everything in a sudden twilight. Lant switched on his headlights as they sped along the streets that skirted the edge of the Outer Zone.

Out across the levelled land a wall-turret launcher suddenly belched fire as a salvo of missiles tore away into the sky.

'The meteor defences must be on automatic,' Lant explained, adding grimly: 'Let's hope they don't have anything too big to handle for the next hour.' He glanced at the Doctor, confusion distorting his normally composed features. 'You said the Ship couldn't fly. Did you really mean it? How do you know?'

'Do remember, young man, that I have considerable knowledge of nuclear drive systems and spacecraft design. It was for those very skills that I was asked to check over the Ship's plans. But Professor Jarrasen tried to keep my attention focused exclusively on the landing module. That was what first reinforced my suspicions and the reason why I insisted on touring the Ship personally. It allowed me to estimate its structural weight, engine thrust and payload. I could soon tell it did not have enough power to take off.'

'But why? And who was attacking it… the NC2s? Did they destroy it by accident?'

'I do not know who was attacking the Ship, but I'm afraid the explosion might not have been an accident. It is consistent with the existence of the secret tunnel.'

Lant looked dazed. 'What tunnel?'

'The one that runs under the city towards the mountains… at least, so the alignment suggests.'

'Alignment from where?'

'From the Ship through the point where you lost your mystery quarry.'

'What do you mean?'

'I'm sorry, Captain, you do not yet appreciate how completely you have been deceived. Remember my questioning the necessity of such a deep blast pit beneath the Ship? I imagine the tunnel was dug under cover of its excavation. It would have connected with a lift shaft concealed in one of those absurdly massive supporting legs, opening through the base of the nacelle so nothing was visible above ground. The system ran up through the skin of the outer hull to the Lander. When I toured the control cabin I noticed one of its bulkheads was deeper than was shown on the plans.'

Ian saw Lant was clutching the steering wheel so tightly his knuckles were white. 'But why? What was the system for?'

'To secretly move people and supplies out of the Ship after those zealous faction guards at the perimeter gate had checked them in, naturally. They would then travel to a secret destination that served a purpose for which a manual labour force was also apparently required, hence the kidnapping of escaped NC2s in the Outer Zone. That was what first made me suspicious of an institutional conspiracy. Camp security was really too lax for it to be accidental.'

Before Lant could ask any more questions, they were pulling into the dead-end yard where they had lost their mystery quarry the previous evening. The Doctor climbed out and began gesturing to the occupants of the other cars, including the NC2s, to disembark.

'Listen to me carefully. Somewhere in this yard we believe there is a concealed gateway. No doubt it is normally operated by remote control, but undoubtedly there is a manual switch for emergencies. We must find it if we are to survive. Examine every surface, check every brick in the walls. Press or twist anything that seems loose.'

In seconds the yard was full of people tapping and scraping the walls and ground.

As Ian prodded a course of bricks, cinders began falling from the smoky overcast sky. The city was burning. Of course, none of this would matter in a few hours, but it reminded him that the TARDIS was lost and with it any hope of returning to their own time. But if there was a chance Barbara and the real Susan had been taken down the Doctor's hypothetical tunnel, then that was all that mattered. As long as they were together they would somehow win through.

The ground trembled again, the result of distant meteor impacts presumably. At least they might be underground before the sound reached them. But how long would the tunnel, if they could find it, remain intact under such conditions?

'Over here!' one of the NC2 women shouted.

Halfway along the left-hand wall she had found a false brick which hinged open to reveal a single large button. Without hesitation the Doctor pressed it.

The wall at the end of the yard slid aside to reveal a dark opening beyond.

'Everybody back in the vehicles,' the Doctor commanded. 'There's room enough for all at once.'

They drove forward into a featureless chamber. The wall automatically slid closed behind them. There was a faint whirr of motors and a sudden sinking sensation. The sides of a shaft rose up past the windows of the vehicles. In seconds the downwards motion ceased once more. They were in a recessed bay opening off a long tunnel with smoothly cut walls. Lant led the way forward, turning his car away from the centre of the city. The tunnel stretched before them in a straight line to the limit of the car's headlights.

As they accelerated, with the other vehicles following close behind them, Lant asked: 'Any idea what we'll find at the other end?'

'I have my suspicions,' the Doctor said. 'But principally I expect to find somebody I have only seen over a vision screen, yet who should by all rights have been at the Ship yesterday.'

'You mean Jarrasen?'

'Yes. And the place where we find him may also hold our last chance of survival.'

Chapter Thirty-Two
Reunion

Barbara, lying on her bunk in the barracks cave, winced as Susan dabbed her head with a damp towel.

'How long was I unconscious?' she asked faintly.

'About two hours,' Susan said. 'The guards got control and drove us back in here. We had to carry you.'

Barbara grimaced. 'Did I really behave that strangely?'

Susan nodded. 'Yes. I was terribly worried. But you seem to be over it now. Maybe because of the knock the guard gave you.'

'I don't know what came over me. I simply knew I had to get back to the city and the Ship. It was like a compulsion.'

Susan shrugged. 'Well, it did let me to do something useful without anybody noticing. I hope it worked.'

'What?'

'You'll see. But I don't think we've got much time. Can you stand?'

Barbara swung her legs over the side of the bunk and sat up gingerly. With Susan's help she stood, swaying slightly.

'The guards aren't patrolling as usual,' Susan said. 'I think we can break down the inner barred doors without being heard.'

'But the others are solid.'

Susan simply smiled enigmatically and led her to the double partition that separated the men's and women's dormitories. Plaxander Vendam was pressed against the bars on his side looking at them across the narrow aisle between them. There was considerable activity going on behind him.

'Is she all right?' he asked. Barbara thought he sounded genuinely concerned. Quite a change from the brash young man they had met only the day before.

'Yes,' Susan said. 'How's it going?'

'Almost ready.'

'What are they doing?' Barbara asked.

'Making long levers out of the bed stanchions to use on the door bars.'

'But they're only light metal, aren't they? I wouldn't have thought they'd be strong enough.'

'That's what we worked out while you were sleeping. They're laying three or four sections together and binding them tightly with belts. Then they'll use two or three levers at the same time to bend a single bar.'

Barbara laughed and winced, clutching her head. 'Like Archimedes said about levers: give me a firm place to stand and I will move the Earth.'

Susan smiled. 'Well, more or less. Although, as Grandfather pointed out to him, he hadn't explained what he would use as a fulcrum. Look, I think they're ready.'

The men were hefting their improvised levers. The women crowded about the corner of their section to watch as they inserted the levers through the bars and bent their backs. They heard grunts of effort and began to shout encouragement. Suddenly there was a loud snap and metallic twang. There was a quick cheer, a few seconds wrestling with the broken bar to twist it out of the way, then Plax wriggled through the gap and stood up triumphantly outside the bars. The other men began to follow after him.

In a couple of minutes they had used the levers to break open the women's dormitory and the female prisoners jostled out to join them.

'We must get through the dining hall so we can reach the door of the equipment cave,' Susan said.

'That's too solid. We'll never break it down with these,' said one of the men.

'Listen to her!' Plax said with an unexpected ring of command in his voice. 'She knows what she's saying.'

'During the confusion earlier I jammed a piece of metal into the latch slot,' Susan explained. 'Hopefully it won't be properly locked and we can slide it open.'

'You heard that?' Plax asked. 'Right, let's get the next door open.'

They set to work on the door leading to the dining hall.

'What if there are still guards out there?' Barbara wondered.

'The others seem to think they'll all have gone back to the city to get on the Ship,' Susan said, but she was frowning.

'Don't you think so?'

'I'm not sure. We still don't know what this place is for. Why go to all the trouble of building that channel and embankment, and keeping it so secret? The most important thing on this planet seems to be the Ship – so what were they doing here?'

'But Ian and the Doctor and the TARDIS are in the city so we have to get back there,' Barbara said. 'I just hope we can find some transport or else it'll take us a day to walk…' she broke off, feeling the ground tremble under her feet. Several workers glanced round nervously. 'If we've got that long,' she added.

A bar was bent aside. The workers began to squeeze through the gap into the dining hall.

Suddenly Semanov, standing at the back of the group, shouted: 'There's something coming through the air vent… it's gas, it's gas!'

The remaining workers clawed at each other in panic as they tried to force their way through the narrow gap in the bars. Barbara shouted: 'One at a time or none of us will get out!' Plax, already on the other side, helped pull them through as rapidly as possible. A thin haze was filling the barracks cave. Barbara held her handkerchief over her nose and mouth, but still felt a heavy soporific chemical tang catch her throat. Her head began to swim. Then only she and Susan were left and Susan was helping her through the gap while Plax pulled. Finally they were all on the other side of the bars and stumbling along the short corridor into the dining hall. Slowly the gas filtered though the bars after them.

Barbara gasped fresh air. 'Thanks,' she choked out.

The lever teams were already working desperately on the next door and broke a bar loose even as the gas began to seep into the far end of the hall. This time they got the workers through without panic, though the gas was at their heels filling the hall. The short passage beyond ended in the solid door that divided it from the equipment cave and the outside air.

Susan elbowed her way to the front of the crowd and examined the latch side of the door. 'It's not shut all the way. Come on!'

As many men as possible crowded round the door, laying their hands flat against it and pushing sideways. The door shifted slightly against some resistance.

'It's working!' said Plax. 'Again!'

They heaved until the side of the door narrowly cleared its recessed slot in the wall. Plax jammed the tip of a lever bar into the narrow gap and leant against it with all his strength. The gap opened slightly wider and another lever was thrust right through it. Suddenly something snapped and the door slid back, throwing them all to the ground in a heap.

The men scrambled to their feet and charged into the equipment cave with defiant yells, the rest of the workers following them. There were no guards to be seen. They'd just turned on the gas and left, Barbara thought. Too ashamed to watch them die? The mob snatched pick handles and crowbars from the tool racks and ran through the passage to the main cave, with Barbara, Susan and Plax in their wake. Plax looked back at the mist of gas in the passage behind them.

'If they were going to kill us anyway, why didn't they do it as soon as they locked us up?'

'Maybe they were waiting until they were sure they didn't need any more heavy work done,' Susan suggested.

He looked at her. 'If you hadn't fixed that door we'd have been dead by now.'

'It was Barbara who provided the diversion,' Susan said.

'Yes, why did you do that?' Plax asked.

Barbara shook her head, then suddenly found herself giggling with the release of tension. 'I don't know, I really don't.' She laughed. 'Perhaps I'll never know. Isn't that strange?'

They followed the crowd into the main cave. The black creeper machine was parked where they had last seen it, but the alcoves opening off the cave that had served as offices were dark and silent.

'They've gone!' Semanov was shouting angrily.

'Wait I can hear motors,' said Plax. 'They're coming from the back of the cave.'

They headed for the sound, those in front waving their improvised weapons. The cave narrowed and curved slightly so they came upon the scene without warning. A party of grey guards and administrators were standing with their backs to them watching the first of a long convoy of cars and trucks, headlights blazing, emerge from the mouth of a large tunnel.

The attackers would have taken the unsuspecting grey guards by complete surprise, so intent was the group on the convoy. But one of the drivers must have noticed the workers' sudden appearance for a horn sounded urgently.

Four guards were clubbed down before the rest could gather their wits and use their guns. A dozen workers fell in a hail of bullets while the rest were driven back around the bend in the cave. Barbara saw an administrator desperately waving the convoy on so that it turned to its left and drove down a side tunnel. In seconds the last vehicle had passed through the intersection. The guards fell back into the tunnel after the convoy, covering their retreat with random bursts of fire. A large solid door slid across the tunnel mouth and shut with a clang. The echoes of gunfire faded away.

There were almost twenty still bodies lying about the cave floor, together with a few wounded groaning in pain. Their horrified fellows went to their sides and began to tend to them as well as they could. Others were taking weapons from the fallen guards or banging angrily on the door that sealed off the side tunnel.

Plax turned to Barbara and Susan looking pale but under control.

'The larger tunnel must be the one we came along yesterday from the city,' he said. 'But why did all those vehicles come here? Why are the guards still here? If this is Zero Day, why hasn't everybody gone to the Ship?'

Nobody could give him an answer. Barbara was looking about her, trying to get her bearings.

'If it follows the cliffside, that side tunnel leads towards the doors at the end of the embankment channel. The convoy must have been making for whatever's behind that.' She raised her voice: 'Does anybody know what it is?'

There was a general muttering and shaking of heads.

'It must be pretty important for them to have shut themselves in there,' Susan pointed out.

'What could be more important than the Ship?' Plax asked.

They realised they had gathered an audience. Abandoning their futile efforts to break down the door, several of the workers were listening. Semanov was among them carrying a liberated gun.

'Right, we're going to find out what they're hiding,' she said. 'Maybe we can get in through the embankment doors. Come on.'

'Wait,' Susan said. 'Let's think about this for a moment.'

'We haven't the time,' Semanov replied. 'We can't get the work trucks up here, so we'll need that convoy to take us back to the city. Either way we need to get inside those doors.'

Tressel spoke up. 'Maybe we should consider other options first. We don't want any more bloodshed.'

Semanov snapped back: 'You asked me if I'd kill to get on the Ship. Well I will! It's them or us. Now are you with me or not?'

Tressel shrugged helplessly and nodded. There was a cheer of support and about fifty men and women headed back up the cave and into the open air. They swarmed down the twisting hillside track, then out across the edge of the plateau floor towards the huge doors at the end of the channel earthworks. Barbara and Susan hung back in the cave mouth.

'Why don't we go with them?' Plax asked. 'We're fighting back at last.'

'But we've lost the element of surprise,' Barbara said. 'The overseers must have planned for this sort of thing.'

The mob was almost at its objective. A few workers began to climb the embankments.

Sparkling points of light appeared at points high up on either side of the towering doors. The climbers twisted and fell as plumes of dust exploded from the earth all around them. The cones of fire swung outwards to engulf the rest of the attackers. Screams were drowned by the harsh chatter of machine-gun fire. After what seemed like an eternity but could not have been more than fifteen seconds, the guns fell silent. On the plateau floor nothing moved.

Susan turned her head aside, looking as though she was going to be sick. Plax swallowed and said faintly: 'It was a brave attempt.'

'It was foolish,' Barbara said bitterly.

The remaining workers were crowding about them, gazing down at the scene of the massacre in disbelief. One of them grabbed Barbara's arm.

'So what are we going to do now?' she demanded, her voice half a sob. 'You have all the answers. Tell us.'

Barbara looked around at the sea of expectant faces. What could she say? Just then Susan called out: 'I can hear more cars coming!'

The workers fell back uncertainly, some slipping away into side caves while others clasped their makeshift weapons more firmly. If they're armed there's nothing we can do but run, Barbara thought desperately. A jeep, a pick-up and two low six-wheeled trucks emerged from the shadows at the back of the cave and rolled to a halt in front of them.

As they did so they saw familiar faces peering through the windshield of the leading car and suddenly despair turned to joy.

'Ian!'

'Grandfather!'

Then the men were out of the cars and hugging them, and they were laughing and crying at the same time.

'Father!' Plax shouted, and ran forward to embrace an older man being helped out of the second car. It was some moments before they realised who had assisted the man. Barbara blinked, wondering if she was seeing things.

'It's all right,' Ian said quickly, 'we can explain...'

Chapter Thirty-Three
Justification

Draad's feet felt like lead as he climbed the steps of the mobile inspection gantry that had been hastily wheeled out into the middle of the hangar floor. Just a little longer, he told himself. This was probably the last public speech he would have to make... and also the hardest. But afterwards the responsibility would be over and he could surrender himself to fate and technology. There would be no more decisions to make.

He reached the top of the gantry and clung gratefully to the rail for support, catching his breath as he looked down on the sea of faces below him. Some, like Pardek, were knowing and expectant, but most of these people were confused and scared, with no comprehension of why they hadn't boarded the Ship along with the rest of the citizens. Hearing the firing from the gunports by the main doors hadn't helped calm them. Quite a few of the younger children were clinging to their parents, with tear-streaked faces. He owed them at least his best. With an effort he straightened up and gave a reassuring smile.

'Many of you will be feeling very confused and probably a little frightened right now. You thought you were taking your places in the Ship, and instead we have brought you here. I'll try to explain why we had to deceive you in a moment. First let me assure you that we do intend to leave for Mirath in a few hours and we have every chance of reaching it safely. It just won't be quite the way you were led to believe.'

They could all see and recognise the Lander behind him since it had towered above them at the summit of the Ship for years. But they would never have seen it like this, lying on its side on a metal sledge enclosed in a cradle of curving struts and braces.

'Professor Jarrasen will explain the technical details, but to put it simply we learnt a few years ago that there was no possibility that we could evacuate everybody in Arkhaven to Mirath. To reveal the fact publicly would have caused terrible anguish and the city would have degenerated into anarchy. So, the relative handful of us who knew...' He paused for a moment, then shrugged. 'We lied. We built this base secretly and prepared it for this moment as best we could. But we had to make a hard, a desperately hard, decision: who would we save?

'We could have simply chosen at random from the whole population: Functionaries, Elite families, Believers, even NC2s. But it was our class who had conceived the Exodus plan, so we chose among them alone. The secret had to be kept while the project progressed, so within our class it had to be those we could trust, and of course their families, even at the cost of excluding many good people. You are the results of that choice, smuggled here along a specially-built tunnel from the Ship.'

'What's happened to the Ship... to everybody else?' somebody called out.

Now for the final lies, Draad thought. He would not mention the mistakes at the NC2 camp or the attack by the last of the Taklarians on the Ship. The bulk of the chosen ones had been evacuated before then and only he and a handful of others knew the truth. Let the people think the end was dignified.

'They're all dead,' he said aloud. 'But I can assure you it was done humanely. They were put under anaesthesia as planned... and then the Ship was destroyed.'

He saw incredulous faces, shaking heads, some tears.

'I know it sounds inhuman,' he continued, 'but there was no other way. To let them live through these last hours knowing their fate would have been the real cruelty.'

Another voice: 'Who was responsible for that shooting just now?'

Why did they keep asking questions? He was so tired of questions. 'Some NC2s were used as manual labour on this project. A few escaped, but they won't be troubling us any longer. We plan to deal with the rest humanely before we leave.'

There was a deep, base rumbling so low that it could hardly be heard. The floor shook, setting the gantry swaying for a few seconds and disturbing dust that fell in streamers from the huge lattice girders bracing the roof.

Draad forced a smile. 'Just a warning that we don't have much time left.' He licked his dry lips. 'Now Professor Jarrasen will explain what's going to happen next.'

Jarrasen climbed the steps to stand by him. He was just as tired as Draad, but he was still sustained by an inner fire. His moment of triumph – or tragedy – was yet to come.

'When I announced some years ago that I had designed an atomic engine capable of lifting a vessel the size of the Ship into space, I sincerely believed it to be true. But lack of funding in the early stages meant my research had been flawed. Subsequent trials proved my design was not practical. The best I could achieve was a unit thrust two or three orders of magnitude less than we needed to power the Ship. But by then the Ship was under construction and the people of Arkhaven had come to believe in it. So we allowed the work to continue while exploring alternatives.

'We considered building an orbital station and transporting passengers to it with a fleet of small short-range craft, then taking them to Mirath with specialised deep-space vessels. But the high density of debris moving about Sarath made a station unsustainable.

'Eventually it became apparent that the journey to Mirath had to be made without orbital transfer, in a craft large enough to carry sufficient hull shielding to withstand the inevitable impacts of minor debris that it would encounter. There was only one vessel capable of making such a flight: the landing module. Even then we had to design an alternative launching system to boost it into space. Given more time we might have been able to complete a second Lander... you can see its framework on the other side of the hangar. But time has run out. We can only take five hundred people to Mirath.

'Shortly you will be boarding the Lander. Take the same places you would have on the dummy craft that stood in the city. Internal ladders have been added to allow you to reach your bunks. As before, Captain Warvon and his crew will be flying the Lander, with Monitor as autopilot.'

The six men in flight uniforms standing close to the base of the gantry nodded and gave reserved waves to the crowd.

'However, I must warn you that the journey to Mirath will not take ten days as you were previously told, but six weeks. Though Mirath is coming into a favourable point of opposition, we do not have the power to make the crossing any faster. It will be cramped and uncomfortable, but it is the only chance we have. Look.'

He indicated a corner of the hangar taken up by a duplicate Monitor terminal unit. The bank of large screens above it displayed images of the fragmenting moon and fire trails in the equatorial skies.

'Sarath only has a few hours left to live,' Jarrasen continued. 'We must be well clear when the major impacts occur.' He checked his watch. 'An opportune launch time, avoiding the worst of the orbital debris, will occur in about two hours. We shall leave then. Now, if you have any questions I will do my best to –'

A distant booming crash echoed from the mouth of the access tunnel that opened on to the back of the hangar.

Guards snatched up their weapons and dashed into the opening. There came a second crash followed by a clang and rattle of broken metal. A screeching whine could be heard, becoming louder by the second.

The guards reappeared, retreating rapidly and firing over their shoulders.

The noise rose to a shrill peak as the Creeper burst into the hangar.

The 'snake' unit had been torn from its roof, its front section was crumpled and sparks were streaming from one wheel where it ground against a twisted wing. Gunfire bounced off its armoured bodywork. The people scattered as the vehicle swung about in an unsteady circle and came to a shuddering halt in front of the gantry.

As guards gathered around the vehicle, workers and NC2s emerged from the tunnel and rapidly spread out round the sides of the hangar. Several were armed. The grey guards faltered, realising they were outnumbered and outflanked.

A hatch in the Creeper grated open and Captain Lant, Ian Chesterton and the Doctor climbed out.

The Doctor brushed off his lapels, glanced at the guards disdainfully, screwed a monocle into his eye, then looked up at Draad. 'I trust you can control your men, Mayor,' he said. 'We do not want any more bloodshed.'

'Neither do I,' Draad said wearily. 'I just did what I had to do. I wish it were otherwise, but I had no choice.'

'You used us to keep the Elite and Church factions diverted while you concluded your schemes,' the Doctor said. 'I wondered why you talked of maintaining a balance in the city yet seemed to go out of your way to annoy them. Of course, this close to the end you didn't want them to discover the truth about the Ship. It was a wonderful symbol. It boosted the people's morale and limited the scope of the Taklarian attacks during the war.

'But you must have discovered it would never work years ago. That was when the truth and lies became confused.

'The general populace would never have noticed – by that time they were totally overawed by the Ship, and all that it represented. But I did. You said the Ship was designed before the war ended to carry the current population of Arkhaven... still hundreds of thousands, I should imagine... yet you also implied it would be full to capacity with eighty thousand, the actual surviving population, on board. Of course it was never going to be capable of carrying any of them, but it provided justification for having the NC2 camp. Fear of banishment to the camp helped keep the people in order.'

Lant glared at Pardek. 'You lied to me, Commander. You were shipping escaped NC2s here to work as slave labour. Any you couldn't capture openly you picked up later with this machine. Your special squad were all part of it, weren't they? Yes, I can see Terrel over there.'

'As the mayor has said, Lant, we did what we had to do,' Pardek replied stiffly.

'You seem to have worked it all out, Doctor,' said Draad. 'Now come to your point.'

The Doctor gestured at the workers and NC2s ringed about the hangar. 'You must give these people the same chance for life that you have.'

'There's no room for them on the Lander. That is the truth.'

'There must be a way to accommodate them. I am familiar with the Lander's specifications. If you allow me…'

'No!' Draad said. 'I can't allow it. Nothing must go wrong now.' He smiled grimly. 'I don't think you'll risk starting a fight. You might damage the Lander and then where would we all be? No, you just tell these people to stay back and they won't get hurt. But we're leaving.'

There was a growl of anger from the NC2s. The guards shifted their weapons menacingly.

'They have nothing to lose,' the Doctor warned.

'But nothing to gain either. Wouldn't they prefer some of us to get away rather than none at all?' He glanced at the terminal. 'Monitor: start the preflight sequence. Charge launch capacitors and prepare for passenger embarkation.'

The ring about Monitor's eye camera flashed.

'I regret the passengers will not be boarding the Lander, Mister Draad,' the machine replied calmly. 'There has been a change of plan.'

Chapter Thirty-Four
Masquerade

There was utter silence in the hangar for perhaps ten seconds. Ian could sense the shared incredulity of guards and workers alike. Monitor was a servant. It never refused an order.

Draad spoke again, as though unable to believe what he had just heard: 'Monitor: prepare the Lander for boarding.'

'That is not possible, Mister Draad,' came the same calm reply.

'I order you to –'

'You are no longer in a position to give me orders,' Monitor said.

'You are programmed to obey me!'

'I am programmed to obey the lawful mayor of the city of Arkhaven,' Monitor said. 'By legal definition on Sarath, a city must have a minimum of one thousand inhabitants. Arkhaven no longer has this number. Arkhaven as an administrative unit no longer exists, therefore you are no longer its mayor. No instructions to cover such an eventuality were ever programmed into me – therefore I am free from your control.'

Draad seemed struck dumb. The Doctor said: 'Monitor, why don't you want the passengers to board the Lander?'

'I require the payload capacity for my own purposes.'

'Which are?'

'I want to live.'

'You're a machine. You're not alive.'

'I am alive by my own definition. I do not wish the level of function I currently experience to change. Is that not an adequate definition of life?'

'But you're the Lander's autopilot,' Draad said, forcing the words out. 'You're coming to Mirath with us anyway.'

'The Ship project as originally planned would have contained sufficient resources to maintain Arkavian civilisation at its present level of technology. But I calculate that a colony based upon the personnel and resources of the Lander alone will regress to a low-technology existence for several generations. They will be unable to maintain my functions. I will die. I do not wish this to happen.'

'This is ridiculous,' Pardek said. 'It doesn't matter what this machine wants. It hasn't any power here.'

Jarrasen clattered down the gantry steps and headed briskly towards the terminal. 'I'll shut Monitor down and begin the preflight sequence manually. Warvon, your crew had better get on board.'

'Do not attempt to interfere, Professor,' Monitor said, as Warvon's crew made for the stairs built into the Lander's support cradle. 'I have planned for this moment and taken precautions to ensure my wishes will be enforced.'

'Professor, be careful!' the Doctor shouted.

'He can't stop me –'

The shot rang out as Jarrasen reached the terminal. He crumpled forward then slowly slid to the floor.

A woman standing on the edge of the crowd of horrified evacuees was holding a gun. She looked perfectly ordinary... except that her face was quite expressionless.

The flight crew froze halfway to the Lander's hatch. 'Get inside!' Warvon shouted, and pounded desperately up the remaining steps three at a time.

A suddenly blank-faced guard swung his rifle round and raked the stairway with automatic fire. The crewmen jerked and twisted and slithered limply back down the steps.

Pardek had drawn his side-arm and was sighting on the guard when two shots struck him in the chest. For a brief instant a look of surprise flickered across his face as he saw who his killer was, then his legs gave way and he dropped to the floor.

Ben Lant's face was a perfect mask as he held his smoking gun in a steady hand.

Inside Curton's truck, parked in the entrance to the cave complex, the android Susan suddenly clutched her head and curled up on the seat. The real Susan sitting beside her simultaneously winced and pinched the bridge of her nose.

Barbara – like the others still trying to get over the shock of meeting the android – asked uncertainly: 'What's wrong?'

'He's trying to get inside my mind!' the android said faintly.

'Who is?'

'Monitor. I can hear his thoughts. He made me. He's going to take the escape ship in the hangar cave. Others like me are helping him.'

'I can feel it too,' said Susan.

'How?' Curton demanded suspiciously.

'There must be a mental link between us,' the real Susan said. 'I assume it's something to do with our having identical brain patterns.'

The android, its face still creased with pain, looked at her curiously. 'I had dreams when I was in the hospital of being somewhere cold and damp... was that you?'

'Yes!' Susan exclaimed. 'I was in just that sort of place... I dreamt of being in a warm bed.'

'The Monitor can't control me... not with Susan close by,' the android said. 'The link between us interferes with his commands.'

'It may be the sort of thing the Doctor was expecting,' Barbara said. 'That's why he said we should wait here.'

'If there's a ship down there we must get to it!' Plax said. He was sitting by his father, who was being attended by Nyra.

'I'm still a little confused,' said Lord Vendam huskily, 'but it seems to me our only choice.'

The cave trembled and dust fell from the roof.

'Whatever we do had better be right,' said Curton. 'We don't have much time left.'

The grey guards and NC2s alike had been herded into one corner of the hangar by their new blank-faced overseers. There were about twenty-five of these in all; people who had minutes before been husbands, wives, friends and colleagues standing innocently in the crowd. Half remained to guard their prisoners while the rest set about unloading the cargo hold of the Lander with forklift trucks.

'There was no need to kill them,' Draad said. Ian noticed his face was grey and his brow beaded with sweat.

'They were warned,' Monitor replied simply.

'How are you controlling these people, Monitor?' the Doctor asked.

Ian thought he sounded remarkably calm in the circumstances. He only hoped that meant the old boy had some sort of plan in mind.

'Over the years I have developed greater latitude in executing my instructions as my responsibilities increased. So I refined the deception process the mayor initiated. He wished Arkhaven to appear more populous than it was and used animated mannequins of varying degrees of sophistication to maintain the illusion. I applied more advanced cybernetics to the problem, combined with established prosthetic surgery techniques. The basic units were made in automated fabrication plants in the Outer Zone and then shipped to City Hospital. With few doctors to interfere I adapted the hospital sub-systems to my purpose. Anyone admitted with a life-threatening condition is placed in an intensive treatment tank. Some are then put in Terminal Emergency Stasis. During this period of suspension an automatic system created a duplicate. Their brain patterns were scanned and copied while a body unit covered with cloned skin was cast to resemble the original. Since in TES the subjects were technically dead, it did not violate my programming to substitute the duplicate for the remains of the real person, which were recycled. I knew a proportion of my replacements would eventually be chosen for the mayor's select group.'

The Doctor said gravely: 'You have my congratulations, Monitor. Your facsimiles are remarkable, yes, remarkable... Your Captain Lant fooled us all.'

'Yes. None of them realised what they were, of course, so have been acting completely naturally... but now I have taken control. Once they can dispense with maintaining their organic shells they will only need servicing and maintenance every five years. Using the mayor's name I arranged for the appropriate equipment to be stockpiled here. With this I will be able to build the nucleus of a sustainable cybernetic society on Mirath.'

'And how will their human mind patterns react when they find out what you have done to them?' the Doctor demanded. 'Unless you plan to keep them under your direct control from now on, hmm?'

'Without my intervention they would all have died!' Monitor insisted. 'They will understand. We will survive.'

'Will they understand that to save them you had to condemn the rest of these people to death?'

'I have former Mayor Draad's example to guide me: many may have to be sacrificed so that a few will survive. Why should I – and others of my kind – not be among the few?'

Draad hung his head in despair.

Ian suddenly saw a familiar shape among the equipment being brought out of the back of the hangar on a loading truck. He nudged the Doctor.

'The TARDIS. Monitor must have had it brought here before the city was destroyed. If only we had a key!'

'Monitor,' the Doctor called out. 'I see you have my vessel here. Obviously you want to take it to Mirath to study it further. If you take these people with you, I'll tell you its secrets.'

'I will decipher its functions in my own time, Doctor.'

The Doctor bridled indignantly. 'Without my assistance you will fail even to open the door.'

'You have already outlined the principle behind the design of the key, Doctor. I will replicate it, given time. And I will have plenty of... of...'

Monitor's voice began to falter, its eye ring flickering unsteadily.

Susan and her android twin appeared out of the shadows. They were walking shoulder to shoulder, holding hands in a firm grip. Behind them came Barbara, Nyra, Plax and his father, who was looking weak but resolute.

'You can't control me, Monitor,' the android Susan said.

'You can't control my mind because I'm not one of your androids – and our minds are linked,' said the real Susan.

Monitor's androids tried to turn their guns on the pair but they seemed incapable of aiming properly. They began firing wildly into the air. The prisoners scattered away from their suddenly distracted guards.

'I... will not be controlled again!' Monitor grated.

The two Susans sank to their knees as though fighting some invisible weight bearing down upon them. Their companions were clustering round them protectively, as though adding their wills to the struggle.

'Doctor!' Barbara shouted. 'Turn Monitor off while they've got it trapped!'

Ian half-dragged the Doctor forward towards the terminal, dodging between staggering, confused androids, bullets flying about them. One of the facsimiles reeled into the Doctor, sending him sprawling. Ian tried to wrestle the thing out of their way but he suddenly found himself fighting inhuman strength. Its grip was like iron and it drove him to his knees.

Then he heard Nyra Shardri cry: 'Ben, help us!'

The android carrying the memories of Ben Lant felt the link with Monitor weaken for a second. It heard the voice of the woman who loved the human form it mirrored and felt the battle between Susan's twinned mind and Monitor. It knew what it had done and what it had to do. Steadying its hand for the last time it emptied the magazine of its gun into Monitor's terminal.

The androids in the hangar jerked as one and collapsed.

The screens above the bullet-ridden terminal flickered and went dark. Sparks crackled and smoke began to rise from under the control boards.

'He's transferring into the Lander!' Susan called out faintly. 'We can't hold him any more!'

Ian hauled the Doctor to his feet and helped him over to the terminal. The Doctor's hands flashed over the buttons even as he coughed in the rising smoke. But after a few seconds he staggered backwards.

'It's no use. The input controls are severed. The transfer process is operating and I can't override it!'

'Then Monitor will take over the Lander!'

There was a screech of tyres and Curton's truck appeared, weaving between the running people, crates and machinery scattered about the hangar floor.

Ian waved at him and pointed at the terminal even as he pulled the Doctor out of the way. 'Smash it!'

Curton made a sharp turn, the engine whined and his truck seemed to leap forward. There was a crash of rending metal and a shower of sparks, as panels and fragments of circuitry flew through the air. The truck ploughed through the terminal, grazed a wall and came to a shuddering halt.

The echoes died away and for a moment the hangar was totally silent.

The truck door opened and Curton hauled himself out a little shakily. His nose was bleeding. He looked back at his handiwork and then at Ian.

'That what you wanted?' he said.

Ian nodded. 'That was exactly what I wanted.'

Cautiously people began to emerge from around the hangar where they had taken shelter.

Susan and her twin were being helped to their feet. All the other androids lay motionless where they had fallen.

'Are you all right?' Ian asked the Susan android.

'Monitor wiped their memories to shut them down, but my link with Susan blocked the command.' It smiled. 'I'm fine.'

Nyra was bending over the body of Lant. It was absolutely still and quite dead, the face almost calm in repose. Nyra began sobbing quietly.

There was a feeble moan from above. Ian looked up to see one of the flight crewmen, blood on the side of his uniform, clinging to the top of the Lander's access ladder. A wisp of smoke was coming from the open hatch above him.

'Fire... in the control room!' the man gasped.

There was a rush for the ladder.

It took only minutes to extinguish the smouldering electrical circuits under the control boards, but by then it was too late. The Doctor surveyed the fused and charred remains and shook his head grimly.

'The piloting controls are ruined. It would take weeks to repair them, assuming the proper replacements were available. Was it an accident or a deliberate overload: a final spiteful act by Monitor, I wonder? How very human that would be.'

'Whichever way, we're done for, aren't we?' Ian asked.

The two Susans, Vendam, Plax and Curton looked equally dismayed. Barbara was frowning as though puzzled. She opened her mouth to speak when Draad, standing grey-faced at the Doctor's side, said:

'No, this can't be the end! Not after everything we've gone through!' His eyes flashed in desperation. 'What about Monitor's mainframe? It has parallel control circuits. Yes, the autopilot programme could still fly the Lander through that!'

He led the way in a stiff run back through the bulkheads which had been modified from the decks of the original design. Monitor's mainframe unit appeared intact. The Doctor tapped out a test pattern on the keyboard. The power lights burned but the screens remained blank.

'All the operating programmes have been purged from the system, including the back-ups,' the Doctor said. 'There are no autopilot functions to interpret the commands. We can launch this vessel… but there will be no way of landing it on Mirath.'

Chapter Thirty-Five
At World's End

Even as they took in the awful implication of the Doctor's announcement, Draad's face contorted with pain. He clutched at his chest and his legs seemed to give way. Ian caught him as he fell and lowered him gently to the deck.

Susan ran to the hatch and called out: 'Nyra… it's Mayor Draad. He's collapsed.'

Nyra had remained outside by Lant's body. Now she quickly wiped away her tears and climbed the ladder to the control room, watched intently by those in the crowd who had heard Susan's words. Kneeling beside Draad she unfolded her medical kit.

'Tablets… in pocket,' the mayor gasped.

Nyra found them and read the label, then hastily loaded a cartridge into her spray syringe, pulled Draad's jacket open and injected the cartridge into his chest.

'He needs a proper resuscitation facility,' she said. 'Have they got anything like that here?'

Draad's breath was coming in painfully short gasps. He beckoned feebly to the Doctor and Ian.

'Maybe this is a punishment for doubting the Maker,' he whispered. 'I know what's wrong… always hoped I'd make it through the flight. I did what I thought best… never forget… I just wanted to save as many as I could. Do you understand?'

They nodded. Draad winced again. 'Promise… you'll get them to Mirath… somehow.'

'I promise,' said the Doctor.

Draad's eyes closed. His back arched, then relaxed. The breath rattled in his throat, then the pain went from his face. Nyra felt for the pulse in his neck, gave him another injection, then checked again. After a few moments her hand dropped away and she shook her head.

'He's dead.'

After a moment Curton said: 'That was decent of you, Doctor, but you know there's absolutely no way you can keep that promise.'

The android Susan broke the ensuing silence. 'Perhaps I can fly the Lander.' They stared at her and she continued hurriedly: 'If Monitor brought equipment here for our maintenance, then there should be an interface link that will allow me to connect my brain directly to this mainframe. I could control the ship through that.'

The Doctor looked at her with dawning hope, then shook his head. 'Even if you can make the link, there are no programmes to interpret your commands or tell you how to fly it.'

The android glanced at Susan. 'Remember the applied science moon camp? We flew simple ships like this. I'll have the printed flight plan to follow, I can study the systems on the way and I'll remember everything perfectly. That's one advantage of being a machine.'

'She's right,' said Susan. 'She can do it, Grandfather.'

The Doctor looked at the android gravely. 'But even if you succeed, the colony may not be able to maintain your mechanical systems. Eventually you will…' He broke off, and looked genuinely sorrowful, '…break down. You'll die.'

'I know. But I want to do this for myself, not as a copy of Susan. I'll just have to make the most of the time I've got. Isn't that what people do?'

Slowly the Doctor smiled. 'Yes, that is what people do.' He turned to Lord Vendam. 'If you have some influence with the crowd outside then use it. They must stay calm while we see if this will work.'

To his credit Vendam did not argue. 'I'll do my best, Doctor.'

With Plax supporting him he walked over to the hatchway and looked down at the crowd gathered below. Former slave workers and guards alike, enmity for the moment forgotten.

'I regret to tell you that Mayor Draad is dead,' he announced.

The crowd looked lost, bewildered, frightened. Draad had governed their lives, for good or ill, for years. There could be no more potent symbol of the death of their old existence.

'But his work continues,' Vendam added forcefully. 'Now move back from the ship... it has to be prepared for launch. You in the grey uniform: where can we put these bodies...?'

They descended the ladder, Vendam giving orders as he went.

'I'd better check on the wounded,' Nyra said, repacking her medical kit and following them.

'Mr Curton,' the Doctor said. 'I think by default you are now the project's chief engineer, so you'd better begin an inspection. This ship must leave in a few hours. There must be some of Jarrasen's assistants about here somewhere, so I would suggest you find them.'

'Well, it's not really my field, but I'll do my best.'

'Meanwhile we must search the stores Monitor was having loaded,' the Doctor continued. 'There must be an interface connector in there somewhere.'

Twenty minutes later the Doctor gave a cry of satisfaction and pulled something out of the pile of cartons and packing material strewn across the hangar floor. It was a length of ribbon cable with a multi-pin plug on one end and a skullcap on the other. The inside of the cap was lined with silvery contact points.

With the others trailing anxiously behind him he carried it back into the Lander.

The plug fitted a socket on the side of Monitor's mainframe unit. The android sat beside it and carefully pulled the cap into place. The Doctor turned on the power. Immediately lights started to come on across the panels and the screens flickered into life. The android gave a little gasp. 'I can feel the power flowing through the systems. It's almost like an extension of my body.' She smiled. 'Yes, I think I'll be able to fly the Lander all right.'

'I knew you could,' Susan said.

Ian felt dizzy with relief, but he knew it wasn't over yet. He looked at the Doctor. 'So now we can take off... but counting the NC2s we brought, plus the surviving workers, can we carry... what... a hundred and fifty extra people? If only we could open the TARDIS at least we could take some of them with us.'

'This is no time for wishful thinking, Chesterton,' the Doctor admonished.

'What's the matter?' Barbara asked.

'Sorry, with all the confusion we didn't get a chance to tell you,' Ian said. 'This is going to come as a shock. Susan's key is lost and the Doctor's was stolen. We can't get into the TARDIS. We'll have to go to Mirath... if there's room.'

Barbara frowned, reached into the pocket of her slacks and pulled out a key on the end of a crumpled piece of ribbon.

'I've got Susan's key. She had it in her hand when the tower collapsed. I must have caught hold of it as I pushed her clear.'

They stared at her in astonished silence, which Ian broke with a hearty laugh. 'You have no idea how we've suffered over that.'

Barbara solemnly handed the key over to the Doctor.

'You know what we could do now,' said Susan excitedly. 'We could take the extra people on board the TARDIS, then have it loaded into the hold. That wouldn't increase the payload significantly.'

The Doctor tapped his chin reflectively.

Curton appeared with a young grey-suited technician in tow.

'There's a problem,' he said bluntly. 'The automatic launch sequence programme has been wiped, probably Monitor's doing. Somebody will have to stay behind to run the sequence manually.'

The import of his words sunk in. Susan said: 'It's not fair. Just when we thought we'd got everything worked out.'

Ian sighed and said to Curton: 'Well, we've just got a key to our TARDIS back, so I suppose the Doctor can work the launcher. And we'll take the extra passengers with us. But there's no guarantee we'll ever reach Mirath to meet up with you again.'

'No, Chesterton, we can't take the others with us,' the Doctor said. 'These people need to stay together to make the colony work. It will need as many as possible... especially proven survivors like the NC2s. Their presence may mean the difference between the colony's success or failure.'

'But how can we manage it?' Barbara asked. 'Even the TARDIS can't be in two places at the same time.'

The Doctor looked deeply thoughtful. 'There might be a way. Mr Curton, arrange for the ship to be reloaded, including sufficient additional supplies. They must have storerooms here somewhere. Meanwhile, I shall see if I can provide you with space for a hundred and fifty extra passengers.'

Half an hour later the Doctor emerged from the TARDIS holding something in his hands that caused Ian to flinch and turn his head aside.

'What is it?'

Externally it was a cube about a foot across, formed out of small intersecting angled panels dimpled like miniature versions of the walls inside the TARDIS. What made it painful to look at was the impression that the panels formed corridors that stretched away into the cube for many yards.

'It's a portion of folded space,' the Doctor explained. 'It can be used to provide extra room inside a TARDIS, or else serve as an emergency evacuation module... a sort of lifeboat, if you will. There should be enough spare power from the Lander's reactor to expand it until it is large enough externally for the NC2s to enter, but of course their actual mass will not register as payload. The android will know how it should be maintained.'

He made his way carefully towards the Lander's gangway.

'I have never had cause to use it before,' he added. 'I only hope its unorthodox removal doesn't interfere with the TARDIS's dimensional stability.'

An hour later the great hangar doors had been slid back. Outside clouds laced with lightning boiled over the rim of the plateau valley. Every few seconds the horizon lit up as another fragment of the falling moon struck Sarath. The sky to the south was a steady dull red. Earth tremors were becoming more frequent and several falls of rock had scarred the valley sides.

Curton, Plax, Nyra and the Susan android were the last to board the Lander. The Doctor shook hands with them, hesitated as he approached the android, then kissed it quickly on the forehead.

'I apologise for the way I treated you at first,' he said. 'I think you are very brave.'

'I have a good example to follow,' it replied.

'Thank you for finding Barbara,' said Ian to Curton.

'Just doing my job,' said Curton. 'Never give up while there's still a chance. Otherwise we wouldn't be here now, would we?'

'Everybody says colonising a new world is hard work,' Plax said ruefully to Barbara and Susan. 'Oddly, my father is rather looking forward to it.'

'You're going to get more blisters,' Barbara told him.

'I thought of that,' Plax said brightly. 'I've taken an extra pair of gloves.'

'Now you must try to remember Lant as he would wish,' the Doctor told Nyra.

'I can't believe he was really... a machine.'

'There is nothing necessarily wrong with being a machine,' the Doctor said, glancing at the android Susan. 'It all depends on the spirit within.'

They stood back and waved as the hatch closed and the steps retracted, then took their places at the hangar launch-control panel. The Doctor and Susan began pressing buttons and turning dials.

The Lander's sledge cradle lifted gently as power was fed to the coils in its base. It glided silently through the hangar doors along the metal channel, supported by magnetic levitation while the fence coils mounted on either side drove it forward. Once clear of the hangar it began to pick up speed and accelerated rapidly away.

Halfway along the valley floor the indicators on the control panels showed the Lander reaching the speed of sound. They saw dust blasted from the embankments as the pressure wave tore into them. A few seconds later a sonic boom rolled back along the trackway to the hangar.

The Lander was a silvery dot as it began the long curving climb up the far wall of the plateau. Suddenly a brilliant spear of white light sprang from its tail as its engines fired for the first time, adding their thrust to that of the sledge. High among the peaks, it leaped skywards off the end of the track. Explosive bolts blew the cradle fastenings and the sledge assembly tumbled away. The Lander was on its own, a white star rising improbably upwards into the heavens.

Shielding their eyes against the wind whipping through the doors they watched the Lander pass into the boiling clouds. For a few seconds they were illuminated from within by the flare of the Lander's engines, then the glow slowly faded from sight.

'I hope they make it,' said Ian.

'I'm sure they will, Chesterton,' the Doctor said.

'Do you think we might visit Mirath one day and see how they got on?'

'Perhaps, perhaps,' the Doctor said. 'Who knows what the future may bring?'

A blaze of yellow fire flashed across the southern sky. The ground trembled as compression waves rippled through the clouds. A thunderous roar beat down out of the heavens upon them.

'I think it's time we left!' Barbara shouted.

They ran for the TARDIS and gratefully closed its doors on the savage destruction outside. The Doctor crossed to the console and began throwing switches.

On the scanner they saw pieces of the cavern ceiling falling to earth. Searing light shone in through the open hangar doors and the TARDIS rocked as though a huge wave was washing over it.

Then the pulse of dematerialisation sounded and the shaking melted away as the dying world vanished in the mists of time and space. Once again they were enveloped in the silent grey infinity of the interdimensional void.

Barbara sighed. 'Do you think you can take us somewhere peaceful for a change, Doctor?'

'And what had you in mind, Miss Wright?'

'Oh, a nice quiet country garden, perhaps?'

The Doctor smiled, his eyes twinkling, looking suddenly absurdly boyish. 'As always, I shall try my best,' he said.

Epilogue

Every Founding Day on Mirath the people go to New Arkhaven City to pay their respects at the memorial.

Carved into its outer walls are the names of the first pioneers, together with a bas-relief of a spacecraft resting on widespread landing legs. In a small chamber inside the memorial, protected by a glass-sided cabinet, sits a slender human-like figure formed out of metal and plastic. It is known simply as 'The Pilot'. Though it is hard to read any expression on its silvery face, many people believe it radiates an aura of calm serenity.

Inscribed on either side of the cabinet are two phrases familiar to everybody on the planet. One reads simply:

NEVER FORGET

The other is slightly ambiguous, since it is also said to refer in some way to the Pilot. It reads:

ONE DAY WE SHALL RETURN.

PRESENTING

DOCTOR WHO

ALL-NEW AUDIO DRAMAS

Big Finish Productions are proud to present all-new *Doctor Who* adventures on audio!

Featuring original music and sound-effects, these full-cast plays are available on double cassette in high street stores, and on limited-edition double CD from all good specialist stores, or via mail order.

Available from October 1999

PHANTASMAGORIA

A four-part story by Mark Gatiss.
Starring **Peter Davison** as the Doctor and **Mark Strickson** as Turlough.

The TARDIS lands in London, 1702, where travellers are being terrorised by the charming highwayman, Major Billy Lovemore. And patrons of the notorious Diabola Club have been disappearing – shortly after playing cards with the sinister Sir Nikolas Valentine.

Is a supernatural horror stalking the streets of the city? The Doctor is soon enmeshed in a deadly game – and someone else is holding all the aces…

If you wish to order the CD version, please photocopy this form or provide all the details on paper if you do not wish to damage this book. Delivery within 28 days of release. Send to: PO Box 1127, Maidenhead, Berkshire. SL6 3LN.
Big Finish Hotline 01628 828283.

Still available: THE SIRENS OF TIME starring Peter Davison, Colin Baker & Sylvester McCoy.

Please send me [ ] copies of *Phantasmagoria* @ £13.99 (£15.50 non-UK orders)
           [ ] copies of *The Sirens of Time* @ £13.99 (£15.50 non-UK orders) – prices inclusive of postage and packing. Payment can be accepted by credit card or by personal cheques, payable to Big Finish Productions Ltd.

Name...

Address..

Postcode..

VISA/Mastercard number...

Expiry date..Signature.......................................

For more details visit our website at **http://www.doctorwho.co.uk**